PENGUIN BOOKS
The History of Love

'A bewitching novel, it brims with all manner of romantic possibility and luminous connection' *Harpers and Queen*

'Vertiginously exciting, vibrantly imagined. Krauss's work is illuminated by the warmth and delicacy of her prose' *The New York Times*

'A real, vivid talent' *Sunday Times*

'Astounding, moving, very funny . . . a joy to read. Leo Gursky is brilliantly drawn' *The Times Literary Supplement*

'Captivating . . . Characters fly off the page and into your consciousness' *Good Housekeeping*

'At least as heartbreaking as it is hilarious . . . Krauss touches the heart' *Washington Post*

'Astonishing' *Scotsman*

'In *The History of Love*, the symptoms of loss are so well-judged and so entertaining that they barely leave room for considerations about the cause' *Observer*

'A new star in the literary firmament . . . one of the most touching stories you are ever likely to read' *In Style*

'Poignant and evocative . . . the writing is beautiful; the voices of the old man and the young girl are as sensitively drawn as each other, and the twists and turns keep you riveted until the last page' *Easy Living*

'Krauss's complex Russian-doll structure demands – and repays – concentration. But the characters are so vivid and human that it never feels like hard work. ****' *Marie Claire*

'Funny, moving, enchanting. There are few books capable of making the heart surge, but *The History of Love* is one of them' *Zembla*

'Beguilingly enigmatic. I have never read a book quite like this, it is beautiful, original and audacious in equal measure. A modern masterpiece' *Leeds Guide*

'Intriguing, engaging' *Evening Standard*

'Krauss beautifully maps a literary labyrinth on which the hopes and desires of her characters depend . . . curiosity and love play a profound role in bringing Krauss's novel to its marvellous close' *San Francisco Chronicle*

'Intricately and carefully constructed. Krauss reveals the characteristics of humanity that transcend time and the experience of living' *Denver Post*

'Brilliant. An achievement of extraordinary depth and beauty' *Newsday*

'The novel's achievement is precisely, and not negligibly, this: to have made a new fiction – alternately delightful and hilarious and deeply affecting – out of what has come before' *LA Weekly*

'A tremendous novel that will wring out our tired hearts' Colm McCann

'An accomplished acrobatic feat' *Boston Sunday Globe*

'Brilliant . . . A most unusual and original piece of fiction – and not to be missed' *Kirkus Reviews*

'Captivating . . . Krauss writes superbly' *Houston Chronicle*

'Krauss has an impressive imagination and considerable talent . . . a memorable feat of storytelling, fine prose and heartbreakingly real characters' *Minneapolis Star-Tribune*

'In her graceful inquiry into the interplay between life and literature, Krauss is winsome, funny and affecting' *Booklist*

'A beautifully constructed, frequently funny and ultimately moving tale' *Time Out New York*

'*The History of Love* by Nicole Krauss is a novel to remind you of the power of fiction -- funny and sad and devastating and hopeful often all at the same time' *Publishers Weekly*

'Extraordinary . . . *The History of Love* is a complex, funny, sad, elegantly constructed meditation on the power of love, language and imagination . . . Krauss's beautifully imagined characters are funny, rueful, smart and sometimes almost unbearably poignant' *Seattle Times*

'A witty, emotional and ambitiously literary work . . . populated with sharp, deeply sympathetic characters' *Rolling Stone*

'The authenticity of the humour contrasted with the sadness is extraordinarily moving. Krauss is the real thing; *The History of Love* is a novel to be read and reread' *Globe and Mail*

'*The History of Love* has perfect pitch and does its dance of time between contemporary New York and the wanderings of the Jews with unsentimental but heartbreaking grace. [Krauss] also happens to write like an angel' Simon Schama, *Guardian*

'A significant novel, genuinely one of the year's best' *New York Magazine*

'Undoubtedly the work of a formidably talented novelist' *Independent*

THE HISTORY OF LOVE

Nicole Krauss

PENGUIN BOOKS

PENGUIN BOOKS

Published by the Penguin Group
Penguin Books Ltd, 80 Strand, London WC2R ORL, England
Penguin Group (USA) Inc., 375 Hudson Street, New York, New York 10014, USA
Penguin Group (Canada), 90 Eglinton Avenue East, Suite 700, Toronto, Ontario,
Canada M4P 2Y3 (a division of Pearson Penguin Canada Inc.)
Penguin Ireland, 25 St Stephen's Green, Dublin 2, Ireland
(a division of Penguin Books Ltd)
Penguin Group (Australia), 250 Camberwell Road,
Camberwell, Victoria 3124, Australia (a division of Pearson Australia Group Pty Ltd)
Penguin Books India Pvt Ltd, 11 Community Centre,
Panchsheel Park, New Delhi – 110 017, India
Penguin Group (NZ), cnr Airborne and Rosedale Roads, Albany,
Auckland 1310, New Zealand (a division of Pearson New Zealand Ltd)
Penguin Books (South Africa) (Pty) Ltd, 24 Sturdee Avenue,
Rosebank, Johannesburg 2196, South Africa

Penguin Books Ltd, Registered Offices: 80 Strand, London WC2R ORL, England

www.penguin.com

First published in the United States of America by
W. W. Norton & Company, Inc. 2005
First published in Great Britain by Viking 2005
Published in Penguin Books 2006
1

Copyright © Nicole Krauss, 2005
Illustrations copyright © Sam Messner, 2005
All rights reserved

The moral right of the author has been asserted

Printed in England by Clays Ltd, St Ives plc

ISBN-13: 978-0-141-02578-0
ISBN-10: 0-141-02578-6

FOR MY GRANDPARENTS,

who taught me the opposite of disappearing

and FOR JONATHAN, *my life*

THE HISTORY OF LOVE

THE LAST WORDS ON EARTH

When they write my obituary. Tomorrow. Or the next day. It will say, *LEO GURSKY IS SURVIVED BY AN APARTMENT FULL OF SHIT.* I'm surprised I haven't been buried alive. The place isn't big. I have to struggle to keep a path clear between bed and toilet, toilet and kitchen table, kitchen table and front door. If I want to get from the toilet to the front door, impossible, I have to go by way of the kitchen table. I like to imagine the bed as home plate, the toilet as first, the kitchen table as second, the front door as third: should the doorbell ring while I am lying in bed, I have to round the toilet and the kitchen table in order to arrive at the door. If it happens to be Bruno, I let him in without a word and then jog back to bed, the roar of the invisible crowd ringing in my ears.

I often wonder who will be the last person to see me alive. If I had to bet, I'd bet on the delivery boy from the Chinese take-out. I order in four nights out of seven. Whenever he comes. I make a big production of finding my wallet. He stands in the door holding the greasy bag while I wonder if this is the night I'll finish off my spring roll, climb into bed, and have a heart attack in my sleep.

I try to make a point of being seen. Sometimes when I'm out, I'll buy a juice even though I'm not thirsty. If the store is crowded I'll even go so far as dropping my change all over the floor, the nickels and dimes skidding in every direction. I'll get down on my knees. It's a big effort for me to get down on my knees, and an even bigger effort to get up. And yet. Maybe I look like a fool. I'll go into the Athlete's Foot and say, *What do you have in sneakers?* The clerk will look me over like the poor schmuck that I am and direct me over to the one pair of Rockports they carry, something in spanking white. *Nah,* I'll say, *I have those already,* and then I'll make my way over to the Reeboks and pick out something that doesn't even resemble a shoe, a waterproof bootie, maybe, and ask for it in size 9. The kid will look again, more carefully. He'll look at me long and hard. *Size 9,* I'll repeat while I clutch the webbed shoe. He'll shake his head and go to the back for them, and by the time he returns I'm peeling off my socks. I'll roll my pants legs up and look down at those decrepit things, my feet, and an awkward minute will pass until it becomes clear that I'm waiting for him to slip the booties onto them. I never actually buy. All I want is not to die on a day when I went unseen.

A few months ago I saw an ad in the paper. It said, *NEEDED: NUDE MODEL FOR DRAWING CLASS. $15/HOUR.* It seemed too good to be true. To have so much looked at. By so many. I called the number. A woman told me to come the following Tuesday. I tried to describe myself, but she wasn't interested. *Anything will do,* she said.

The days passed slowly. I told Bruno about it, but he misunderstood and thought I was signing up for a drawing class in order to see nude girls. He didn't want to be corrected. *They show their boobs?* he asked. I shrugged. *And down there?*

After Mrs. Freid on the fourth floor died, and it took three days before anyone found her, Bruno and I got into the habit of checking on each other. We'd make little excuses—*I ran out of toilet paper*, I'd say when Bruno opened the door. A day would pass. There would be a knock on my door. *I lost my TV Guide,* he'd explain, and I'd go and find him mine, even though I knew his was right there where it always was on his couch. Once he came down on a Sunday afternoon. *I need a cup of flour,* he said. It was clumsy, but I couldn't help myself. *You don't know how to cook.* There was a moment of silence. Bruno looked me in the eye. *What do you know,* he said, *I'm baking a cake.*

When I came to America I knew hardly anyone,

only a second cousin who was a locksmith, so I worked for him. If he had been a shoemaker I would have become a shoemaker; if he had shoveled shit I, too, would have shoveled. But. He was a locksmith. He taught me the trade, and that's what I became. We had a little business together, and then one year he got TB, they had to cut his liver out and he got a 106 temperature and died, so I took it over. I sent his wife half the profits, even after she got married to a doctor and moved to Bay Side. I stayed in the business for over fifty years. It's not what I would have imagined for myself. And yet. The truth is I came to like it. I helped those in who were locked out, others I helped keep out what couldn't be let in, so that they could sleep without nightmares.

Then, one day I was looking out the window. Maybe I was contemplating the sky. Put even a fool in front of the window and you'll get a Spinoza. The afternoon passed, darkness sifted down. I reached for the chain on the bulb and suddenly it was as if an elephant had stepped on my heart. I fell to my knees. I thought: I didn't live forever. A minute passed. Another minute. Another. I clawed at the floor, pulling myself along toward the phone.

Twenty-five percent of my heart muscle died. It took time to recover and I never went back to work. A year went by. I was aware of time passing for the sake of itself. I stared out the window. I watched fall

turn into winter. Winter into spring. Some days Bruno
came downstairs to sit with me. We've known each
other since we were boys; we went to school together.
He was one of my closest friends, with thick glasses,
reddish hair that he hated, and a voice that cracked
when he was emotional. I didn't know he was still alive
and then one day I was walking down East Broadway
and I heard his voice. I turned around. His back was
to me, he was standing in front of the grocer's asking
for the price of some fruit. I thought: You're hearing
things, you're such a dreamer, what is the likelihood—
your boyhood friend? I stood frozen on the sidewalk.
He's in the ground, I told myself. Here you are in the
United States of America, there's McDonald's, get a
grip. I waited just to make sure. I wouldn't have recognized his face. But. The way he walked was unmistakable. He was about to pass me, I put my arm out. I
didn't know what I was doing, maybe I was seeing
things, I grabbed his sleeve. *Bruno*, I said. He stopped
and turned. At first he seemed scared and then
confused. *Bruno*. He looked at me, his eyes began to
fill with tears. I grabbed his other hand, I had one
sleeve and one hand. *Bruno*. He started to shake. He
touched his hand to my cheek. We were in the middle
of the sidewalk, people were hurrying past, it was a
warm day in June. His hair was thin and white. He
dropped the fruit. *Bruno*.

A couple of years later his wife died. It was too

much to live in the apartment without her, everything reminded him, so when an apartment opened up in the floor above me he moved in. We often sit together at my kitchen table. The whole afternoon might go by without our saying a word. If we do talk, we never speak in Yiddish. The words of our childhood became strangers to us—we couldn't use them in the same way and so we chose not to use them at all. Life demanded a new language.

Bruno, my old faithful. I haven't sufficiently described him. Is it enough to say he is indescribable? No. Better to try and fail than not to try at all. The soft down of your white hair lightly playing about your scalp like a half-blown dandelion. Many times, Bruno, I have been tempted to blow on your head and make a wish. Only a last scrap of decorum keeps me from it. Or perhaps I should begin with your height, which is very short. On a good day you barely reach my chest. Or shall I start with the eyeglasses you fished out of a box and claimed as your own, enormous round things that magnify your eyes so that your permanent response appears to be a 4.5 on the Richter? They're women's glasses, Bruno! I've never had the heart to tell you: Many times I've tried. And something else. When we were boys you were the greater writer. I had too much pride to tell you then. But. I knew. Believe me when I say, I knew it then as I know it now. It pains me to think how I never told you, and also to think of all you could have been. Forgive me, Bruno. My oldest friend. My best. I haven't done you justice. You have given me such company at the end of my life. You, especially you, who might have found the words for it all.

Once, it was a long time ago, I found Bruno lying in the middle of the living room floor next to an empty bottle of pills. He'd had enough. All he wanted was to sleep forever. Taped to his chest was a note with three words: *GOODBYE, MY LOVES*. I shouted out. *NO, BRUNO, NO, NO, NO, NO, NO, NO, NO!* I slapped his face. At last his eyes fluttered open. His gaze was blank and dull. *WAKE UP, YOU DUMKOP!* I shouted. *LISTEN TO ME NOW: YOU HAVE TO WAKE UP!* His eyes drifted closed again. I dialed 911. I filled a bowl with cold water and threw it on him. I put my ear to his heart. Far off, a vague rustle. The ambulance came. At the hospital they pumped his stomach. *Why did you take all those pills?* the doctor asked. Bruno, sick, exhausted, coolly raised his eyes. *WHY DO YOU THINK I TOOK ALL THOSE PILLS?* he shrieked. The recovery room turned silent; everyone stared. Bruno groaned and turned toward the wall. That night I put him to bed. *Bruno*, I said. *So sorry*, he said. *So selfish*. I sighed and turned to go. *Stay with me!* he cried.

We never spoke of it after that. Just as we never spoke of our childhoods, of the dreams we shared and lost, of everything that happened and didn't happen.

Once we were sitting silently together. Suddenly one of us began to laugh. It was contagious. There was no reason for our laughter, but we began to giggle and the next thing we were rocking in our seats and howling, *howling* with laughter, tears streaming down our cheeks. A wet spot bloomed in my crotch and that made us laugh harder, I was banging the table and fighting for air, I thought: Maybe this is how I'll go, in a fit of laughter, what could be better, laughing and crying, laughing and singing, laughing so as to forget that I am alone, that it is the end of my life, that death is waiting outside the door for me.

When I was a boy I liked to write. It was the only thing I wanted to do with my life. I invented imaginary people and filled notebooks with their stories. I wrote about a boy who grew up and got so hairy people hunted him for his fur. He had to hide in the trees, and he fell in love with a bird who thought she was a three-hundred-pound gorilla. I wrote about Siamese twins, one of which was in love with me. I thought the sex scenes were purely original. And yet. When I got older I decided I wanted to be a real writer. I tried to write about real things. I wanted to describe the world, because to live in an undescribed world was too lonely. I wrote three books before I was twenty-one, who knows what happened to them. The first was about Slonim, the town where I lived which was sometimes Poland and sometimes Russia. I drew a map of it for the frontispiece, labeling the houses and shops, here was Kipnis the butcher, and here Grodzenski the tailor, and here lived Fishl Shapiro who was either a great *tzaddik* or an idiot, no one could decide, and here the square and the field where we played, and here was where the river got wide and here narrow, and here the forest began, and here stood the tree from which Beyla Asch hanged herself, and here and here. And yet. When I gave it to the only person in Slonim whose opinion I cared about, she just shrugged and said she liked it better when I made things up. So I wrote a second book, and I made up everything. I filled it with men who grew wings, and trees with their roots growing into the sky, people who forgot their own names and people who couldn't forget anything; I even made up words. When it was finished I ran all the way to her house. I raced through the door, up the stairs, and handed it to the only person in Slonim whose opinion I cared about. I leaned against the wall and watched her face as she read. It grew dark out, but she kept reading. Hours went by. I slid to the floor. She read and read. When she finished she looked up. For a long time she didn't speak. Then she said maybe I shouldn't make up *everything*, because that made it hard to believe *anything*.

Another person might have given up. I started again. This time I didn't write about real things and I didn't write about imaginary things. I wrote about the only thing I knew. The pages piled up. Even after the only person whose opinion I cared about left on a boat for America, I continued to fill pages with her name.

After she left, everything fell apart. No Jew was safe. There were rumors of unfathomable things, and because we couldn't fathom them we failed to believe them, until we had no choice and it was too late. I was working in Minsk, but I lost my job and went home to Slonim. The Germans pushed east. They got closer and closer. The morning we heard their tanks approaching, my mother told me to hide in the woods. I wanted to take my youngest brother, he was only thirteen, but she said she would take him herself. Why did I listen? Because it was easier? I ran out to the woods. I lay still on the ground. Dogs barked in the distance. Hours went by. And then the shots. So many shots. For some reason, they didn't scream. Or maybe I couldn't hear their screams. Afterwards, only silence. My body was numb, I remember I tasted blood in my mouth. I don't know how much time passed. Days. I never went back. When I got up again, I'd shed the only part of me that had ever thought I'd find words for even the smallest bit of life.

And yet.

A couple of months after my heart attack, fifty-seven years after I'd given it up, I started to write again. I did it for myself alone, not for anyone else, and that was the difference. It didn't matter if I found the words, and more than that, I knew it would be impossible to find the right ones. And because I accepted that what I'd once believed was possible was in fact impossible, and because I knew I would never show a word of it to anyone, I wrote a sentence:

Once upon a time there was a boy.

It remained there, staring up from the otherwise blank page for days. The next week I added another. Soon there was a whole page. It made me happy, like talking aloud to myself, which I sometimes do.

Once I said to Bruno, *Take a guess, how many pages do you think I have?*

No idea, he said.

Write a number, I said, *and slip it across the table.* He shrugged and took a pen out of his pocket. He thought for a minute or two, studying my face. *A ballpark guess,* I said. He hunched over his napkin, scrawled a number, and turned it over. I wrote down the real number, 301, on my own napkin. We pushed the napkins across the table. I picked up Bruno's. For reasons I can't explain he had written 200,000. He picked up my napkin and turned it over. His face fell.

At times I believed that the last page of my book and the last page of my life were one and the same, that when my book ended I'd end, a great wind would sweep through my rooms carrying the pages away, and when the air cleared of all those fluttering white sheets the room would be silent, the chair where I sat would be empty.

Every morning, I wrote a little more. Three-hundred and one, it's not nothing. Now and then, when I'd finished, I'd go to the movies. It's always a big event for me. Maybe I buy some popcorn and— if people are around who'll look—spill it. I like to sit up front, I like for the screen to fill my whole view so that there is nothing to distract me from the moment. And then I want the moment to last forever. I can't tell you how happy it makes me to watch it up there, blown up. I would say *larger than life*, but I've never understood that expression. What is larger than life? To sit in the front row and look up at a beauti-ful girl's face two stories high and have the vibrations of her voice massaging your legs is to be reminded of the size of life. So I sit in the front row. If I leave with a crick in my neck and a fading hard-on it was a good seat. I'm not a dirty man. I'm a man who wanted to be as large as life.

There are passages of my book I know by heart.

By heart, this is not an expression I use lightly.

My heart is weak and unreliable. When I go it will be my heart. I try to burden it as little as possible. If something is going to have an impact, I direct it else-where. My gut for example, or my lungs, which might seize up for a moment but have never yet failed to take another breath. When I pass a mirror and catch a glimpse of myself, or I'm at the bus stop and some kids come up behind me and say, *Who smells shit?*—small daily humiliations—these I take, generally speaking, in my liver. Other damages I take in other places. The pancreas I reserve for being struck by all that's been lost. It's true that there's so much, and the organ is so small. But. You would be surprised how much it can take, all I feel is a quick sharp pain and then it's over. Sometimes I imagine my own autopsy. Disappointment in myself: right kidney. Disappointment of others in me: left kidney. Personal failures: *kishkes*. I don't mean to make it sound like I've made a science of it. It's not that well thought out. I take it where it comes. It's just that I notice certain patterns. When the clocks are turned back and the dark falls before I'm ready, this, for reasons I can't explain, I feel in my wrists. And when I wake up and my fingers are stiff, almost certainly I was dreaming of my childhood. The field where we used to play, the field in which everything was discovered and everything was possible. (We ran so hard we thought we would spit blood: to me that is the sound of childhood, heavy breathing and shoes scraping the hard earth.) Stiffness of the fingers is the dream of childhood as it's been returned to me at the end of my life. I have to run them under the hot water, steam clouding the mirror, outside the rustle of pigeons. Yesterday I saw a man kicking a dog and I felt it behind my eyes. I don't know what to call this, a place before tears. The pain of forgetting: spine. The pain of remembering: spine. All the times I have suddenly realized that my parents are dead, even now, it still surprises me, to exist in the world while that which made me has ceased to exist: my knees, it takes half a tube of Ben-Gay and a big production just to bend them. To everything a season, to every time I've woken only to make the mistake of believing for a moment that someone was sleeping beside me: a hemorrhoid. Loneliness: there is no organ that can take it all.

Every morning, a little more.

Once upon a time there was a boy. He lived in a village that no longer exists, in a house that no longer exists, on the edge of a field that no longer exists, where everything was discovered and everything was possible. A stick could be a sword. A pebble could be a diamond. A tree a castle.

Once upon a time there was a boy who lived in a house across the field from a girl who no longer exists. They made up a thousand games. She was Queen and he was King. In the autumn light, her hair shone like a crown. They collected the world in small handfuls. When the sky grew dark they parted with leaves in their hair.

Once upon a time there was a boy who loved a girl, and her laughter was a question he wanted to spend his whole life answering. When they were ten he asked her to marry him. When they were eleven he kissed her for the first time. When they were thirteen they got into a fight and for three weeks they didn't talk. When they were fifteen she showed him the scar on her left breast. Their love was a secret they told no one. He promised her he would never love another girl as long as he lived. *What if I die?* she asked. *Even then,* he said. For her sixteenth birthday he gave her an English dictionary and together they learned the words. *What's this?* he'd ask, tracing his index finger around her ankle, and she'd look it up. *And this?* he'd ask, kissing her elbow. *Elbow! What kind of word is that?* and then he'd lick it, making her giggle. *What about this?* he asked, touching the soft skin behind her ear. *I don't know,* she said, turning off the flashlight and rolling over, with a sigh, onto her back. When they were seventeen they made love for the first time, on a bed of straw in a shed. Later—when things happened that they could never have imagined—she wrote him a letter that said: *When will you learn that there isn't a word for everything?*

Once upon a time there was a boy who loved a girl whose father was shrewd enough to scrounge together all the zloty he had to send his youngest daughter to America. At first she refused to go, but the boy also knew enough to insist, swearing on his life that he'd earn some money and find a way to follow her. So she left. He got a job in the nearest city, work-

ing as a janitor in a hospital. At night he stayed up
writing his book. He sent her a letter into which he'd
copied eleven chapters in tiny handwriting. He wasn't
even sure the mail would get through. He saved all
the money he could. One day he was laid off. No one
said why. He returned home. In the summer of 1941,
the *Einsatzgruppen* drove deeper east, killing hundreds
of thousands of Jews. On a bright, hot day in July,
they entered Slonim. At that hour, the boy happened
to be lying on his back in the woods thinking about
the girl. You could say it was his love for her that saved
him. In the years that followed, the boy became a man
who became invisible. In this way, he escaped death.

Once upon a time a man who had become invisible arrived in America. He'd spent three and a half
years hiding, mostly in trees, but also cracks, cellars,
holes. Then it was over. The Russian tanks rolled in.
For six months he lived in a Displaced Persons camp.
He got word to his cousin who was a locksmith in
America. In his head, he practiced over and over the
only words he knew in English. *Knee. Elbow. Ear.*
Finally his papers came through. He took a train to a
boat, and after a week he arrived in New York Harbor.
A cool day in November. Folded in his hand was the
address of the girl. That night he lay awake on the
floor of his cousin's room. The radiator clanged and
hissed, but he was grateful for the warmth. In the
morning his cousin explained to him three times how

to take the subway to Brooklyn. He bought a bunch
of roses but they wilted because though his cousin had
explained the way three times he still got lost. At last
he found the place. Only as his finger pressed the
doorbell did the thought cross his mind that perhaps
he should have called. She opened the door. She wore
a blue scarf over her hair. He could hear the broad-
cast of a ball game through the neighbor's wall.

Once upon a time, the woman who had been a
girl got on a boat to America and threw up the whole
way, not because she was seasick but because she was
pregnant. When she found out, she wrote to the boy.
Every day she waited for a letter from him, but none
came. She got bigger and bigger. She tried to hide it
so she wouldn't lose her job at the dress factory where
she worked. A few weeks before the baby was born,
she got news from someone who heard they were
killing Jews in Poland. *Where?* she asked, but no one
knew where. She stopped going to work. She
couldn't bring herself to get out of bed. After a week,
the son of her boss came to see her. He brought her
food to eat, and put a bouquet of flowers in a vase by
her bed. When he found out she was pregnant, he
called a midwife. A baby boy was born. One day the
girl sat up in bed and saw the son of her boss rocking her child in the sunlight. A few months later, she
agreed to marry him. Two years later, she had another
child.

The man who had become invisible stood in her living room listening to all of this. He was twenty-five years old. He had changed so much since he last saw her and now part of him wanted to laugh a hard, cold laugh. She gave him a small photograph of the boy, who was now five. Her hand was shaking. She said: *You stopped writing. I thought you were dead.* He looked at the photograph of the boy who would grow up to look like him, who, although the man didn't know it then, would go to college, fall in love, fall out of love, become a famous writer. *What's his name?* he asked. She said: *I called him Isaac.* They stood for a long time in silence as he stared at the picture. At last he managed three words: *Come with me.* The sound of children shouting came from the street below. She squeezed her eyes shut. *Come with me*, he said, holding out his hand. Tears rolled down her face. Three times he asked her. She shook her head. *I can't*, she said. She looked down at the floor. *Please*, she said. And so he did the hardest thing he'd ever done in his life: he picked up his hat and walked away.

And if the man who once upon a time had been a boy who promised he'd never fall in love with another girl as long as he lived kept his promise, it wasn't because he was stubborn or even loyal. He couldn't help it. And having hidden for three and a half years, hiding his love for a son who didn't know he existed didn't seem unthinkable. Not if it was what the only woman he would ever love needed him to do. After all, what does it mean for a man to hide one more thing when he has vanished completely?

THE NIGHT BEFORE I was scheduled to model for the art class I was nervous and excited. I unbuttoned my shirt and took that off. Then I unbuckled my pants and took off those. My undershirt. The underpants. I stood in front of the hall mirror in my socks. I could hear the cries of children in the playground across the street. The string for the bulb was overhead, but I didn't pull it. I stood looking at myself in what light was left. I've never thought of myself as handsome.

As a child my mother and my aunts used to tell me that I would grow up to *become* handsome. It was clear to me that I wasn't anything to look at then, but I believed that some measure of beauty might come to me eventually. I don't know what I thought: that my ears, which stuck out at an undignified angle, would recede, that my head would somehow grow to fit them? That my hair, not unlike a toilet brush in texture, would, with time, unkink itself and reflect light? That my face, which held so little promise— eyelids as heavy as a frog's, lips on the thin side— would somehow transform itself into something not regrettable? For years I would wake up in the morning and go to the mirror, hoping. Even when I was

too old to continue hoping, I still did. I grew older
and there was no improvement. If anything, things
went downhill when I entered adolescence and was
abandoned by the pleasant attractiveness that all children have. The year of my Bar Mitzvah I was visited
by a plague of acne that stayed four years. But still I
continued to hope. As soon as the acne cleared my
hairline began to recede, as if it wanted to disassóci-
ate itself from the embarrassment of my face. My ears,
pleased with the new attention they now enjoyed,
seemed to strain farther into the spotlight. My eyelids
drooped—some muscle tension had to give to support
the struggle of the ears—and my eyebrows took on a
life of their own, for a brief period achieving all anyone
could have hoped for them, and then surpassing those
hopes and approaching Neanderthal. For years I
continued to hope that things would turn out differently, but I never looked in the mirror and confused
what I saw for anything but what it was. With time I
thought about it less and less. Then hardly at all. And
yet. It's possible that some small part of me has never
stopped hoping—that even now there are moments
when I stand in front of the mirror, my wrinkled *pischer*
in my hand, and believe my beauty is yet to come.

The morning of the class, September 19th, I woke
in a state of excitement. I got dressed and ate my
breakfast bar of Metamucil, then went to the bathroom and waited in anticipation. Nothing for half an

hour, but my optimism didn't wane. Then I managed
a series of pellets. Full of hope, I waited some more.
It's not impossible that I will die sitting on the toilet,
pants around my ankles. After all, I spend so much
time there, all of this raising another question, namely:
who will be the first person to see me dead?

I gave myself a sponge bath and dressed. The day
crawled on. When I'd waited as long as I could, I took
a bus across town. The newspaper ad was folded into
a square in my pocket and I took it out a few times
to look at the address, even though I knew it by heart.
It took me a while to find the right building. At first
I thought there was some mistake. I passed it three
times until I realized it had to be the one. It was an
old warehouse. The front door was rusted and held
open with a cardboard box. For a moment I let myself
imagine that I'd been lured there to be robbed and
killed. I pictured my body on the floor in a pool of
blood.

The sky had gotten dark and it was starting to
rain. I felt grateful for the feel of wind and the drops
on my face, thinking I had little time to live. I stood
there, unable to go forward, unable to turn back.
Finally I heard laughter coming from inside. See,
you're being ridiculous, I thought. I reached for the
handle on the door and just then it swung open. A
girl wearing a sweater too big for her came out. She
pushed up her sleeves. Her arms were thin and pale.

Do you need help? she asked. There were tiny holes in the sweater. It came down to her knees, and under it she was wearing a skirt. Her legs were bare, despite the chill. *I'm looking for a drawing class. There was an ad in the paper, maybe I have the wrong place*—I fumbled in my coat pocket for the ad. She gestured upstairs. *Second floor, first room on the right. But it doesn't start for another hour.* I looked up at the building. I said, *I thought I might get lost so I came early.* She was shivering. I took off my raincoat. *Here, wear this. You'll get sick.* She shrugged, but didn't move to take it. I held my arm outstretched until it was clear she wasn't going to.

There was nothing more to say. There were steps, so I went up them. My heart was beating. I considered turning back: past the girl, down the rubbish-filled street, through the city, to my apartment where there was work to be done. What kind of fool was I, to think they wouldn't turn away when I took off my shirt and dropped my pants and stood naked before them? To think that they would observe my varicose-veined legs, my hairy, sagging *knedelach* and, what—start to sketch? And yet. I didn't turn back. I gripped the banister and climbed the stairs. I could hear the rain on the skylight. A dirty light filtered through. At the top of the stairs there was a hallway. To the left was a room where a man was painting a large canvas. The room on the right was empty. There was a block covered in a length of black velvet, and a disorganized circle of folding chairs and easels. I went in and sat down to wait.

  After half an hour people started to wander in. A woman asked me who I was. *I'm here about the ad*, I told her. *I called and spoke to someone.* To my relief, she seemed to understand. She showed me where to change, a corner where a makeshift curtain had been hung. I stood there and she pulled it around me. I heard her footsteps move away, and still I stood there. A minute passed and then I removed my shoes. I lined them up neatly. I took off my socks and put those into the shoes. I unbuttoned my shirt and took that off; there was a hanger, so I hung it. I heard chairs scraping and then laughter. Suddenly I didn't care anymore about being seen. I would have liked to grab my shoes and slip out of the room, down the stairs, and away from there. And yet. I unzipped my pants. Then it occurred to me: what, exactly, did "nude" mean?

  Did they really mean no underwear? I deliberated. What if they expected underwear and I came out with my you-know-whats swinging? I reached for the ad in the pocket of my pants. *NUDE MODEL*, it said. Don't be an idiot, I told myself. These aren't amateurs. The underwear was down around my knees when the woman's footsteps returned. *Are you all right in there?* Someone opened a window and a car splashed past in the rain. *Fine, fine. I'll be out in a moment.* I looked down. There was a tiny smear. My bowels. They never cease to appall me. I stepped out of my underwear and crumpled it into a ball.

I thought: Maybe I've come here to die after all. Wasn't it true that I had never seen the warehouse before? Maybe these were what they called angels. The girl outside, of course, how could I have not noticed, she had been so pale. I stood without moving. I was starting to get cold. I thought: So this is how death takes you. Naked in an abandoned warehouse. Tomorrow Bruno would come downstairs and knock on my door and there would be no answer. Forgive me, Bruno. I would have liked to say goodbye. I'm sorry to have disappointed you with so few pages. Then I thought: My book. Who would find it? Would it be thrown away, along with the rest of my things? Even though I thought I'd been writing it for myself, the truth was that I wanted someone to read it.

I closed my eyes and inhaled. Who would wash my body? Who would say the Mourner's Kaddish? I thought: My mother's hands. I pulled back the curtain. My heart was in my throat. I stepped forward. Squinting in the light, I stood before them.

I was never a man of great ambition.

I cried too easily.

I didn't have a head for science.

Words often failed me.

While others prayed I only moved my lips.

Please.

The woman who'd shown me where to change pointed to the box draped in velvet.

Stand here.

I walked across the floor. There were maybe twelve of them, sitting in chairs holding their drawing pads. The girl in the big sweater was there.

Anything that feels comfortable.

I didn't know which way to face. They were in a circle, someone was going to have to face my rectal side no matter which way you cut it. I chose to remain as I was. I let my arms hang at my sides and focused on a spot on the floor. They lifted their pencils.

Nothing happened. Instead I felt the plush cloth under the soles of my feet, the hairs rising on my arms, my fingers like ten small weights pulling downward. I felt my body waking under twelve pairs of eyes. I lifted my head.

Try to keep still, the woman said.

I stared at a crack in the concrete floor. I could hear their pencils moving across the pages. I wanted to smile. Already my body was starting to revolt, the knees beginning to shake and the back muscles straining. But. I didn't care. If need be, I would stand there all day. Fifteen, twenty minutes passed. Then the woman said: *Why don't we take a quick break and then we'll start again with a different pose.*

I sat. I stood. I rotated so that those who hadn't

gotten my rectal side now got it. Pages turned. It went
on, I don't know how long. Once I thought I would
pass out. I cycled through feeling to numbness to
feeling to numbness. My eyes watered with pain.

Somehow I got back into my clothes. I couldn't
find my underwear and was too tired to look. I made
it down the stairs, clutching the banister. The woman
came down after me, she said, *Wait, you forgot the fifteen
dollars*. I took it, and when I went to put it into my
pocket I felt the ball of underwear there. *Thank you*.
I meant that. I was exhausted. But happy.

I want to say somewhere: I've tried to be forgiving.
And yet. There were times in my life, whole years,
when anger got the better of me. Ugliness turned me
inside out. There was a certain satisfaction in bitterness. I courted it. It was standing outside, and I invited
it in. I scowled at the world. And the world scowled
back. We were locked in a stare of mutual disgust. I
used to let the door slam in people's faces. I farted
where I wanted to fart. I accused cashiers of cheating
me out of a penny, while holding the penny in my
hand. And then one day I realized I was on my way
to being the sort of schmuck who poisons pigeons.
People crossed the street to avoid me. I was a human
cancer. And to be honest: I wasn't really angry. Not
anymore. I had left my anger somewhere long ago.
Put it down on a park bench and walked away. And
yet. It had been so long, I didn't know any other way

of being. One day I woke up and said to myself: *It's not too late.* The first days were strange. I had to practice smiling in front of the mirror. But it came back to me. It was as if a weight had been lifted. I let go, and something let go of me. A couple of months later, I found Bruno.

When I got home from the art class, there was a note from Bruno on my door. It said: *WARE ARE YOU?* I was too tired to climb the stairs to tell him. Inside it was dark and I pulled the string for the bulb in the hallway. I saw myself in the mirror. My hair, what was left of it, stuck up in the back like a wave at its crest. My face looked shriveled like something left out in the rain.

I fell into bed still wearing my clothes minus the underwear. It was past midnight when the telephone rang. I awoke from a dream in which I was teaching my brother Josef how to pee in an arc. Sometimes I have nightmares. But this wasn't one. We were in the woods, the cold bit at our behinds. Steam rose from the snow. Josef turned to me, smiling. A beautiful child, blond with gray eyes. Gray, like the ocean on a sunless day, or the elephant I saw in the town square when I was his age. Plain as day, standing in the dusty sunlight. Later no one could remember having seen it, and because it was impossible to understand how an elephant would have arrived in Slonim, no one believed me. But I saw it.

A siren sounded in the distance. Just as my brother opened his mouth to speak, the dream broke off and I woke up in the darkness of my bedroom, the rain pit-pattering on the glass. The telephone continued to ring. Bruno, no doubt. I would have ignored it if I hadn't been afraid he'd call the police. Why doesn't he just tap on the radiator with his walking stick like he always does? Three taps means ARE YOU ALIVE?, two means YES, one, NO. We only do it at night, during the day there are too many other noises, and anyway, it isn't foolproof since usually Bruno falls asleep wearing his Walkman.

I threw off the sheets and stumbled across the floor, banging into a table leg. *HELLO?* I shouted into the phone, but the line was dead. I hung up, went to the kitchen, and took a glass down from the cabinet. The water gurgled in the pipes and splattered out in a burst. I drank some down and then remembered my plant. I've had it for almost ten years. It's barely alive, but it is alive. More brown than green. There are parts that have withered. But still it lives, leaning always to the left. Even when I rotate it so that what faced the sun no longer faces the sun, it stubbornly leans to the left, choosing against physical need in favor of an act of creativity. I poured the rest of my water into its pot. What does it mean, anyway, *to flourish?*

A moment later the phone rang again. *OK, OK,* I said, picking up the receiver. *No need to wake the whole building.* There was silence on the other end. I said: *Bruno?*

Is this Mr. Leopold Gursky?

I assumed it was someone trying to sell me something. They're always calling to sell. Once they said if I sent in a check for $99 I'd be pre-approved for a credit card, and I said, *Right, sure, and if I step under a pigeon I'm preapproved for a load of shit.*

But the man said he wasn't trying to sell me anything. He'd locked himself out of his house. He'd called Information for the number of a locksmith. I told him I was retired. The man paused. He seemed unable to believe his bad luck. He'd already called three other people and no one answered. *It's pouring out here,* he said.

Couldn't you stay somewhere else for the night? In the morning it'll be easy to find a locksmith. They're a dime a dozen.

No, he said.

All right, I mean, if it's too much . . . he began, then paused, waiting for me to speak up. I didn't. *OK, then.* I could hear the disappointment in his voice. *Sorry to have disturbed you.*

And yet he didn't hang up and neither did I. I was filled with guilt. I thought: What do I need with sleep? There will be time. Tomorrow. Or the next day.

OK, OK, I said, even though I didn't want to say it. I'd have to dig up my tools. I might as well be looking for a needle in a haystack or a Jew in Poland. *Hold on a second, will you—I'm getting a pen.*

He gave me an address all the way uptown. Only after I hung up did I remember I could wait forever before a bus came at that hour. I had the card in the kitchen drawer for Goldstar Car Service, not that I ever call it. But. You never know. I ordered a car and started digging through the hall closet for my toolbox. Instead, I found the box of old eyeglasses. Who knows where I got them. Someone probably selling it on the street with some mismatched china and a doll with no head. From time to time I try on a pair. Once I cooked an omelet wearing a pair of ladies' reading glasses. It was a mammoth omelet, it struck fear in my heart just to look at it. I fished around in the box and pulled out a pair. They were square and flesh-colored, with lenses half an inch thick. I slipped them on. The floor dropped from under me, and when I tried to take a step it lurched upwards. I staggered toward the hall mirror. In an effort to gain some focus I zoomed in, but miscalculated and banged into the glass. The buzzer rang. When your pants are down around your ankles, that's when everyone arrives. *I'll be down in a minute,* I shouted into the speaker. When I took off the glasses, the toolbox was there under my nose. I ran my hand across its battered top. Then I grabbed my raincoat off the floor, smoothed down my hair in the mirror, and went out.

LAUGHING & CRYING

I studied it for a few minutes. It wasn't right. I added another word.

day, but no wallet. Both pockets of the coat, No, No. I must have left it home in the rush. Then I remembered my fee from the art class. I dug past the peppermints, the note, the underwear, and came up with it. *Sorry*, I said. *How embarrassing. All I have on me is fifteen.* I admit I was reluctant to part with the bills, hard-earned wasn't the word for them but something else, more bittersweet. But after a brief pause the turban bobbed and the money was accepted.

The man was standing under the doorway. Of course he hadn't expected me in a limousine, and out I'd popped like Mr. Locksmith to the Stars. I was humiliated, I wanted to explain, *Believe me, I'd never mistake myself for anyone special.* But it was pouring still, and I thought he needed me more than he needed any explanation of how I got there. His hair was matted down from the rain. He thanked me three times for coming. *It's nothing*, I said. And yet. I knew I almost hadn't come.

It was a tricky lock. The man stood above me, holding my flashlight. The rain was dripping down the back of my neck. I felt how much depended on my unlocking that lock. The minutes passed. I tried and failed. Tried and failed. And then at last my heart started to race. I turned the handle and the door slipped open.

We stood dripping in the hallway. He took off his shoes, so I took off mine. He thanked me again, and went to change into dry clothes and call me a car. I tried to protest, saying I could take the bus or hail a taxi, but he wouldn't hear of it, what with the rain. He left me in the living room. I wandered into the dining room, and from there I caught sight of a roomful of books. I'd never seen so many books in one place that wasn't a library. I walked in.

I, too, like to read. Once a month I go to the local branch. For myself I pick a novel and for Bruno with his cataracts a book on tape. At first he was doubtful. *What am I supposed to do with this?* he said, looking at the box set of *Anna Karenina* like I'd handed him an enema. And yet. A day or two later I was going about my business when a voice from above bellowed, *ALL HAPPY FAMILIES RESEMBLE ONE ANOTHER*, nearly giving me a conniption. After that he listened to whatever I brought him at top volume, then returned it to me without comment. One afternoon I came back from the library with *Ulysses*. The next morning I was in the bathroom when, *STATELY PLUMP BUCK MULLIGAN*, rang out from above. For a month straight he listened. He had a habit of pressing the stop button and rewinding when he hadn't fully understood something. *INELUCTABLE MODALITY OF THE VISIBLE: AT LEAST THAT.* Pause, rewind. *INELUCTABLE MODALITY OF THE.* Pause, rewind. *INELUCTABLE MODALITY.* Pause. *INELUCT.* When the due date approached he wanted it renewed. By then I'd had it with his stopping and starting, so I went to The Wiz and got him a Sony Sportsman, and now he schleps it around clipped to his belt. For all I know he just likes the sound of an Irish accent.

I busied myself looking through the man's shelves. Out of habit I looked to see if there was anything by my son, Isaac. Sure enough there was. And not just one book, but four. I ran my finger along their spines. I stopped on *Glass Houses* and took it off the shelf. A beautiful book. Stories. I've read them I don't know how many times. There's one—the title story. It's my favorite, not that I don't love them all. But this one stands alone. Not alone, but apart. It's short, but every time I read it I cry. It's about an angel who lives on Ludlow Street. Not far from me, just across Delancey. He's lived there for so long he can't remember why God put him on earth. Every night the angel talks aloud to God, and every day he waits for some word from Him. To pass the time, he walks through the city. In the beginning he's in the habit of marveling at everything. He starts a collection of pebbles. Teaches himself difficult math. And yet. With each day that passes he's blinded a little less by the beauty of the world. At night the angel lies awake listening to the footsteps of the widow who lives above him, and every morning on the stairs he passes the old man, Mr. Grossmark, who spends his days dragging himself upstairs and down, upstairs and down, muttering,

Who's there? So far as he can tell that's all he ever says, except for once when out of nowhere he turned to the angel as he passed on the stairs and said, *Who am I?* which so startled the angel who never speaks and is never spoken to that he said nothing, not even: *You're Grossmark, the human being.* The more sadness he sees, the more his heart begins to turn against God. He starts to roam the streets at night, stopping for anyone who looks like they need an ear. The things he hears— it's too much. He can't understand it. When he asks God why He's made him so useless, the angel's voice cracks trying to hold back angry tears. Eventually he stops talking to God altogether. One night he meets a man under a bridge. They share the vodka the man has in a brown bag. And because the angel is drunk and lonely and angry with God, and because, without his even knowing it, he feels the urge, familiar among humans, to confide in someone, he tells the man the truth: that he's an angel. The man doesn't believe him, but the angel insists. The man asks him to prove it, and so the angel lifts his shirt despite the cold and shows the man the perfect circle on his chest, which is the mark of an angel. But that means nothing to the man, who doesn't know from the mark of angels, so he says, *Show me something God can do,* and the angel, naïve like all angels, points to the man. And because the man thinks he's lying, he punches the angel in the stomach, sending him tottering backwards off the pier and plunging into the dark river. Where he drowns, because one thing about angels is that they can't swim.

Alone in that roomful of books, I held my son's book in my hands. It was the middle of the night. Past the middle. I thought: Poor Bruno. By now he's probably called the morgue to find out if anyone brought in an old man with an index card in his wallet that says: *MY NAME IS LEO GURSKY I HAVE NO FAMILY PLEASE CALL PINELAWN CEMETERY I HAVE A PLOT THERE IN THE JEWISH PART THANK YOU FOR YOUR CONSIDERATION.*

I turned my son's book over to look at his photograph. We met once. Not met, but stood face to face. It was at a reading at the 92nd Street Y. I bought tickets four months in advance. Many times in my life I'd imagined our meeting. I as his father, he as my son. And yet. I knew it never could happen, not the way I wanted. I'd accepted that the most I could hope for was a place in the audience. But during the reading something came over me. Afterwards, I found myself standing in line, my hands shaking as I pressed into his the scrap of paper on which I'd written my name. He glanced at it and copied it into a book. I tried to say something but there was no sound. He smiled and thanked me. And yet. I didn't budge. *Is there something else?* he asked. I flapped my hands. The woman behind me gave me an impatient look and pushed forward to greet him. Like a fool I flapped.

What could he do? He signed the woman's book. It was uncomfortable for everyone. My hands danced on. The line had to move around me. Occasionally he looked up at me, bewildered. Once, he smiled at me the way you smile at an idiot. But my hands fought to tell him everything. At least as much as they could before a security guard firmly grasped my elbow and escorted me out the door.

It was winter. Fat white flakes drifted down under the street lamps. I waited for my son to come out but he never came. Maybe there was a back door, I don't know. I took the bus home. I walked down my snow-covered street. Out of habit I turned and checked for my footsteps. When I arrived at my building I looked for my name on the buzzers. And because I know that sometimes I see things that aren't there, after dinner I called Information to ask if I was listed. That night before I went to sleep, I opened the book, which I'd put on my bedside table. *TO LEON GURSKY*, it said.

I was still holding the book when the man whose door I'd unlocked came up behind me. *You know it?* he asked. I dropped it and it landed with a thud at my feet, my son's face staring up. I didn't know what I was doing. I tried to explain. *I'm his father*, I said. Or maybe I said: *He's my son.* Whatever it was, I got the point across because the man looked shocked and then he looked surprised and then he looked like he didn't

believe me. Which was fine with me, because after all
who did I think I was, showing up in a limousine, picking a lock, and then claiming to be the progenitor of
a famous writer?

Suddenly I was tired, more tired than I'd been in
years. I leaned over, picked the book up, and put it
back on the shelf. The man kept looking at me, but
just then the car honked outside which was lucky
because I'd had enough of being looked at for one day.
Well, I said, making my way toward the front door, *I'd
better be going*. The man reached for his wallet, took
out a hundred-dollar bill, and handed it to me. *His
father?* he asked. I pocketed the money and handed
him a complimentary peppermint. I stuffed my feet
into my wet shoes. *Not really his father*, I said. And
because I didn't know what else to say, I said: *More
like his uncle*. This seemed to confuse him enough, but
just in case I added: *Not exactly his uncle*. He raised his
eyebrows. I picked up my toolbox and stepped out into
the rain. He tried to thank me again for coming but
I was already on my way down the stairs. I got into
the car. He was still standing in the doorway, looking
out. To prove that I was off my rocker, I gave him the
Queen's wave.

It was three in the morning when I got home. I
climbed into bed. I was exhausted. But I couldn't sleep.
I lay on my back, listening to the rain and thinking
about my book. I'd never given it a title, because what

does a book need with a title unless someone is going to read it?

I got out of bed and went to the kitchen. I keep my manuscript in a box in the oven. I took it out, set it on the kitchen table, and rolled a sheet of paper into the typewriter. For a long time I sat looking at the blank page. With two fingers I picked out a title:

Bruno's note was still taped to the door. I crumpled it into my pocket.

A black limousine idled in the street, rain falling in the headlights. Other than that, there were only a few empty cars parked along the curb. I was about to go back into the building, but the limousine driver rolled down the window and called my name. He wore a purple turban. I walked up to the window. *There must be a mistake*, I said. *I ordered a car.*

OK, he said.

But this is a limousine, I pointed out.

OK, he repeated, motioning me in.

I can't pay extra.

The turban bobbed. He said: *Get in before you get soaking.*

I ducked inside. There were leather seats, and a pair of crystal liquor bottles along the sideboard. It was bigger than I'd imagined. The soft exotic music coming from up front and the gentle rhythm of the windshield wipers only barely reached me. He pointed the nose of the car into the street and we headed into the night. The traffic lights bled into the puddles. I opened a crystal bottle but it was empty. There was a little jar of peppermints and I filled my pockets. When I looked down my fly was open.

I sat up and cleared my throat.

Ladies and gentlemen, I'll do my best to keep this brief, you've all been so patient. The truth is I'm shocked, really, I'm pinching myself. An honor I could have only dreamed of, the Goldstar Lifetime Achievement Award, I'm practically speechless. . . . Has it really been? And yet. Yes. All of the evidence suggests. A lifetime.

We made our way through the city. I've walked through all of those neighborhoods, my business took me all over the city. They even knew me in Brooklyn, I went everywhere. Picking locks for the Hasids. Locks for the *shvartzers*. Sometimes I even walked for pleasure, a whole Sunday I might have spent just walking. Once, years ago, I found myself in front of the Botanical Garden and went in to see the cherry trees. I bought some Cracker Jacks, and watched the fat lazy goldfish swimming in their pool. There was a wedding party taking photographs under a tree, the white blossoms made it look as if it alone had been caught in a snowstorm. I found my way to the tropical greenhouse. It was another world inside, wet and warm, like the breath of people making love had been trapped there. With my finger I wrote on the glass *LEO GURSKY*.

The limousine came to a stop. I put my face up to the window. *Which one?* The driver pointed to a townhouse. It was beautiful, with steps up to the door and leaves carved in stone. *Seventeen dollars*, the driver said. I felt in my pocket for my wallet. No. Other pocket. Bruno's note, my underwear from earlier that

LAUGHING & CRYING & WRITING

Then another:

LAUGHING & CRYING & WRITING & WAITING

I crumpled it into a ball and dropped it on the floor. I put the water on to boil. Outside the rain had stopped. A pigeon cooed on the windowsill. It puffed up its body, marched back and forth, and took flight. Free as a bird, so to speak. I fed another page into the machine and typed:

WORDS FOR EVERYTHING

Before I could change my mind again, I rolled it
out, laid it on top of the stack, and closed the lid of
the box. I found some brown paper and packaged it
up. On the front I wrote my son's address, which I
know by heart.

I waited for something to happen, but nothing did.
No wind that swept everything away. No heart attack.
No angel at the door.

It was five in the morning. It would be hours before
the post office opened. To pass the time, I dragged the
slide projector out from under the sofa. It's something
I do on special occasions, my birthday, say. I prop the
projector up on a shoebox, plug it in, and flip the
switch. A dusty beam lights up the wall. The slide I
keep in a jar on the kitchen shelf. I blow on it, drop
it in, advance. The picture comes into focus. A house
with a yellow door at the edge of a field. It's the end
of autumn. Between the black branches the sky is turning orange, then dark blue. Wood smoke rises from
the chimney, and through the window I can almost see
my mother leaning over a table. I run toward the house.
I can feel the cold wind against my cheeks. I reach out
my hand. And because my head is full of dreams, for
a moment I believe I can open the door and go right
through it.

Outside, it was already getting light. Before my eyes, the house of my childhood dissolved to almost nothing. I turned off the projector, ate a Metamucil bar, and went to the bathroom. When I did all I was going to do, I gave myself a sponge bath and dug through the closet for my suit. I found the galoshes I'd been looking for, and an old radio. At last, crumpled on the floor, the suit, a white summer suit, passable if you ignored the brownish stain down the front. I dressed myself. I spat into my palm and forced my hair into submission. I sat fully dressed with the brown paper package on my lap. I checked and rechecked the address. At 8:45 I put my raincoat on and tucked the package under my arm. I looked at myself in the hall mirror one last time. Then I went out the door and into the morning.

MY MOTHER'S SADNESS

1. MY NAME IS ALMA SINGER

When I was born my mother named me after every girl in a book my father gave her called *The History of Love*. She named my brother Emanuel Chaim after the Jewish historian Emanuel Ringelblum, who buried milk cans filled with testimony in the Warsaw Ghetto, and the Jewish cellist Emanuel Feuermann, who was one of the great musical prodigies of the twentieth century, and also the Jewish writer of genius Isaac Emmanuilovich Babel, and her uncle Chaim, who was a joker, a real clown, made everyone laugh like crazy, and who died by the Nazis. But my brother refused to answer to it. When people asked him his name, he made something up. He went through fifteen or twenty names. For a month he referred to himself in the third person as Mr. Fruit. On his sixth birthday he took a running leap out of a second-floor window and tried to fly. He broke his arm and got a permanent scar on his fore-head, but from then on nobody ever called him anything but Bird.

2. WHAT I AM NOT

My brother and I used to play a game. I'd point to a chair. "THIS IS NOT A CHAIR," I'd say. Bird would point to the table. "THIS IS NOT A TABLE." "THIS IS NOT A WALL," I'd say. "THAT IS NOT A CEILING." We'd go on like that. "IT IS NOT RAINING OUT." "MY SHOE IS NOT UNTIED!" Bird would yell. I'd point to my elbow. "THIS IS NOT A SCRAPE." Bird would lift his knee. "THIS IS ALSO NOT A SCRAPE!" "THAT IS NOT A KETTLE!" "NOT A CUP!" "NOT A SPOON!" "NOT DIRTY DISHES!" We denied whole rooms, years, weathers. Once, at the peak of our shouting, Bird took a deep breath. At the top of his lungs, he shrieked: "I! HAVE NOT! BEEN! UNHAPPY! MY WHOLE! LIFE!" "But you're only seven," I said.

3. MY BROTHER BELIEVES IN GOD

When he was nine and a half, he found a little red volume called *The Book of Jewish Thoughts* inscribed to our father, David Singer, on the occasion of his Bar Mitzvah. In it, Jewish thoughts are gathered under subheadings such as "Every Israelite Holds the Honor of His Entire People in His Hands," "Under the Romanoffs," and "Immortality." Soon after he found it, Bird started to wear a black velvet *kippah* around everywhere, not caring that it didn't fit right and puffed up in the back giving him a dopey look. He also got in the habit of following Mr. Goldstein, the janitor at Hebrew School who mumbled in three languages, and whose hands left behind more dust than they cleaned away. There were rumors that Mr. Goldstein slept only an hour a night in the basement of the shul; that he had been in a labor camp in Siberia, that his heart was weak, that a loud noise could kill him, that snow made him cry. Bird was drawn to him. He followed him around after Hebrew School while Mr. Goldstein vacuumed between the rows of seats, cleaned the toilets, and rubbed curses off the blackboard. It was Mr. Goldstein's job to take out of circulation the old *siddur*s that were torn or ripped, and one afternoon, with two crows as big as dogs

watching from the trees, he pushed a wheelbarrow
full of them out behind the synagogue, bumping
over rocks and tree roots, dug a hole, said a prayer,
and buried them. "Can't just throw them away,"
he told Bird. "Not if it has on it God's name. Has
to be buried properly."

The next week Bird started to write the four
Hebrew letters of the name no one is allowed to
pronounce and no one is allowed to throw away
on the pages of his homework. A few days later I
opened the hamper and found it written in
permanent marker on the label of his underwear.
He wrote it in chalk across our front door, scrib-
bled it across his class photograph, on the bathroom wall, and, before it came to an end, carved
it with my Swiss Army knife as high as he could
reach on the tree in front of our house.

Maybe it was because of that, or his habit of
putting his arm over his face and picking his nose
as if people couldn't tell what he was doing, or
the way he sometimes made strange noises like a
video game, but that year the couple of friends
he'd had stopped coming by to play.

Every morning he wakes early to *daven*
outside, facing Jerusalem. When I watch him from
the window, I regret having taught him to sound
out the Hebrew letters when he was only five. It
makes me sad, knowing it can't last.

4. MY FATHER DIED WHEN I WAS SEVEN

What I remember, I remember in parts. His ears. The wrinkled skin on his elbows. The stories he used to tell me about his childhood in Israel. How he used to sit in his favorite chair listening to music, and liked to sing. He spoke to me in Hebrew, and I called him *Abba*. I've forgotten almost everything, but sometimes words will come back to me, *kum-kum*, *shemesh*, *chol*, *yam*, *etz*, *neshika*, *motek*, their meanings worn off like the faces of old coins. My mother, who is English, met him while she was working on a kibbutz not far from Ashdod, the summer before she started Oxford. He was ten years older than she was. He'd been in the army, and afterwards traveled through South America. Then he went back to school and became an engineer. He liked to camp outside, and always kept a sleeping bag and two gallons of water in his trunk, and could start a fire with a piece of flint if he had to. He picked my mother up on Friday nights while the other kibbutzniks lay on blankets under a giant movie screen on the grass, petting dogs and getting high. He drove her to the Dead Sea where they floated strangely.

5. THE DEAD SEA IS THE LOWEST PLACE ON EARTH

6. NO TWO PEOPLE LOOKED LESS ALIKE THAN MY MOTHER AND FATHER

When my mother's body turned brown, and my father laughed and said she was getting to look more like him every day, it was a joke because where he was six-foot-three with bright green eyes and black hair, my mother is pale, and so small that even now, at forty-one, if you saw her from across the street you could mistake her for a girl. Bird is small and fair like her, and I am tall like my father. I am also black-haired, gap-toothed, skinny in a bad way, and fifteen.

7. THERE IS A PHOTOGRAPH OF MY MOTHER THAT NO ONE HAS EVER SEEN

In the fall, my mother went back to England to start university. Her pockets were full of sand from the lowest place on earth. She weighed 104 pounds. There's a story she sometimes tells about the train ride from Paddington Station to Oxford when she met a photographer who was almost completely blind. He wore dark sunglasses, and said he'd damaged his retinas a decade ago on a trip to Antarctica. His suit was perfectly pressed, and he held his camera in his lap. He said he saw the world differently now, and it wasn't necessarily bad. He asked if he could take a picture of her. When he raised up the lens and looked through it, my mother asked what he saw. "The same thing I always see," he said. "Which is?" "A blur," he said. "Then why do it?" she asked. "In case my eyes ever heal," he said. "So I'll know what I've been looking at." In my mother's lap there was a brown paper bag with a chopped liver sandwich my grandmother had made for her. She offered the sandwich to the almost completely blind photographer. "Aren't you hungry?" he asked. She told him that she was, but that she'd never told her mother that she hated chopped liver, and eventually it became too late to tell her, having said nothing for years. The train pulled into Oxford Station, and my mother got off, leaving behind her a trail of sand. I know there is a moral to this story, but I don't know what it is.

8. MY MOTHER IS THE MOST STUBBORN PERSON I KNOW

After five minutes, she decided that she hated Oxford. The first week of term my mother did nothing but sit in her room in a drafty stone building, watching the rain fall on the cows in Christ Church Meadow, feeling sorry for herself. She had to heat up water for tea on a hot plate. To see her tutor, she had to climb fifty-six stone stairs and bang on the door until he woke up from the cot in his study where he slept under a pile of papers. She wrote to my father in Israel almost every day on expensive French stationery, and when she ran out of that she wrote to him on graph paper torn out of a notebook. In one of these letters (which I found hidden in an old Cadbury's tin under the sofa in her study), she wrote: *The book you gave me is sitting on my desk, and every day I learn to read it a little more.* The reason she had to learn to read it was because it was written in Spanish. She watched her body turn pale again in the mirror. During the second week of term, she bought a used bicycle and rode around tacking up posters that said *WANTED: HEBREW TUTOR*, because languages came easily to her, and she wanted to be able to understand my father. A few people applied, but only one didn't back out when my mother explained that she couldn't pay, a pimply boy named Nehemia from Haifa who was in his first year and as miserable as my mother, and who felt—according to a letter she wrote to my father—the company of a girl was reason enough to agree to meet twice a week at the King's Arms for nothing more than the price of his beer. My mother was also teaching herself Spanish out of a book called *Teach Yourself Spanish*. She spent a lot of time in the Bodleian Library reading hundreds of books and not making any friends. She ordered up so many books that whenever the clerk who worked at the desk saw her coming, he tried to hide. At the end of the year, she got a First on her exams and, despite her parents' objections, dropped out of university and went to live with my father in Tel Aviv.

9. WHAT FOLLOWED WERE THE HAPPIEST YEARS OF THEIR LIVES

They lived in a sunny house covered with bougainvillea in Ramat Gan. My father planted an olive tree and a lemon tree in the garden, and dug a little trench around each for water to collect. At night they listened to American music on his shortwave radio. When the windows were open, and the wind was blowing in the right direction, they could smell the sea. Eventually they got married on the beach in Tel Aviv, and for their honeymoon they spent two months traveling in South America. When they returned, my mother started translating books into English—first from Spanish, and later from Hebrew, too. Five years passed like that, and then my father got offered a job he couldn't turn down, working for an American company in the aerospace industry.

10. THEY MOVED TO NEW YORK AND HAD ME

While my mother was pregnant with me she read three gazillion books on a wide variety of subjects. She didn't like America, but she didn't hate it, either. Two and a half years and eight gazillion books later, she had Bird. Then we moved to Brooklyn.

11. I WAS SIX WHEN MY FATHER WAS DIAGNOSED WITH PANCREATIC CANCER

That year my mother and I were driving together

in the car. She asked me to pass her bag. "I don't have it," I said. "Maybe it's in the back," she said. But it wasn't in the back. She pulled over and searched the car, but the bag was nowhere to be found. She put her head in her hands and tried to remember where she'd left her bag. She was always losing things. "One of these days," she said, "I'm going to lose my head." I tried to picture what would happen if she lost her head. In the end, though, it was my father who lost everything: weight, his hair, various internal organs.

12. HE LIKED TO COOK AND LAUGH AND SING, COULD START A FIRE WITH HIS HANDS, FIX THINGS THAT WERE BROKEN, AND EXPLAIN HOW TO LAUNCH THINGS INTO SPACE, BUT HE DIED WITHIN NINE MONTHS

13. MY FATHER WAS NOT A FAMOUS RUSSIAN WRITER

At first my mother kept everything exactly as he left it. According to Misha Shklovsky, that's what they do with famous writers' houses in Russia. But my father wasn't a famous writer. He wasn't even Russian. Then one day I came home from school and every obvious sign of him was gone. The closets were cleared of his clothes, his shoes were gone from by the door, and out in the street, next to a pile of garbage bags, stood his old chair. I went up to my bedroom and watched it through the window. The wind sent leaves cartwheeling past it on the sidewalk. An old man passed by and sat in it. I went out and fished his sweater out of the trash bin.

14. AT THE END OF THE WORLD

After my father died, Uncle Julian, my mother's brother, who is an art historian and lives in London, sent me a Swiss Army knife that he said had belonged to Dad. It had three different blades, a corkscrew, a little scissors, a pair of tweezers, and a toothpick. In the letter Uncle Julian sent with it, he said Dad had once lent it to him when he'd gone camping in the Pyrenees, and that he'd forgotten about it completely until now, and thought I might want it. *You have to be careful,* he wrote, *because the blades are sharp. It's made to help you survive in the wilderness. I wouldn't know because Aunt Frances and I checked into a hotel after it rained on us the first night and we turned into prunes. Your dad was a much better outdoorsman than I. Once, in the Negev, I saw him collect water with a funnel and a tarp. He also knew the name of every plant and if it was edible. I know it isn't much consolation, but if you come to London I will tell you the names of all of the curry places in Northwest London and if they are edible. Love, Uncle Julian. PS. Don't tell your mum that I gave this to you, because she'd probably get angry at me and say you're too young.* I examined the different parts, picking each one out with my thumbnail, and testing the blades against my finger.

I decided I would learn to survive in the wild like my father. It would be good to know in case anything happened to Mom, leaving Bird and me to fend for ourselves. I didn't tell her about the knife because Uncle Julian had meant for it to be a secret, and besides, why would my mother let me camp alone in the woods if she hardly even let me go halfway down the block?

15. WHENEVER I WENT OUT TO PLAY, MY MOTHER WANTED TO KNOW EXACTLY WHERE I WAS GOING TO BE

When I'd come in, she'd call me into her bedroom,

take me in her arms, and cover me with kisses.
She'd stroke my hair and say, "I love you so much,"
and when I sneezed she'd say, "Bless you, you
know how much I love you, don't you?" and when
I got up for a tissue she'd say, "Let me get it for
you I love you so much," and when I looked for
a pen to do my homework she'd say, "Use mine,
anything for you," and when I had an itch on my
leg she'd say, "Is this the spot, let me hug you,"
and when I said I was going up to my room she'd
call after me, "What can I do for you I love you
so *much*," and I always wanted to say, but never
said: Love me less.

16. EVERYTHING IS REMADE AS REASON

One day my mother got up from the bed she had
been lying in for almost a year. It seemed like the
first time we had seen her not through all the
water glasses that had collected around her bed,
and which, in his boredom, Bird would sometimes
try to make sing with a wet finger around the rims.
She made macaroni and cheese, one of the few
things she knows how to cook. We pretended it
was the best thing we'd ever eaten. One afternoon
she took me aside. "From now on," she said, "I'm

going to treat you like an adult." I'm only eight, I wanted to say, but didn't. She started to work again. She roamed the house in a kimono printed with red flowers, and wherever she went a trail of crumpled pages followed. Before Dad died, she used to be neater. But now if you wanted to find her all you had to do was follow the pages of crossed-out words, and at the end of the trail she'd be there, looking out the window or into a glass of water as if there were a fish in it that only she could see.

17. CARROTS

With my allowance I bought a book called *Edible Plants and Flowers in North America*. I learned that you could leach the bitterness out of acorns by boiling them in water, that wild roses are edible, and that you should avoid anything that smells of almond, has a three-leaved growth pattern, or has milky sap. I tried to identify as many plants as I could in Prospect Park. Because I knew it would be a long time before I'd be able to recognize every plant, and because there was always the chance that I'd have to survive in someplace other than North America, I also memorized the Universal Edibility Test. It's a good idea to know, since some poisonous plants, like hemlock, can look similar to some edible plants, like wild carrots and parsnips. To do the test, you have to first not eat for eight hours. Then you separate the plant into its different parts—root, leaf, stem, bud, and flower—and test a small piece of one on the inside of your wrist. If nothing happens, touch it to the inside of your lip for three minutes, and if nothing happens after that, hold it on your tongue for fifteen minutes. If nothing still happens, you can chew it without swallowing, and hold that in your mouth for fifteen minutes, and if nothing happens after that, swallow and wait eight hours, and if nothing happens after that, eat a quarter of a cup's worth, and if nothing happens after that: it's edible.

I kept *Edible Plants and Flowers in North America* under my bed in a backpack that also had my father's Swiss Army knife, a flashlight, a plastic tarp, a compass, a box of granola bars, two bags of peanut M&M's, three cans of tuna, a can opener, Band-Aids, a snakebite kit, a change of underwear, and a New York City subway map. It really should have also had a piece of _flint_, but when I tried to buy one at the hardware store they wouldn't sell it to me, either because I was too young or because they thought I was a <u>pyromaniac</u>. In an emergency, you can also strike a spark using a hunting knife and a piece of jasper, agate, or jade, but I

didn't know where to find jasper, agate, or jade.
Instead, I took some matches from the 2nd Street
Café and put them in a zip-lock bag to protect
them from the rain.

For Chanukah I asked for a sleeping bag. The
one my mother got me had pink hearts on it, was
made of flannel, and would keep me alive for about
five seconds in subzero temperatures before I died
of hypothermia. I asked her if we could take it
back and get a heavyweight down bag instead.
"Where are you planning to sleep, the Arctic
Circle?" she asked. I thought, There or maybe the
Peruvian Andes, since that's where Dad once
camped. To change the subject, I told her about
hemlock, wild carrots, and parsnip, but that turned
out to be a bad idea because her eyes got teary
and when I asked her what was wrong she said
nothing, it just reminded her of the carrots Dad
used to grow in the garden in Ramat Gan. I wanted
to ask her what else he used to grow aside from
an olive tree, a lemon tree, and carrots, but I didn't
want to make her even sadder.

I started to keep a notebook called *How to
Survive in the Wild*.

18. MY MOTHER NEVER FELL OUT OF LOVE WITH MY FATHER

She's kept her love for him as alive as the summer they first met. In order to do this, she's turned life away. Sometimes she subsists for days on water and air. Being the only known complex life-form to do this, she should have a species named after her. Once Uncle Julian told me how the sculptor and painter Alberto Giacometti said that sometimes just to paint a head you have to give up the whole figure. To paint a leaf, you have to sacrifice the whole landscape. It might seem like you're limiting yourself at first, but after a while you realize that having a quarter-of-an-inch of something you have a better chance of holding on to a certain feeling of the universe than if you pretended to be doing the whole sky.

My mother did not choose a leaf or a head. She chose my father, and to hold on to a certain feeling, she sacrificed the world.

19. THE WALL OF DICTIONARIES BETWEEN MY MOTHER AND THE WORLD GETS TALLER EVERY YEAR

Sometimes pages of the dictionaries come loose

and gather at her feet, *shallon, shalop, shallot, shallow, shalom, sham, shaman, shamble*, like the petals of an immense flower. When I was little, I thought that the pages on the floor were words she would never be able to use again, and I tried to tape them back in where they belonged, out of fear that one day she would be left silent.

20. MY MOTHER HAS ONLY BEEN ON TWO DATES SINCE MY FATHER DIED

The first was five years ago, when I was ten, with a fat English editor at one of the houses that publishes her translations. On his left pinky he wore a ring with a family crest that may or may not have been his own. Whenever he was talking about himself, he waved that hand. A conversation occurred in which it was established that my mother and this man, Lyle, had been at Oxford at the same time. On the strength of this coincidence he'd asked her out. Plenty of men have asked my mother out and she always said No. For some reason, this time she agreed. On Saturday night she appeared in the living room with her hair swept up, wearing the red shawl my father bought for her in Peru. "How do I look?" she asked. She looked beautiful, but somehow it didn't seem fair to wear it. There wasn't time to say anything because right then Lyle arrived at the front door, panting. He made himself comfortable on the sofa. I asked him if he knew anything about wilderness survival, and he said, "Absolutely." I asked him if he knew the difference between hemlock and wild carrots, and he gave me a blow-by-blow account of the final moments of an Oxford regatta during which his boat pulled forward to win during the last three seconds. "Holy cow," I said, in a way that could have been interpreted as sarcastic. Lyle also recalled fond memories of punting on the Cherwell. My mother said she wouldn't know since she never punted on the Cherwell. I thought, Well I'm not surprised.

After they left, I stayed up watching a TV program about the albatrosses of Antarctica: they can go years without touching the ground, sleep aloft in the sky, drink sea water, cry out the salt, and return year after year to raise babies with the same mate. I must have fallen asleep because when I heard my mother's key in the lock it was almost one AM. A few curls had fallen down around her neck and her mascara was smudged, but when I asked her how it went she said she knew orang-utans with whom she could carry on more exciting conversations.

About a year later Bird fractured his wrist trying to leap off our neighbor's balcony, and the tall, stooped doctor who treated him in the emergency room asked my mother on a date. Maybe it was because he made Bird smile even though his hand was turned at a terrible angle from his wrist, but for the second time since my father died my mother said Yes. The doctor's name was Henry Lavender, which I thought boded well (Alma Lavender!). When the doorbell rang, Bird streaked down the stairs naked but for his cast, put "That's Amore" on the record player, and streaked back up. My mother shot down the stairs not wearing her red shawl and pulled up the needle. The record gave out a screech. It spun noiselessly on the turntable while Henry Lavender came in and accepted a glass of cold white wine, and told us about his collection of seashells, many of which he'd dove for himself on trips to the Philippines. I imagined our future together in which he would take us on diving expeditions, the four of us smiling at each other through our masks under the sea. The next morning, I asked my mother how it had gone. She said he was a perfectly nice man. I saw this as a positive thing, but when Henry Lavender called that afternoon my mother was at the supermarket and didn't call him back. Two days later he made another attempt. This time my mother was going for a walk in the park. I said, "You're not going to call him back, are you?" and she said, "No." When Henry Lavender called a third time, she was engrossed in a book of stories, repeatedly exclaiming that the author should be given a Posthumous Nobel. My mother is always giving out Posthumous Nobels. I slipped into the kitchen with the portable. "Dr. Lavender?" I said. And then I told him that I thought my mother actually liked him and even though a normal person would probably be very happy to talk to him and even go out again, I'd known my mother for eleven and a half years and she'd never done anything normal.

21. I THOUGHT IT WAS JUST THAT SHE HADN'T MET THE RIGHT PERSON

The fact that she stayed home all day in her pajamas translating books by mostly dead people didn't seem to help matters much. Sometimes she would get stuck on a certain sentence for hours and go around like a dog with a bone until she'd shriek out, "I'VE GOT IT!" and scurry off to her desk to dig a hole and bury it. I decided to take things into my own hands. One day a veterinarian named Dr. Tucci came to speak to my sixth-grade class.

He had a nice voice and a green parrot named Gordo who perched on his shoulder and stared moodily out the window. He also had an iguana, two ferrets, a box turtle, tree frogs, a duck with a broken wing, and a boa constrictor named Mahatma who'd recently shed his skin. He kept two llamas in his backyard. After class, while everyone else was handling Mahatma, I asked if he was married and when, with a puzzled expression, he said No, I asked for his business card. It had a picture of a monkey on it, and a few kids lost interest in the snake and started demanding business cards, too.

That night I found an attractive snapshot of my mother in a bathing suit to send to Dr. Frank Tucci, along with a typed list of her best qualities. These included HIGH IQ, BIG READER, ATTRAC-TIVE (SEE PHOTO), FUNNY. Bird looked over the list and after some thought suggested I add OPIN-IONATED, which was a word I'd taught him, and also STUBBORN. When I said I didn't think those were her best or even good qualities, Bird said if they were on the list it might make it seem like they were good, and then if Dr. Tucci agreed to meet her he wouldn't be put off. This seemed like a fair argument at the time so I added OPINION-ATED and STUBBORN. At the bottom I wrote our telephone number. Then I mailed it.

A week passed and he didn't call. Three days went by and I wondered if maybe I shouldn't have written OPINIONATED and STUBBORN.

The next day the telephone rang and I heard my mother say, "Frank who?" There was a long silence. "Excuse me?" Another silence. Then she started laughing hysterically. She got off the phone and came to my room. "What was that all about?" I asked innocently. "What was what all about?" my mother asked even more innocently. "The person who just called," I said. "Oh, *that*," she said. "I hope you don't mind, I arranged a double date, me and the snake charmer and you and Herman Cooper."

Herman Cooper was an eighth-grade nightmare who lived on our block, called everyone Penis, and hooted at the huge balls on our neighbor's dog.

"I'd rather lick the sidewalk," I said.

22. THAT YEAR I WORE MY FATHER'S SWEATER FOR FORTY-TWO DAYS STRAIGHT

On the twelfth day I passed Sharon Newman and her friends in the hall. "WHAT'S UP WITH THAT DISGUSTING SWEATER?" she said. Go eat some hemlock, I thought, and decided to wear Dad's sweater for the rest of my life. I made it almost to the end of the school year. It was alpaca wool, and by the middle of May it was unbearable. My mother thought it was belated grieving. But I wasn't trying to set any records. I just liked the way it felt.

23. MY MOTHER KEEPS A PHOTOGRAPH OF MY FATHER ON THE WALL NEXT TO HER DESK

Once or twice I passed her door and heard her talking aloud to it. My mother is lonely even when we're around her, but sometimes my stomach hurts when I think about what will happen to her when I grow up and go away to start the rest of my life. Other times I imagine I'll never be able to leave at all.

24. ALL THE FRIENDS I EVER HAD ARE GONE

On my fourteenth birthday, Bird woke me up by jumping on my bed and singing "For She's a Jolly Good Fellow." He gave me a melted Hershey's

bar and a red woolen hat that he took from the
Lost and Found. I picked a curly blond hair off it
and wore it around the rest of the day. My mother
gave me an anorak tested by Tenzing Norgay, the
Sherpa who climbed Mt. Everest with Sir Edmund
Hillary, and also an old leather pilot's hat like the
kind worn by Antoine de Saint-Exupéry, who is a
hero of mine. My father read me *The Little Prince*
when I was six, and told about how Saint-Ex was
a great pilot who risked his life to open mail routes
to remote places. In the end he was shot down by
a German fighter, and he and his plane were lost
forever in the Mediterranean Sea.

Along with the jacket and the pilot's hat, my
mother also gave me a book by someone named
Daniel Eldridge who she said would deserve a
Nobel if they gave them to paleontologists. "Is he
dead?" I asked. "Why do you ask?" "No reason,"
I said. Bird asked what a paleontologist was and
Mom said that if he took a complete, illustrated
guide to the Metropolitan Museum of Art, shred
it into a hundred pieces, cast them into the wind
from the museum's steps, let a few weeks pass,
went back and scoured Fifth Avenue and Central
Park for as many surviving scraps as he could find,
then tried to reconstruct the history of painting,
including schools, styles, genres, and names of
painters from his scraps, that would be like being

a paleontologist. The only difference is that paleontologists study fossils in order to figure out the origin and evolution of life. Every fourteen-year-old should know something about where she comes from, my mother said. It wouldn't do to go around without the faintest clue of how it all began. Then, very quickly, as if it weren't the point of everything, she said the book had belonged to Dad. Bird hurried over and touched the cover.

It was called *Life as We Don't Know It*. On the back cover was a picture of Eldridge. He had dark eyes with thick lashes and a beard, and was holding up a fossil of a scary-looking fish. Underneath it said he was a professor at Columbia. That night I started to read it. I thought Dad might have written some notes in the margins, but he hadn't. The only sign of him was his name on the inside cover. The book was about how Eldridge and some other scientists had gone down to the bottom of the ocean in a submersible and discovered hydrothermal vents at the places where tectonic plates met, which spewed mineral-rich gases reaching up to 700 degrees. Until that point, scientists thought the ocean floor was a wasteland with little or no life. But what Eldridge and his colleagues observed in the headlights of their submersible were hundreds of organisms never before seen by human eyes—a whole ecosystem that they realized was very, very old. They called it the dark biosphere. There were a lot of hydrothermal vents down there, and pretty soon they figured out that there were microorganisms living on the rock around the vents in temperatures hot enough to melt lead. When they brought some of the organisms to the surface, they smelled of rotten eggs. They realized that these strange organisms were subsisting on the hydrogen sulfide spewed from the vents, and breathing out sulfur the way plants on land produce oxygen. According to Dr. Eldridge's book, what they had found was no less than a window onto the chemical pathways that billions of years ago led to the dawn of evolution.

The idea of evolution is so beautiful and sad. Since the earliest life on earth, there have been somewhere between five and fifty billion species, only five to fifty million of which are alive today. So, ninety-nine percent of all the species that have ever lived on earth are extinct.

25. MY BROTHER, THE MESSIAH

That night while I was reading, Bird came into my room and climbed into bed with me. At eleven and a half, he was small for his age. He pressed his little cold feet into my leg. "Tell me something about Dad," he whispered. "You forgot to cut your toenails," I said. He kneaded the balls of his feet into my calf. "Please?" he begged. I tried to think, and because I couldn't remember anything I hadn't already told him a hundred times, I made up something. "He liked to rock-climb," I said. "He was a good climber. Once he climbed up a rock that was, like, two hundred feet tall. Somewhere in the Negev, I think." Bird breathed his hot breath on my neck. "Masada?" he asked. "Could be," I said. "He just liked it. It was a hobby," I said. "Did he like to dance?" Bird asked. I had no idea if he liked to dance, but I said, "He loved it. He could even do the tango. He learned it in Buenos Aires. He and Mom danced all the time. He'd move the coffee table against the wall and use the whole room. He used to lift her and dip her and sing in her ear." "Was I there?" "Sure you were," I said. "He used to throw you up in the air and catch you." "How'd he know he wouldn't drop me?" "He just knew." "What did he call me?" "Lots of things. Buddy, Little Guy, Punch." I was making it up as I went. Bird looked unimpressed. "Judah the Maccabee," I said. "Plain Maccabee. Mac." "What's the thing he called me the *most*?" "I guess it was Emmanuel." I pretended to think. "No, wait. It was Manny. He used to call you Manny."

"*Manny*," Bird said, testing it out. He cuddled closer. "I want to tell you a secret," he whispered. "Because it's your birthday." "What?" "First you have to promise to believe me." "OK." "Say 'I promise.'" "I promise." He took a deep breath. "I think I might be a *lamed vovnik*." "A what?" "One of the *lamed vovniks*," he whispered. "The thirty-six holy people." "*What* thirty-six holy people?" "The ones that the existence of the world depends on." "Oh, *those*. Don't be—" "You promised," Bird said. I didn't say anything. "There are always thirty-six at any time," he whispered. "No one knows who they are. Only their prayers reach God's ear. That's what Mr. Goldstein says." "And you think you might be one of them," I said. "What else does Mr. Goldstein say?" "He says that when the Messiah comes, he's going to be one of the *lamed vovniks*. In every generation there's one person who has the potential to be the Messiah. Maybe he lives up to it, or maybe he doesn't. Maybe the world is ready for him, or maybe it isn't. That's all." I lay in the dark trying to think of the right thing to say. My stomach began to hurt.

26. THE SITUATION VERGED ON CRITICAL

The next Saturday I put *Life as We Don't Know It* into my backpack and took the subway up to Columbia University. I wandered around the campus for forty-five minutes until I found Eldridge's office in the Earth Sciences building. When I got there the secretary eating take-out said Dr. Eldridge wasn't around. I said I would wait, and he said maybe I should come back another time since Dr. Eldridge wouldn't be in for a few hours. I told him I didn't mind. He went back to his food. While I waited, I read one issue of *Fossil* magazine. Then I asked the secretary, who was laughing out loud about something on his computer, if he thought Dr. Eldridge would be back soon. He stopped laughing and looked at me like I'd just ruined the most important moment of his life. I went back to my seat and read one issue of *Paleontologist Today*.

I got hungry, so I went down the hall and got a package of Devil Dogs from a vending machine. Then I fell asleep. When I woke up the secretary was gone. The door of Eldridge's office was open, and the lights were on. Inside, a very old man with white hair was standing next to a filing cabinet under a poster that said: HENCE WITHOUT PARENTS, BY SPONTANEOUS BIRTH, RISE THE FIRST SPECKS OF ANIMATED EARTH— *ERASMUS DARWIN.*

"Well to be honest I hadn't thought of that option," the old man said into the phone. "I doubt he'd even want to apply. Anyway, I think we already have our man. I'll have to talk to the department, but let's just say things are looking good." He saw me standing at the door and made a gesture that he'd be off in a moment. I was about to say it was OK, I was waiting for Dr. Eldridge, but he turned his back and gazed out the window. "Good, glad to hear it. I better run. Right, then. All the best. 'Bye now." He turned to me. "Terribly sorry," he said. "What can I help you with?" I scratched my arm and noticed the dirt under my fingernails. "You're not Dr. Eldridge are you?" I asked. "I am," he said. My heart sank. Thirty years must have passed since the photograph on the book was taken. I didn't have to think for very long to know that he couldn't help me with the thing I had come about, because even if he deserved a Nobel for being the greatest living paleontologist, he also deserved one for being the oldest.

I didn't know what to say. "I read your book," I managed, "and I'm thinking of becoming a paleontologist." He said: "Well don't sound so disappointed."

27. ONE THING I AM NEVER GOING TO DO WHEN I GROW UP

Is fall in love, drop out of college, learn to subsist on water and air, have a species named after me, and ruin my life. When I was little my mother used to get a certain look in her eyes and say, "One day you're going to fall in love." I wanted to say, but never said: Not in a million years.

The only boy I'd ever kissed was Misha Shklovsky. His cousin taught him in Russia, where he lived before he moved to Brooklyn, and he taught me. "Not so much tongue," was all he said.

28. A HUNDRED THINGS CAN CHANGE YOUR LIFE; A LETTER IS ONE

Five months passed and I'd almost given up on finding someone to make my mother happy. Then it happened: in the middle of last February a letter arrived, typed on blue airmail paper and postmarked from Venice, forwarded to my mother from her publisher. Bird saw it first, and brought it to Mom to ask if he could have the stamps. We were all in the kitchen. She opened it and read it standing up. Then she read it a second time, sitting down. "This is amazing," she said. "What?" I asked. "Someone wrote to me about *The History of Love*. The book Dad and I named you after." She read the letter aloud to us.

> Dear Ms. Singer,
> I just finished your translation of the poems of Nicanor Parra, who, as you say, "wore on his lapel a little Russian astronaut, and carried in his pockets the letters of a woman who left him for another." It's sitting here next to me on the table in my room in a pensione overlooking the Grand Canal. I don't know what to say about it, except that it moved me in a way one hopes to be moved each time he begins a book. What I mean is, in some way I'd find almost impossible to describe, it changed me. But I won't go on about that. The truth is, I'm writing not to thank you, but to make what might seem like an odd request. In your introduction, you mentioned in passing a little-known writer, Zvi Litvinoff, who escaped from Poland to Chile in 1941, and whose single published work, written in Spanish, is called *The History of Love*. My question is: would you consider translating it? It would be solely for my personal use;

I don't have any intention of publishing it, and the rights would remain yours if you wished to do so yourself. I'd be willing to pay whatever you think is a fair price for the work. I always find these matters awkward. Could we say, $100,000? There. If that strikes you as too little, please let me know.

I'm imagining your response as you read this letter —which by then will have spent a week or two sitting in this lagoon, then another month riding the chaos of the Italian mail system, before finally crossing the Atlantic and being passed over to the US Post Office, who will have transferred it into a sack to be pushed along in a cart by a mailman who'll have slugged through rain or snow in order to slip it through your mail slot where it will have dropped to the floor, to wait for you to find it. And having imagined it, I'm prepared for the worst, in which you take me for some sort of lunatic. But maybe it doesn't need to be that way. Maybe if I tell you that a very long time ago someone once read to me as I was falling asleep a few pages from a book called *The History of Love*, and that all these years later I haven't forgotten that night, or those pages, you'd understand.

I'd be grateful if you could send your response to me here, care of the above address. In case I've already gone by the time it arrives the concierge will forward my mail.

Yours eagerly,
Jacob Marcus

I thought, Holy cow! I could hardly believe our luck, and considered writing back to Jacob Marcus myself with the excuse of explaining that it was Saint-Exupéry who'd established the last southern section of the mail route to South America in 1929, all the way to the tip of the continent. Jacob Marcus seemed interested in mail, and, anyway, once my mother had pointed out that it was in part because of Saint-Ex's courage that Zvi Litvinoff, the author of *The History of Love*, could later receive the final letters from his family and friends in Poland. At the end of the letter I would add something about my mother being single. But I thought better of it, in case she somehow found out, spoiling what had begun so well, and without any meddling. A hundred thousand dollars was a lot of money. But I knew that even if Jacob Marcus had offered almost nothing, my mother would have still agreed to do it.

29. MY MOTHER USED TO READ TO ME FROM *THE HISTORY OF LOVE*

"*The first woman may have been Eve, but the first girl will always be Alma*," she'd say, the Spanish book open on her lap while I lay in bed. This was when I was four or five, before Dad got sick and the book was put away on a shelf. "Maybe the first time you saw her you were ten. She was standing in the sun scratching her legs. Or tracing letters in the dirt with a stick. Her hair was being pulled. Or she was pulling someone's hair. And a part of you was drawn to her, and a part of you resisted—wanting to ride off on your bicycle, kick a stone, remain uncomplicated. In the same breath you felt the strength of a man, and a self-pity that made you feel small and hurt. Part of you thought: Please don't look at me. If you don't, I can still turn away. And part of you thought: Look at me.

"If you remember the first time you saw Alma, you also remember the last. She was shaking her head. Or disappearing across a field. Or through your window. *Come back, Alma!* you shouted. *Come back! Come back!*

"But she didn't.

"And though you were grown up by then, you felt as lost as a child. And though your pride was broken, you felt as vast as your love for her. She was gone, and all that was left was the space where you'd grown around her, like a tree that grows around a fence.

"For a long time, it remained hollow. Years, maybe. And when at last it was filled again, you knew that the new love you felt for a woman would have been impossible without Alma. If it weren't for her, there would never have been an empty space, or the need to fill it.

"Of course there are certain cases in which the boy in question refuses to stop shouting at the top of his lungs for Alma. Stages a hunger strike. Pleads. Fills a book with his love. Carries on until she has no choice but to come back. Every time she tries to leave, knowing it's what has to be done, the boy stops her, begging like a fool. And so she always returns, no matter how often she leaves or how far she goes, appearing soundlessly behind him and covering his eyes with her hands, spoiling for him anyone who could ever come after her."

30. THE ITALIAN POST TAKES SO LONG; THINGS GET LOST AND LIVES ARE RUINED FOREVER

It must have taken another few weeks for my

mother's reply to arrive in Venice, and by then Jacob Marcus had most likely gone, leaving instructions for his mail to be forwarded. In the beginning, I pictured him as very tall and thin with a chronic cough, speaking the few words of Italian he knew with a terrible accent, one of those sad people who are never at home anywhere. Bird imagined him as John Travolta in a Lamborghini with a suitcase of cash. If my mother imagined him at all, she didn't say.

But his second letter came at the end of March, six weeks after his first, postmarked from New York and handwritten on the back of an old black-and-white postcard of a zeppelin. My idea of him evolved. Instead of a cough, I gave him a cane he'd had since a car accident in his early twenties, and decided his sadness was because of his parents who'd left him alone too much as a child, then died, leaving him all of their money. On the back of the postcard, he wrote:

Dear Ms. Singer,
I was overjoyed to receive your response, and to hear that you'll be able to begin work on the translation. Please send the details of your bank account, and I'll wire the first $25,000 immediately. Would you agree to sending me the book in quarters,

as you translate it? I hope you'll forgive
my impatience, and attribute it to my
anticipation and excitement about finally
getting to read Litvinoff's book, and yours.
Also to my fondness for receiving mail,
and to extending, for as long as possible,
an experience that I expect to move me
deeply.

Yours truly,
J.M.

31. EVERY ISRAELITE HOLDS THE HONOR OF HIS ENTIRE PEOPLE IN HIS HANDS

The money arrived a week later. To celebrate, my
mother took us to a French movie with subtitles
about two girls who run away from home. The
theater was empty aside from three other people.
One of them was the usher. Bird finished his Milk
Duds during the opening credits, and tore up and
down the aisles in a sugar high until he fell asleep
in the front row.

Not long after that, during the first week of
April, he climbed up onto the roof at Hebrew
School, fell, and sprained his wrist. To console

himself, he set up a card table outside the house, and painted a sign that said *FRESH LEMON-AID 50 CENTS PLEASE POUR YOURSELF (SPRAINED WRIST)*. Rain or shine, he was out there with his pitcher of lemonade and a shoebox for collecting money. When he'd exhausted the clientele on our street, he moved a few blocks away and set up in front of a vacant lot. He started to spend more and more time there. When business was slow, he'd abandon the card table and wander around, playing in the lot. Each time I passed he'd done something to improve it: dragged the rusted fencing off to one side, hacked down the weeds, filled a garbage bag with trash. When it got dark he'd come home with his legs scratched, his *kippah* lopsided on his head. "What a mess," he'd say. But when I asked what he was planning to do there, he just shrugged. "A place belongs to anyone who has a use for it," he told me. "Thank you Mr. Dali Lamed Vovnik. Did Mr. Goldstein tell you that?" "No." "Well what's the big use you have for it?" I called after him. Instead of answering, he walked to the doorframe, reached up to touch something, kissed his hand, and went up the stairs. It was a plastic mezuzah; he'd stuck them on every doorframe in the house. There was even one on the door to the bathroom.

The next day I found the third volume of *How*

to Survive in the Wild in Bird's room. He'd scrawled God's name in permanent marker across the top of every page. "WHAT DID YOU DO TO MY NOTEBOOK?" I shouted. He was silent. "YOU RUINED IT." "No, I didn't. I was careful—" "Careful? *Careful?* Who said you could even *touch* it? Ever heard the word PRIVATE?" Bird stared at the notebook in my hand. "When are you going to start acting like a normal person?" "What's going on down there?" Mom called from the top of the stairs. "Nothing!" we said together. After a minute we heard her go back to her study. Bird put his arm over his face and picked his nose. "Holy shit, Bird," I whispered through my teeth. "At least try to be normal. You have to at least *try*."

32. FOR TWO MONTHS MY MOTHER HARDLY LEFT THE HOUSE

One afternoon, during the last week before summer vacation, I came home from school and found my mother in the kitchen, holding a package addressed to Jacob Marcus at an address in Connecticut. She'd finished translating the first quarter of *The History of Love,* and wanted me to take it to the post office. "Sure," I said, tucking it under my arm. Instead, I walked to the park and worked my thumbnail under the seal. On top was a letter, one sentence, written in my mother's tiny English handwriting:

> Dear Mr. Marcus,
> I hope these chapters are all you hoped for; anything less is my fault entirely.
> Yours,
> Charlotte Singer

My heart sank. Fifteen boring words without even the slightest hint of romance! I knew I should send it, that it wasn't up to me, that it isn't fair to meddle in other people's business. But then, there are a lot of things that aren't fair.

33. *THE HISTORY OF LOVE*, CHAPTER 10

During the Age of Glass, everyone believed some part of him or her to be extremely fragile. For some it was a hand, for others a femur, yet others believed it was their noses that were made of glass. The Age of Glass followed the Stone Age as an evolutionary corrective, introducing into human relations a new sense of fragility that fostered compassion. This period lasted a relatively short time in the history of love—about a century—until a doctor named Ignacio da Silva hit on the treatment of inviting people to recline on a couch and giving them a bracing smack on the body part in question, proving to them the truth. The anatomical illusion that had seemed so real slowly disappeared and—like so much we no longer need but can't give up—became vestigial. But from time to time, for reasons that can't always be understood, it surfaces again, suggesting that the Age of Glass, like the Age of Silence, never entirely ended.

Take for example that man walking down the street. You wouldn't notice him necessarily, he's not the sort of man one notices; everything about his clothes and his demeanor ask not to be picked out from a crowd. Ordinarily—he would tell you this himself—he would be overlooked. He carries nothing. At least he appears to carry nothing, not an umbrella even though it looks like rain, or a briefcase though it's rush hour, and around him, stooped against the wind, people are making their way home to their warm houses at the edge of the city where their children lean over their homework at the kitchen table, the smell of dinner in the air, and probably a dog, because there is always a dog in such houses.

One night when this man was still young, he decided to go to a party. There, he ran into a girl he'd gone up through the grades with since elementary school, a girl he'd always been a little in love with even though he was sure she didn't know he existed. She had the most beautiful name he'd ever heard: Alma. When she saw him standing by the door her face lit up, and she crossed the room to talk to him. He couldn't believe it.

An hour or two went by. It must have been a good conversation, because the next thing he knew Alma had told him to close his eyes. Then she kissed him. Her kiss was a question he wanted to spend his whole life answering. He felt his body shaking. He was scared he was about to lose control of his muscles. For anyone else, it was one thing, but for him it wasn't so easy, because this man believed—and had believed for as long as he could remember—that part of him was made of glass. He imagined a wrong move in which he fell and shattered in front of her.

He pulled away, even though he didn't want to. He smiled at Alma's feet, hoping she'd understand. They talked for hours.

That night he went home full of joy. He couldn't sleep, so excited was he for the next day, when he and Alma had a date to go to the movies. He picked her up the following evening and gave her a bunch of yellow daffodils. At the theater, he fought—and triumphed over!—the perils of sitting. He watched the whole movie leaning forward, so that his weight was resting on the underside of his thighs and not on the part of him that was made of glass. If Alma noticed she didn't say. He moved his knee a little, and a little more, until it was resting against hers. He was sweating. When the movie was over, he had no idea what it had been about. He suggested they take a walk through the park. This time it was he who stopped, took Alma in his arms, and kissed her. When his knees started to shake and he pictured himself lying in splinters of glass, he fought the urge to pull away. He ran his fingers down her spine over her thin blouse, and for a moment he forgot the danger he was in, grateful for the world

which purposefully puts divisions in place
so that we can overcome them, feeling the
joy of getting closer, even if deep down we
can never forget the sadness of our insur-
mountable differences. Before he knew it,
he was shaking violently. He seized his
muscles to try to stop. Alma felt his hesitation. She leaned back and looked at him
with something like hurt, and then he
almost but didn't say the two sentences
he'd been meaning to say for years: *Part
of me is made of glass*, and also, *I love you.*

He saw Alma one last time. He had no
idea it would be the last. He thought everything was just beginning. He spent the
afternoon making her a necklace of tiny
birds out of folded paper strung together
with thread. Right before he went out the
door, he grabbed a needlepoint cushion
from his mother's couch on an impulse,
and stuffed it into the seat of his pants as
a protective measure. As soon as he did,
he wondered why he hadn't thought of it
before.

That night—after he gave Alma the
necklace, tying it gently around her neck
while she kissed him, feeling only a little
tremor, nothing so terrible, as she ran *her*

fingers down *his* spine, and paused for a moment before slipping her hand into the seat of his pants, only to pull back as a look came over her that teetered between laughter and horror, a look that reminded him of a kind of pain he'd never not known—he told her the truth. At least he tried to tell the truth, but what came out was only half of the truth. Later, much later, he found that he was unable to relieve himself of two regrets: one, that when she leaned back he saw in the lamplight that the necklace he made had scratched her throat, and, two, that in the most important moment of his life he had chosen the wrong sentence.

For a long time I sat there reading the chapters my mother had translated. When I finished the tenth, I knew what I had to do.

34. THERE WAS NOTHING LEFT TO LOSE

I crumpled my mother's letter and threw it in the trash. I ran home, and went up to my bedroom to draft a new letter to the one man I believed could make my mother change. I worked on it for hours. Late that night, after she and Bird had already gone to sleep, I got out of bed, tiptoed down the hall, and carried my mother's typewriter into my room, the one she still likes to use for letters that are more than fifteen words. I had to type it a lot of times before I managed to do one without any mistakes. I read it over a last time. Then I signed my mother's name and went to sleep.

FORGIVE ME

Almost everything known about Zvi Litvinoff comes from the introduction his wife wrote in the volume of *The History of Love* reissued a few years after he died. The tone of her prose, tender and effacing, is colored by the devotion of one who has dedicated her life to another's art. It begins, *I met Zvi in Valparaíso, in the fall of 1951, soon after I turned twenty. I'd seen him often at the cafés along the water that I used to frequent with my friends. He wore a coat even in the warmest months, and stared moodily out at the view. He was almost twelve years older than I, but there was something about him I was drawn to. I knew he was a refugee because I'd heard his accent on the few occasions when someone he knew, also from that other world, would pause for a moment at his table. My parents had immigrated to Chile from Kraków when I was very young, so there was something about him that was familiar and moving to me. I would make my coffee last, watching him read through the newspaper. My friends laughed at me, calling him* un viéjon, *and one day a girl named Gracia Stürmer challenged me to go speak to him.*

And so Rosa did. She spoke to him for almost three hours that day as the afternoon lengthened and the cool air came in off the water. And Litvinoff, for his part—pleased with the attention of this young woman with a pale face and dark hair, delighted that she understood bits of Yiddish, suddenly filled with a longing he hadn't known he'd been carrying around inside of him for years—came to life, entertaining her with stories and quoting from poetry. That evening, Rosa went home filled with a giddy joy. Among the cocky, self-absorbed boys at the university with their pomaded hair and empty talk of philosophy, and the melodramatic few who had professed their love to her at the sight of her naked body, there was not one with even half as much experience as Litvinoff. The next afternoon, after her classes, Rosa hurried back to the café. Litvinoff was there waiting for her, and again they talked excitedly for hours: about the sound of the cello, silent films, and the memories they both associated with the smell of salt water. This went on for two weeks. They had a lot in common, but between them hung a dark and heavy difference that drew Rosa closer, in an effort to grasp even the smallest bit of it. But Litvinoff rarely talked about his past and all he'd lost. And not once did he mention the thing he'd begun to work on in the evenings at the old drafting table in the room where he lodged, the book that would become his masterpiece. All he said was that he taught part-time in a Jewish school. It was hard for Rosa to imagine the man sitting across from her— dark as a crow in his coat, and touched with the solemnity of an old photograph—surrounded by a class of laughing, squirming children. *It wasn't until two months later*, Rosa writes, *during the first moments of sadness that seemed to slip in through the open window without our noticing, disturbing the rarefied atmosphere that comes with the beginning of love, that Litvinoff read to me the first pages of the* History.

They were written in Yiddish. Later, with Rosa's help, Litvinoff would translate them into Spanish. The original Yiddish manuscript, written in longhand, was lost when the Litvinoffs' house was flooded while they were away in the mountains. All that remains is a single page that Rosa rescued from where it was floating on the surface of the water that had reached the height of two feet in Litvinoff's study. *At the bottom I caught sight of the gold cap of the pen he always carried in his pocket*, she writes, *and had to plunge my arm in up to the shoulder to reach it*. The ink had run, and in some places the writing was illegible. But the name he had given her in his book, the name that belonged to every woman in the *History*, could still be made out in Litvinoff's sloping handwriting at the bottom of the page.

Unlike her husband, Rosa Litvinoff wasn't a writer, and yet the introduction is guided along by a natural intelligence, and shadowed throughout, almost intuitively, with pauses, suggestions, ellipses, whose total effect is of a kind of half-light in which the reader can project his or her own imagination. She describes the open window and how Litvinoff's voice trembled with feeling as he read to her from the beginning, but says nothing about the room itself—which we are left to assume must have been Litvinoff's, with the drafting table that had once belonged to his landlady's son and into the corner of which was carved the words of the most important of all Jewish prayers, *Shema yisrael adonai elohanu adonai echad*, so that every time Litvinoff sat down to write at its sloped surface he would consciously or unconsciously utter a prayer—nothing of the narrow bed in which he slept, or the socks he'd washed and wrung out the night before, now draped like two exhausted animals over the back of a chair, nothing of the single framed photograph, turned at an angle so that it faced the peeling wallpaper (which Rosa must have looked at when Litvinoff excused himself to go down the hall to the bathroom), of a boy and a girl standing with their arms hanging stiffly by their sides, hands clasped, knees bare, stalled in place, while out the window, seen in the far corner of the frame, the afternoon was slowly getting away from them. And though Rosa describes how with time she married her dark crow, how her father died and the large house of her childhood with its sweet-smelling gardens was sold and somehow they had money, how they bought a small white bungalow on the cliffs above the water outside Valparaíso, and Litvinoff was able to give up his job at the school for a while and write most afternoons and evenings, she says nothing of Litvinoff's persistent cough which would often send him out onto the terrace in the middle of the night where he'd stand gazing out at the black water, nothing of his long silences, or the way his hands sometimes shook, or how she was watching him grow old before her eyes, as if time were passing more quickly for him than for everything around him.

As for Litvinoff himself, we know only what is written on the pages of the one book he wrote. He kept no diary and wrote few letters. Those he did write were either lost or destroyed. Aside from a few shopping lists and personal notes and the single page of the Yiddish manuscript Rosa managed to salvage from the flood, there is only one known surviving letter, a postcard from 1964 addressed to a nephew in London. By then, the *History* had been published in a modest run of a couple of thousand copies, and Litvinoff was teaching again, this time—because of the bit of esteem gained from his recent publication—a course on literature at the university. The postcard can be viewed in a display case lined with worn blue velvet in the dusty museum of the city's history that is almost always closed when anybody thinks to visit it. On the back it says, simply:

> Dear Boris,
> I was so happy to hear that you'd passed the exams. Your mother, may her memory be a blessing, would be so proud. A real doctor! You'll be busier now than ever, but if you want to visit there is always the extra room. Stay for as long as you like. Rosa is a good cook. You could sit by the sea and turn it into a real vacation. How about girls? Just a question. You should never be too busy for that. Sending my love and congratulations.
>
> Zvi

The front of the postcard, a hand-colored photo of the sea, is reproduced on the wall placard, along with the words, *Zvi Litvinoff, author of* The History of Love, *was born in Poland, and lived in Valparaíso for thirty-seven years until his death in 1978. This postcard was written to his oldest sister's son, Boris Perlstein.* In smaller letters, printed in the lower left corner, it says: *Gift of Rosa Litvinoff.* What it does not say is that his sister, Miriam, was shot in the head by a Nazi officer in the Warsaw Ghetto, or that aside from Boris, who escaped

on a *kindertransport* and lived out the remaining years
of the War, and his childhood, in an orphanage in
Surrey, and later Boris's children, who were at times
smothered by the desperation and fear that accompan-
ied their father's love, Litvinoff had no surviving
relatives. It also doesn't say that the postcard was never
sent, but any observant viewer can see that the stamp
isn't canceled.

What is *not* known about Zvi Litvinoff is endless.
It is not known, for example, that on his first and
last trip to New York City in the fall of 1954—where
Rosa insisted they go to show some editors his manuscript —he pretended to get lost from his wife in a
crowded department store, wandered outside,
crossed the street, and stood blinking in the sunlight
in Central Park. That while she searched for him
among the displays of stockings and leather gloves,
he was walking through an avenue of elm trees. That
by the time Rosa found a manager and an announcement was made over the loudspeaker—*Mr Z Litvinoff,
calling Mr Z Litvinoff. Would you please meet your wife
in Ladies' Footwear*—he had reached a pond, and was
watching as a boat rowed by a young couple floated
towards the reeds behind which he was standing, and
the girl, thinking she was hidden, unbuttoned her
shirt to reveal two white breasts. That the sight of
these breasts had filled Litvinoff with regret, and he
hurried back through the park to the department

store, where he found Rosa—her face flushed and
her hair damp at the nape of her neck—talking to a
pair of policemen. That when she threw her arms
around him, telling him he'd scared her half to death
and asking where on earth he'd been, Litvinoff
answered that he had gone to the bathroom and
gotten locked inside the stall. That later, in a hotel
bar, the Litvinoffs met the one editor who would
agree to see them, a nervous man with a thin laugh
and nicotine-stained fingers who told them that
though he liked the book very much, he could not
publish it because no one would buy it. As a token
of his appreciation, he made them a gift of a book
his publishing house had just brought out. After an
hour he excused himself saying he had a dinner to
attend, and hurried out, leaving the Litvinoffs with
the check.

That night, after Rosa had fallen asleep, Litvinoff
locked himself in the bathroom for real. He did this
almost every night because he was embarrassed that
his wife should have to smell his business. While he
sat on the toilet, he read the first page of the book
the editor had given them. Also, he cried.

It is not known that Litvinoff's favorite flower was
the peony. That his favorite form of punctuation was
the question mark. That he had terrible dreams and
could only fall asleep, if he could fall asleep at all, with
a glass of warm milk. That he often imagined his own

death. That he thought the woman who loved him
was wrong to. That he was flat-footed. That his
favorite food was the potato. That he liked to think
of himself as a philosopher. That he questioned all
things, even the most simple, to the extent that when
someone passing him on the street raised his hat and
said, "Good day," Litvinoff often paused so long to
weigh the evidence that by the time he'd settled on
an answer the person had gone on his way, leaving
him standing alone. These things were lost to obliv-
ion like so much about so many who are born and die
without anyone ever taking the time to write it all
down. That Litvinoff had a wife who was so devoted
is, to be frank, the only reason anyone knows anything
about him at all.

A few months after the book was published by a
small publishing house in Santiago, Litvinoff received
a package in the mail. At the moment the postman
rang the bell, Litvinoff's pen had been poised above
a blank piece of paper, his eyes watery with revela-
tion, filled with the feeling that he was on the verge
of understanding the essence of something. But when
the bell rang the thought was lost, and Litvinoff, ordin-
ary again, dragged his feet down the dark hallway and
opened the door where the mailman stood in the
sunlight. "Good day," the mailman said, handing him
a large, neatly wrapped brown envelope, and Litvinoff
did not have to weigh the evidence for long to come

to the conclusion that while a moment ago the day had verged on being excellent, more than he could have hoped for, it suddenly had changed like the direction of a squall on the horizon. This was further confirmed when Litvinoff opened the package and found the typeset of *The History of Love*, along with the following brief note from his publisher: *The enclosed dead matter is no longer needed by us and is being returned to you.* Litvinoff winced, not knowing it was a custom to return the galley proofs to the author. He wondered if this would affect Rosa's opinion of the book. Not wanting to find out, he burned the note along with the matter, watching the embers sputter and curl in the fireplace. When his wife returned from her shopping, threw open the windows to let in the light and fresh air, and asked why he'd lit a fire on such a beautiful day, Litvinoff shrugged and complained of a chill.

Of the two thousand original copies printed of *The History of Love*, some were bought and read, many were bought and not read, some were given as gifts, some sat fading in bookstore windows serving as landing docks for flies, some were marked up with pencil, and a good many were sent to the paper compactor, where they were shredded to a pulp along with other unread or unwanted books, their sentences parsed and minced in the machine's spinning blades. Staring out the window, Litvinoff imagined the two thousand copies of *The History of Love* as a flock of two thousand homing pigeons that could flap their wings and return to him to report on how many tears shed, how many laughs, how many passages read aloud, how many cruel closings of the cover after reading barely a page, how many never opened at all.

He couldn't have known it, but among the original run of *The History of Love* (there was a flare of interest following Litvinoff's death, and the book was briefly returned to print with Rosa's introduction), at least one copy was destined to change a life—more than one life. This particular book was one of the last of the two thousand to be printed, and sat for longer than the rest in a warehouse in the outskirts of Santiago, absorbing the humidity. From there it was finally sent to a bookstore in Buenos Aires. The careless owner hardly noticed it, and for some years it languished on the shelves, acquiring a pattern of mildew across the cover. It was a slim volume, and its position on the shelf wasn't exactly prime: crowded on the left by an overweight biography of a minor actress, and on the right by the once-bestselling novel of an author that everyone had since forgotten, it hardly left its spine visible to even the most rigorous browser. When the store changed owners it fell victim to a massive clearance, and was trucked off to another warehouse, foul, dingy, crawling with daddy longlegs, where it remained in the dark and damp before finally being sent to a small secondhand bookstore not far from the home of the writer Jorge Luis Borges. By then, Borges was completely blind and had no reason to visit the bookshop—because he could no longer read, and because over the course of his life he'd read so much, memorized such vast portions of Cervantes, Goethe, and Shakespeare, that all he had to do was sit in the darkness and reflect. Often visitors who loved the writer Borges would look up his address and knock on his door, but when they were shown in they'd find the reader Borges, who would lay his fingers on the spines of his books until he located the one he wished to hear, and would hand it to the visitor, who had no choice but to sit and read it aloud to him. Occasionally he left Buenos Aires to travel with his friend María Kodama, dictating to her his thoughts on the felicity of a hot air balloon ride or the beauty of the tiger. But he did not visit the secondhand bookstore, even though while he could still see, he had been on friendly terms with the owner.

The owner took her time unpacking the books she'd bought cheaply and in bulk from the warehouse. One morning, going through the boxes, she discovered the mildewed copy of *The History of Love*. She'd never heard of it, but the title caught her eye. She put it aside, and during a slow hour in the shop she read the opening chapter, called "The Age of Silence":

The first language humans had was gestures. There was nothing primitive about this language that flowed from people's hands, nothing we say now that could not be said in the endless array of movements possible with the fine bones of the fingers and wrists. The gestures were complex and subtle, involving a delicacy of motion that has since been lost completely.

During the Age of Silence, people communicated more, not less. Basic survival demanded that the hands were almost never still, and so it was only during sleep (and sometimes not even then) that people were not saying something or other. No distinction was made between the gestures of language and the gestures of life. The labor of building a house, say, or preparing a meal was no less an expression than making the sign for *I love you* or *I feel serious*. When a hand was used to shield one's face when frightened by a loud noise something was being said, and when fingers were used to pick up what someone else had dropped something was being said; and even when the hands were at rest, that, too, was saying something. Naturally, there were misunderstandings. There were times when a finger might have been lifted to scratch a nose, and if casual eye contact was made with one's lover just then, the lover might accidentally take it to be the gesture, not at all dissimilar, for *Now I realize I was wrong to love you.* These mistakes were heartbreaking. And yet, because people knew how easily they could happen, because they didn't go around with the illusion that they understood perfectly the things other people said, they were used to interrupting each other to ask if they'd understood correctly. Sometimes these misunderstandings were even desirable, since they gave people a reason to say, *Forgive me, I was only scratching my nose. Of course I know I've always been right to love you.* Because of the frequency of these mistakes, over time the gesture for asking forgiveness evolved into the simplest form. Just to open your palm was to say: Forgive me.

Aside from one exception, almost no record exists of this first language. The exception, on which all knowledge of the subject is based, is a collection of seventy-nine fossil gestures, prints of human hands frozen in midsentence and housed in a small museum in Buenos Aires. One holds the gesture for *Sometimes when the rain*, another for *After all these years*, another for *Was I wrong to love you?* They were found in Morocco in 1903 by an Argentine doctor named Antonio Alberto de Biedma. He was hiking in the High Atlas Mountains when he discovered the cave where the seventy-nine gestures were pressed into the shale. He studied them for years without getting any closer to understanding, until one day, already suffering the fever of the dysentery that would kill him, he suddenly found himself able to decipher the meanings of the delicate motions of fists and fingers trapped in stone. Soon afterwards he was taken to a hospital in Fez, and as he lay dying his hands moved like birds forming a thousand gestures, dormant all those years.

If at large gatherings or parties, or around people with whom you feel distant, your hands sometimes hang awkwardly at the ends of your arms—if you find yourself at a loss for what to do with them, overcome with sadness that comes when you recognize the foreignness of your own body—it's because your hands remember a time when the division between mind and body, brain and heart, what's inside and what's outside, was so much *less*. It's not that we've forgotten the language of gestures entirely. The habit of moving our hands while we speak is left over from it. Clapping, pointing, giving the thumbs-up: all artifacts of ancient gestures. Holding hands, for example, is a way to remember how it feels to say nothing together. And at night, when it's too dark to see, we find it necessary to gesture on each other's bodies to make ourselves understood.

The owner of the secondhand bookstore lowered the volume of the radio. She flipped to the back flap of the book to find out more about the author, but all it said was that Zvi Litvinoff had been born in Poland and moved to Chile in 1941, where he still lived today. There was no photograph. That day, in between helping customers, she finished the book. Before locking up the shop that evening, she placed it in the window, a little wistful about having to part with it.

The next morning, the first rays of the rising sun fell across the cover of *The History of Love*. The first of many flies alighted on its jacket. Its mildewed pages began to dry out in the heat as the blue-gray Persian cat who lorded over the shop brushed past it to lay claim to a pool of sunlight. A few hours later, the first of many passersby gave it a cursory glance as they went by the window.

The shop owner did not try to push the book on any of her customers. She knew that in the wrong hands such a book could easily be dismissed or, worse, go unread. Instead she let it sit where it was in the hope that the right reader might discover it.

And that's what happened. One afternoon a tall young man saw the book in the window. He came into the shop, picked it up, read a few pages, and brought it to the register. When he spoke to the owner, she couldn't place his accent. She asked where he was from, curious about the person who was taking the book away. Israel, he told her, explaining that he'd recently finished his time in the army and was traveling around South America for a few months. The owner was about to put the book in a bag, but the young man said he didn't need one, and slipped it into his backpack. The door chimes were still tinkling as she watched him disappear, his sandals slapping against the hot, bright street.

That night, shirtless in his rented room, under a fan lazily pushing around the hot air, the young man opened the book and, in a flourish he had been fine-tuning for years, signed his name: *David Singer*.

Filled with restlessness and longing, he began to read.

A JOY FOREVER

I don't know what I expected, but I expected something. My fingers shook whenever I went to unlock the mailbox. I went Monday. Nothing. I went Tuesday and Wednesday. There was nothing on Thursday, either. Two and a half weeks after I put my book in the mail, the telephone rang. I was sure it was my son. I'd been dozing in my chair, there was drool on my shoulder. I jumped to answer it. *HELLO?* But. It was only the teacher from the art class saying she was looking for people for a project she was doing at a gallery, and she thought of me, because of my quote unquote compelling presence. Naturally I was flattered. At any other time it would have been reason enough to splurge on spare ribs. And yet. *What kind of project?* I asked. She said all I had to do was sit naked on a metal stool in the middle of the room and then, if I felt like it, which she was hoping I would, dip my body into a vat of kosher cow's blood and roll on the large white sheets of paper provided.

I may be a fool but I'm not desperate. There's only so far I'm willing to go, so I thanked her very much for the offer but said I was going to have to turn it down since I was already scheduled to sit on my thumb and rotate in accordance with the movements of the earth around the sun. She was disappointed. But she seemed to understand. She said if I wanted to come in and see the drawings the class had done of me I could come to the show they were putting up in a month. I wrote down the date and hung up the phone.

I'd been in the apartment all day. It was already getting dark, so I decided to go out for a walk. I'm an old man. But I can still get around. I hoofed it past Zafi's Luncheonette and the Original Mr. Man Barber and Kossar's Bialys where sometimes I'll go for a hot bagel on a Saturday night. They didn't used to make bagels. Why should they? If it's called Bialys, then it's bialys. And yet.

I kept walking. I went into the drugstore and knocked over a display of KY jelly. But. My heart wasn't in it. When I passed the Center, there was a big banner that said DUDU FISHER THIS SUNDAY NIGHT BUY TICKETS NOW. Why not? I thought. I don't go in for the stuff myself, but Bruno loves Dudu Fisher. I went in and bought two tickets.

I didn't have any destination in mind. It started

to get dark but I persevered. When I saw a Starbucks I went in and bought a coffee because I felt like a coffee, not because I wanted anyone to notice me. Normally I would have made a big production, *Give me a Grande Vente, I mean a Tall Grande, Give me a Chai Super Vente Grande, or do I want a Short Frappe?* and then, for punctuation, I would've had a small mishap at the milk station. Not this time. I poured the milk like a normal person, a citizen of the world, and sat down in an easy chair across from a man reading the newspaper. I wrapped my hands around the coffee. The warmth felt good. The next table over there was a girl with blue hair leaning over a notebook and chewing on a ballpoint pen, and at the table next to her was a little boy in a soccer uniform sitting with his mother who told him, *The plural of elf is elves.* A wave of happiness came over me. It felt giddy to be part of it all. To be drinking a cup of coffee like a normal person. I wanted to shout out: *The plural of elf is elves! What a language! What a world!*

There was a pay phone by the restrooms. I felt in my pocket for a quarter and dialed Bruno's number. It rang nine times. The girl with blue hair passed me on the way to the bathroom. I smiled at her. Amazing! She smiled back. On the tenth ring he picked up.

Bruno?

Yes?

Isn't it good to be alive?

No thank you, I don't want to buy anything.

I'm not trying to sell you anything! It's Leo. Listen. I was sitting here drinking a coffee in Starbucks and suddenly it hit me.

Who hit you?

Ach, listen! It hit me how good it is to be alive. Alive! And I wanted to tell you. *Do you understand what I'm saying? I'm saying life is a thing of beauty, Bruno. A thing of beauty and a joy forever.*

There was a pause.

Sure, whatever you say Leo. Life is a beauty.

And a joy forever, I said.

All right, Bruno said. *And a joy.*

I waited.

Forever.

I was about to hang up when Bruno said, *Leo?*

Yes?

Did you mean human life?

I worked on my coffee for half an hour, making the most of it. The girl closed her notebook and got up to leave. The man neared the end of his newspaper. I read the headlines. I was a small part of something larger than myself. Yes, *human life*. Human! Life! Then the man turned the page and my heart stopped.

It was a photo of Isaac. I'd never seen it before. I collect all his clippings, if there was a fan club I'd be the president. For twenty years I've subscribed to the magazine where occasionally he publishes. I thought I'd seen every photo of him. I've studied them all a thousand times. And yet. This one was new to me. He was standing in front of a window. His chin was down, head tilted to the side. He might have been thinking. But his eyes were looking up, as if someone had called his name right before the shutter clicked. I wanted to call out to him. It was only a newspaper, but I wanted to holler it at the top of my lungs. *Isaac! Here I am! Can you hear me, my little Isaac?* I wanted him to turn his eyes to me just as he had to whomever had just shaken him from his thoughts. But. He couldn't. Because the headline said, ISAAC MORITZ, NOVELIST, DEAD AT 60.

> *Isaac Moritz, acclaimed author of six novels including* The Remedy, *which won the National Book Award, died Tuesday night. The cause of death was Hodgkin's disease. He was 60.*
>
> *Mr. Moritz's novels are defined by their humor and compassion, and the hope they search for amid despair. From the first, he had his ardent supporters. These included Philip Roth, one of the judges for the National Book Award in 1972, awarded to Mr. Moritz for his first novel. "At the center of* The Remedy *is a live human heart, fierce and imploring," Roth said in a press release announcing the prize. Another of Mr. Moritz's fans, Leon Wieseltier, speaking on the telephone*

this morning from the offices of the New Republic *in Washington, D.C., called Mr. Moritz "one of the most important and undervalued writers of the late twentieth century. To call him a Jewish writer," he added, "or, worse, an experimental writer, is to miss entirely the point of his humanity, which resisted all categorization."*

Mr. Moritz was born in 1940 in Brooklyn to immigrant parents. A quiet and serious child, he filled notebooks with detailed descriptions of scenes from his own life. One of these—an entry about watching a dog being beaten by a gang of children, written at the age of twelve—later inspired the most famous scene in The Remedy, *when the protagonist, Jacob, leaves the apartment of a woman to whom he has just made love for the first time, and, standing in the shadows of a street lamp in the freezing cold, watches a dog being brutally kicked to death by two men. At that moment, overcome with the tender brutality of physical existence—with "the insoluble contradiction of being animals cursed with self-reflection, and moral beings cursed with animal instincts"— Jacob launches into a lament, a single, ecstatic paragraph, unbroken over five pages, that* Time *magazine called one of the most "incandescent, haunting passages" in contemporary literature.*

Aside from winning him an avalanche of

praise and the National Book Award, The Remedy *also made Mr. Moritz a household name. In its first year of publication it sold 200,000 copies, and was a* New York Times *bestseller.*

His sophomore attempt was awaited with eager anticipation, but when Glass Houses, *a book of stories, was finally published five years later it was met with mixed reviews. While some critics saw it as a boldly innovative departure, others, such as Morton Levy, who wrote a scathing attack in* Commentary, *called the collection a failure.* "Mr. Moritz," *wrote Levy,* "whose debut novel was emboldened by his eschatological speculations, has here shifted his focus to pure scatology." *Written in a fragmented and at times surreal style, the stories in* Glass Houses *range in subject from angels to garbage collectors.*

Reinventing his voice yet again, Mr. Moritz's third book, Sing, *was written in a stripped-down language described in the* New York Times *as* "taut as a drum." *Though in his more recent two novels he continued to search for new means of expressing them, Mr. Moritz's themes were consistent. At the root of his art was a passionate humanism and an unflinching exploration of man's relationship with his God.*

Mr. Moritz is survived by his brother, *Bernard Moritz.*

I sat in a daze. I thought of my son's five-year-old face. Also the time I watched him tie his shoe from across the street. Finally a Starbucks employee with a ring in his eyebrow came up to me. *We're closing,* he said. I looked around. It was true. Everyone was gone. A girl with painted nails was dragging a broom across the floor. I got up. Or I tried to get up but my legs buckled under me. The Starbucks employee looked at me as if I were a cockroach in the brownie mix. The paper cup I held was crushed to a damp pulp in my palm. I handed it to him and started to make my way across the floor. Then I remembered the newspaper. The employee had already thrown it into the trash bin he was rolling across the floor. I fished it out, smeared as it was with uneaten Danish, while he looked on. Because I am not a beggar, I handed him the tickets for Dudu Fisher.

I don't know how I got home. Bruno must have heard me unlock the door, because a minute later he came downstairs and knocked. I didn't answer. I was sitting in the dark in the chair by the window. He kept knocking. Finally I heard him go back upstairs. An hour or more passed and then I heard him on the stairs again. He slid a piece of paper under the door. It said: *LIFE IS BUTIFUL.* I pushed it back out. He pushed it back in. I pushed it out, he pushed it in. Out, in, out, in. I stared at it. *LIFE IS BUTIFUL.* I thought, Perhaps it is. Perhaps that is the word for life. I heard Bruno breathing on the other side of the door. I found a pencil. I scrawled: *AND A JOKE FOREVER.* I pushed it back under the door. A pause while he read it. Then, satisfied, he made his way up the stairs.

It's possible I cried. What's the difference.

I fell asleep near dawn. I dreamed I was standing in a railway station. The train came in and my father got off. He was wearing a camel-hair coat. I ran to him. He didn't recognize me. I told him who I was. He shook his head no. He said: *I only had daughters.* I dreamed my teeth crumbled, that my blankets suffocated me. I dreamed of my brothers, there was blood everywhere. I'd like to say: I dreamed that the girl I loved and I grew old together. Or I dreamed of a yellow door and an open field. I'd like to say, I dreamed that I'd died and my book was found among my things, and in the years that followed the end of my life, I became famous. And yet.

I picked up the newspaper and cut out the photograph of my Isaac. It was wrinkled, but I smoothed it out. I put it in my wallet, in the plastic part made for a photo. I opened and closed the Velcro a few times to look at his face. Then I noticed that underneath where I cut it out it said, *A memorial service will be—*I couldn't read the rest. I had to take the photograph out and piece the two parts together. *A memorial service will be held Saturday, October 7, at 10 AM at Central Synagogue.*

It was Friday. I knew I shouldn't stay in, so I made myself go out. The air felt different in my lungs. The world no longer looked the same. You change and then you change again. You become a dog, a bird, a plant that leans always to the left. Only now that my son was gone did I realize how much I'd been living for him. When I woke up in the morning it was because he existed, and when I ordered food it was because he existed, and when I wrote my book it was because he existed to read it.

I took the bus uptown. I told myself I couldn't go to my own son's funeral in the wrinkled *shmatta* I call a suit. I didn't want to embarrass him. More than that, I wanted to make him proud. I got off on Madison Avenue and walked along, looking in the windows. My handkerchief was cold and wet in my hand. I didn't know which store to go into. Finally, I just chose one that looked nice. I fingered the material on a jacket. A giant *shvartzer* in a shiny beige suit and cowboy boots approached me. I thought he was going to throw me out. *I'm just feeling the fabric*, I said. *You want to try it on?* he asked. I was flattered. He asked me my size. I didn't know. But he seemed to understand. He looked me over, showed me into a dressing room, and hung the suit on the hook. I took my clothes off. There were three mirrors. I was exposed to parts of myself I hadn't seen in years. Despite my grief, I took a moment to examine them. Then I put on the suit.

The pants were stiff and narrow and the jacket practically came down to my knees. I looked like a clown. The *shvartzer* ripped aside the curtain with a smile. He straightened me out and buttoned me up and spun me around. We both looked into the mirror. *Fits you like a glove*, he announced. *If you wanted*, he said, pinching some material at the back, *we could take it in a drop here. But you don't need it. Looks like it was made for you.* I thought: What do I know from fashion? I asked him the price. He reached into the back of my pants and dug around in my *tuchas. This one's . . . a thousand*, he announced. I looked at him. *A thousand what?* I said. He laughed politely. We stood in front of the three mirrors. I folded and refolded my wet hanky. With a last shred of composure, I plucked my underwear from where it had lodged between my cheeks. There should be a word for this. The one-string harp.

Out on the street, I kept walking. I knew the suit didn't matter. But. I needed to do something. To steady myself.

There was a shop on Lexington that advertised passport pictures. I like to go sometimes. I keep them in a little album. Mostly they're of me, except for one, which is of Isaac, aged five, and another of my cousin, the locksmith. He was an amateur photographer and one day he showed me how to make a pinhole camera. This was the spring of 1947. I stood in the back of his tiny shop watching him fix the photographic paper inside the box. He told me to sit, and shone a lamp on my face. Then he removed the cover over the pinhole. I sat so still I was hardly breathing. When it was finished we went into the darkroom and dropped it in the developing pan. We waited. Nothing. Where I should have been there was only a scratchy grayness. My cousin insisted we do it again, so we did it again, and again, nothing. Three times he tried to take a picture of me with the pinhole camera, and three times I failed to appear. My cousin couldn't understand it. He cursed the man who sold him the paper, thinking he'd been given a bad batch. But I knew he hadn't. I knew that the way others had lost a leg or an arm, I'd lost whatever the thing is that makes people indelible. I told my cousin to sit in the chair. He was reluctant, but finally he agreed. I took a photograph of him, and as we watched the paper in the developing pan his face appeared. He laughed. And I laughed, too. It was I who'd taken the picture, and if it was proof of his existence, it was also proof of my own. He let me keep it. Whenever I took it out of my wallet and looked at him, I knew I was really looking at me. I bought an album, and fixed it to the second page. On the first page, I put the photo of my son. A few weeks later I passed a drugstore with a photo booth. I went in. From then on, every time I had some spare money I'd go to the booth. In the beginning it was always the same. But I kept trying. Then one day I accidentally moved as the shutter clicked. A shadow appeared. The next time I saw the outline of my face, and a few weeks later my face itself. It was the opposite of disappearing.

When I opened the door of the camera shop a bell tinkled. Ten minutes later I stood on the sidewalk clutching four identical photos of myself. I looked at them. You could call me plenty of things. But. Handsome isn't one of them. I tucked one in my wallet, next to the picture of Isaac from the newspaper. The rest I threw in the trash.

I looked up. Across the street was Bloomingdale's. I'd been there once or twice in my day to get a little *shpritz* from one of the perfume ladies. What can I say, it's a free country. I rode the escalator up and down until I found the suit department on the lower level. This time I looked at the prices first. There was a dark blue suit hanging on the rack that was on sale for two hundred dollars. It looked like it was my size. I took it to the dressing room and tried it on. The pants were too long, but that was to be expected. Same with the sleeves. I walked out of the cubicle. A tailor with a tape measure around his neck motioned me up onto the block. I stepped forward, and as I did I remembered the time my mother sent me to the tailor to pick up my father's new shirts. I was nine, maybe ten. In the dim interior, the dummies stood together in the corner as if waiting for a train. Grodzenski the

tailor was bent over his machine, his foot pedaling. I
watched him, fascinated. Every day under his touch,
with only the dummies as witness, drab bolts of cloth
grew collars, cuffs, ruffles, pockets. *You want to try?* he
asked. I sat down in his seat. He showed me how to
bring the machine to life. I watched the needle leap
up and down, leaving behind it a miraculous path of
blue stitches. While I pedaled, Grodzenski brought
out my father's shirts wrapped in brown paper. He
motioned me to come behind the counter. He brought
out another package wrapped in the same brown paper.
Carefully, he removed a magazine. It was a few years
old. But. In perfect condition. He handled it with the
tips of his finger. Inside were black and silver photographs of women with soft, white skin, as if they were
lit from the inside. They modeled dresses of a kind
I'd never seen: dresses of pure pearl, of feathers and
fringe, dresses that revealed legs, arms, the curve of a
breast. A single word slid from Grodzenski's lips: *Paris.*
Silently he turned the pages, and silently I watched.
Our breath condensed on the glossy photos. Maybe
Grodzenski was showing me, with his quiet pride, the
reason he hummed a little while he worked. At last
he closed the magazine, slipping it back into the paper.
He went back to work. If someone had told me then
that Eve had eaten the apple just so that the
Grodzenskis of the world could exist, I would have
believed it.

Grodzenski's poor relation buzzed around me with chalk and pins. I asked if it would be possible for him to hem the suit while I waited. He looked at me like I had two heads. *I gottahundred suits back there to take-cara, and you wannme ta do yours now?* He shook his head. *Minimum, two weeks.*

It's for a funeral, I said. *My son.* I tried to steady myself. I reached for my handkerchief. Then I remembered it was in the pocket of my pants crumpled on the dressing room floor. I stepped off the block and hurried back to my cubicle. I knew I'd made a fool of myself in that clown suit. A man should buy a suit for life, not for death. Wasn't that what Grodzenski's ghost was telling me? I couldn't embarrass Isaac and I couldn't make him proud. Because he didn't exist.

And yet.

That evening, I went home with the hemmed suit in a plastic garment bag. I sat at the kitchen table and made a single rip in the collar. I would have liked to shred the whole thing. But I restrained myself. Fishl the *tzaddik* who might have been an idiot once said: *A single rip is harder to bear than a hundred rips.*

I bathed myself. Not a bird bath with a sponge, but the real thing, darkening the ring around the tub another shade. I dressed myself in the new suit, and brought the vodka down off the shelf. I took a drink, wiping my mouth with the back of my hand, repeating the gesture that was made a hundred times by my

father and his father and his father's father, eyes half
closed as the sharpness of the alcohol replaced the
sharpness of grief. And then, when the bottle was gone,
I danced. Slowly at first. But getting faster. I stomped
my feet and kicked my legs, joints cracking. I
pounded my feet and crouched and kicked in the dance
my father danced, and his father, tears sliding down
my face as I laughed and sang, danced and danced,
until my feet were raw and there was blood under my
toenail, I danced the only way I knew how to dance:
for life, crashing into the chairs, and spinning until I
fell, so that I could get up and dance again, until dawn
broke and found me prostrate on the floor, so close
to death I could spit into it and whisper: *L'chaim.*

I woke up to the sound of a pigeon ruffling its
feathers on the windowsill. One arm of the suit was
torn, my head was pounding, there was dried blood
on my cheek. But I'm not made of glass.

I thought: Bruno. Why hadn't he come? I might
not have answered had he knocked. Still. No doubt
he'd heard me, unless he had on his Walkman. Even
then. A lamp had crashed to the floor, and I'd overturned all the chairs. I was about to go up and knock
on his door when I looked at the clock. It was already
quarter past ten. I like to think the world wasn't ready
for me, but maybe the truth is that I wasn't ready for
the world. I've always arrived too late for my life. I
ran to the bus stop. Or rather, hobbled, hiked up

trouser legs, did a little skip-scamper-stop-and-pant, hiked up trouser legs, stepped, dragged, stepped, dragged, etcetera. I caught the bus uptown. We sat in traffic. *Doesn't this thing go any faster?* I said loudly. The woman next to me got up and moved to another seat. Maybe I slapped her thigh in my effusiveness, I don't know. A man in an orange jacket and snakeskin-print pants stood up and started to sing a song. Everyone turned to look out the window until they realized he wasn't asking for money. He was just singing.

By the time I got to the shul the service was already over, but the place was still crowded with people. A man in a yellow bow tie and a white jacket, what was left of his hair lacquered across his scalp, said, *Of course we knew, but when it finally happened none of us were ready*, to which a woman standing next to him replied, *Who can be ready?* I stood alone by a large potted plant. My palms were damp, I felt myself getting dizzy. Perhaps it had been a mistake to come.

I wanted to ask where he'd been buried; the newspaper hadn't said. Suddenly I was filled with regret that I'd bought my own plot so prematurely. If I'd known, I could have joined him. Tomorrow. Or the next day. I'd been afraid of being left to the dogs. I'd gone to Mrs. Freid's stone setting at Pinelawn, and it had seemed like a nice place. A Mr. Simchik showed me around and gave me a pamphlet. I'd been imagining something under a tree, a weeping willow perhaps, maybe a little bench. But. When he told me the price my heart sank. He showed me my options, a few plots that were either too close to the road or where the grass was balding. *Nothing at all with a tree?* I asked. Simchik shook his head. *A bush?* He licked a finger and rustled through his papers. He hemmed and hawed, but finally he gave in. *We may have something,* he said, *it's more than you were planning to spend but you can pay in installments.* It was at the far end, in the suburbs of the Jewish part. It wasn't exactly under a tree but it was near one, near enough that during the fall some of its leaves might drift down on me. I thought it over. Simchik told me to take my time and went back to the office. I stood in the sunlight. Then. I got down on the grass and rolled onto my back. The ground was hard and cold under my raincoat. I watched the clouds pass above. Maybe I fell asleep. The next thing I knew, Simchik was standing above me. *Nu? You'll take it?*

Out of the corner of my eye I saw Bernard, my son's half-brother. A huge oaf, the spitting image of his father, may his memory be a blessing. Yes, even his. His name was Mordecai. She called him Morty. Morty! He's been in ground three years. I consider it a small victory that he kicked the bucket first. And yet. When I remember, I light a *yartzeit* candle for him. If not me, who?

My son's mother, the girl I fell in love with when I was ten, died five years ago. I expect to join her soon, at least in that. Tomorrow. Or the next day. Of that I am convinced. I thought it would be strange to live in the world without her in it. And yet. I'd gotten used to living with her memory a long time ago. Only at the very end did I see her again. I snuck into her room in the hospital and sat with her every day. There was a nurse, a young girl, and I told her—not the truth. But. A story not unlike the truth. This nurse let me come after hours, when there was no chance of my running into anyone. She was hooked to a life support, tubes up her nose, one foot in the other world. Whenever I looked away, I half expected that when I turned back she would be gone. She was tiny and wrinkled and deaf as a doorknob. There was so much I should have said. And yet. I told her jokes. I was a regular Jackie Mason. Sometimes I thought I saw the hint of a smile. I tried to keep things light. I said: *Would you believe, this thing here where your arm bends, this they call an elbow*. I said: *Two rabbis diverged in a yellow wood*. I said: *Moshe goes to the doctor. Doctor, he says*, etcetera, etcetera. Many things I did not say. Example. *I waited so long*. Other example. *And were you happy? With that nebbish that clod that numbskull schlemiel you call a husband?* The truth was I'd given up waiting long ago. The moment had passed, the door between the lives we could have led and the lives we led had shut in our faces. Or better to say, in *my* face.

Grammar of my life: as a rule of thumb, wherever there appears a plural, correct for singular. Should I ever let slip a royal *We*, put me out of my misery with a swift blow to the head.

Are you all right? You're looking a little pale.

It was the man I'd seen earlier, the one in the yellow bow tie. When your pants are down around your ankles that's when everyone arrives, never a moment before when you might have been in a position to receive them. I tried to steady myself against the potted plant.

Fine, fine, I said.

And how did you know him? he asked, giving me the once-over.

We were—I wedged my knee between the pot and the wall, hoping it would give me some balance. *Related.*

Family! So sorry, forgive me. I thought I'd met all the mishpocheh! The way he pronounced it was *mishpoky.*

Of course, I should have guessed. He looked me up and down again, running a palm over his hair to make sure it was securely positioned. *I thought you were one of the fans,* he said, gesturing toward the thinning crowd. *Which side, then?*

I took hold of the thickest part of the plant. I tried to focus on the man's bow tie while the room around me swayed.

Both, I said.

Both? he repeated, incredulous, as he looked down at the roots struggling to keep their grip in the earth.

I'm— I began. But with a sudden jerk the plant came free. I lurched forward, only my leg was still wedged such that the unsupported leg was forced to spring forward alone, leaving the lip of the pot no place to go except jammed into my groin, and my hand no choice but to grind the clod of dirt dangling from the roots into the face of the man in the yellow bow tie.

Sorry, I said, pain shooting up my groin and electrocuting my *kishkes.* I tried to stand up straight. My mother, may her memory be a blessing, used to say, *Don't slump.* Dirt rained from the man's nostrils. As a final touch, I pulled my cruddy hanky out and pressed it into his nose. He swatted my hand away and pulled out his own, freshly laundered and pressed into a neat square. He shook it loose. A flag of surrender. An awkward moment passed as he cleaned himself up and I nursed my nether region.

Next thing I knew, I was standing face to face with my son's half-brother, my sleeve between the teeth of the pit bull in a bow tie. *Look what I rustled up,* he barked. Bernard raised his eyebrows. *Says he's mishpoky.*

Bernard smiled politely as he eyed first the rip in my collar, then the tear in my arm. *Forgive me,* he said. *I don't remember you. Have we met?*

The pit bull visibly salivated. A fine dusting of soil

shifted in the crease of his shirt. I glanced at the sign marked EXIT. I might have made a run for it had I not been severely wounded in the privates. A wave of nausea came over me. And yet. Sometimes you need a stroke of genius and, lo and behold, genius comes and strokes you.

De rets Yiddish? I whispered hoarsely.

Pardon?

I grabbed Bernard's sleeve. The dog had mine and I had Bernard's. I brought my face close to his. His eyes were bloodshot. He may have been an oaf but he was a good man. And yet I had no choice.

I raised my voice. *DE RETS YIDDISH?* I could taste the stale alcohol on my breath. I grabbed his collar. The veins in his neck popped out as he recoiled backwards. *FARSHTAIST?*

Sorry. Bernard shook his head. *I don't understand.*

Good, I continued in Yiddish, *because this here dumbbell,* I said, gesturing at the man in the bow tie, *this here putz has inserted himself up my tuchas and it's only because I can't crap of my own free will that he has not been ejected. Would you kindly ask him to take his paws off me before I am forced to plug his schnoz with another plant, and this time I won't bother to de-pot it.*

Robert? Bernard struggled to understand. He seemed to grasp that I was talking about the man hanging on to my elbow with his teeth. *Robert was Isaac's editor. You knew Isaac?*

The pit bull tightened his hold. I opened my mouth. And yet.

Sorry, Bernard said. *I wish I spoke Yiddish, but. Well, thank you for coming. It's been moving to see how many people have come out. Isaac would have been pleased.* He took my hand between his own and shook it. He turned to go.

Slonim, I said. I hadn't planned on it. And yet.

Bernard turned back.

Pardon?

I said it again.

I come from Slonim, I said.

Slonim? he repeated.

I nodded.

He looked suddenly like a child whose mother has been late to pick him up, and only now that she's arrived allows himself to give in to tears.

She used to tell us about it.

Who's she? demanded the dog.

My mother. He comes from the same town as my mother, Bernard said. *I've heard so many stories.*

I meant to pat his arm but he moved to brush something from his eye, the result being that I ended up patting his man-breast. Not knowing what else to do, I gave it a squeeze.

The river, right? Where she used to swim, Bernard said.

The water was freezing. We would take our clothes

off and dive off the bridge screaming bloody murder. Our hearts would stop. Our bodies would turn to stone. For a moment we felt we were drowning. When we scrambled back onto the bank, gasping for air, our legs would be heavy, pain shooting up the ankles. Your mother was skinny, with small pale breasts. I would fall asleep drying in the sun, and wake to the shock of ice-cold water on my back. And her laughter.

Did you know her father's shoe shop? Bernard asked.

Every morning I picked her up there so we could walk together to school. Except for the time we got in a fight and didn't talk for three weeks, hardly a day passed that we didn't walk together. In the cold, her wet hair would freeze into icicles.

I could go on and on, all the stories she told us. The field where she used to play.

Ya, I said, patting his hand. *Ze field.*

Fifteen minutes later I was sandwiched between the pit bull and a young woman in the back of a stretch limousine, you would think I was making a habit of it. We were going to Bernard's house for a small gathering of family and friends. I would have preferred to go to my son's house, to mourn among his things, but I had to content myself with going to his half-brother's. Sitting in the seat opposite me in the limousine were two others. When one nodded and smiled in my direction, I nodded and smiled back. *A relative of Isaac's?* he asked. *Apparently,* the dog replied, groping for a lock of hair snapping in the draft from the window the woman had just lowered.

It took almost an hour to get to Bernard's house. Somewhere in Long Island. Beautiful trees. I'd never seen such beautiful trees. Out in the driveway, one of Bernard's nephews had slit his pants legs to the knee and was running up and down in the sunlight, watching how they caught the breeze. Inside the house, people stood around a table piled with food talking about Isaac. I knew I didn't belong there. I felt like a fool and an imposter. I stood by the window, making myself invisible. I didn't think it would be so painful. And yet. To hear people talk about the son I'd only been able to imagine as if he were as familiar to them as a relative was almost too much to bear. So I slipped away. I wandered through the rooms of Isaac's half-brother's house. I thought: My son walked on this carpet. I came to a guest bedroom. I thought: From time to time, he slept in this bed. This very bed! His head on these pillows. I lay down. I was tired, I couldn't help myself. The pillow sank under my cheek. And as he lay here, I thought, he looked out this very window, at that very tree.

You're such a dreamer, Bruno says, and maybe I am. Maybe I was also dreaming this, in a moment the doorbell would ring, I'd open my eyes, and Bruno would be standing there asking if I had a roll of toilet paper.

I must have fallen asleep because the next thing I knew, Bernard was standing above me.

Sorry! Didn't realize anyone was in here. Are you sick?

I sprang up. If the word *spring* can be used in reference to my movements at all, this was the moment. And that's when I saw it. It was on a shelf right behind his shoulder. In a silver picture frame. I would say *plain to see*, but I've never understood that expression. What could be less plain than seeing?

Bernard turned.

Oh, that, he said taking it down off the shelf. *Let's see. This is my mother when she was a child. My mother, see? Did you know her then, the way she looked in this picture?*

("Let's stand under a tree," she said. "Why?" "Because it's nicer." "Maybe you should sit on a chair, and I'll stand above you, like they always do with husbands and wives." "That's stupid." "Why's it stupid?" "Because we're not married." "Should we hold hands?" "We can't." "But why?" "Because, people will know." "Know what?" "About us." "So what if they know?" "It's better when it's a secret." "Why?" "So no one can take it from us.")

Isaac found it in her things after she died, Bernard said. *It's a nice photograph, isn't it? Don't know who he is. She didn't have much from over there. A couple of photos of her parents and her sisters, that's all. Of course, she had no idea she wouldn't see them again, so she didn't bring much. But I never saw this one until one day Isaac found it in a drawer in her apartment. It was inside an envelope with some letters. They were all in Yiddish. Isaac thought they were from someone she used to be in love with in Slonim. I doubt it, though. She never mentioned anyone. You can't understand a word I'm saying, can you?*

("If I had a camera," I said, "I'd take a picture of you every day. That way I'd remember how you looked every single day of your life." "I look exactly the same." "No, you don't. You're changing all the time. Every day a tiny bit. If I could, I'd keep a record of it all." "If you're so smart, how did I change today?" "You got a fraction of a millimeter taller, for one thing. Your hair grew a fraction of a millimeter longer. And your breasts grew a fraction of a—" "They did not!" "Yes, they did." "Did NOT." "Did too." "What else, you big pig?" "You got a little happier and also a little sadder." "Meaning they cancel each other out, leaving me exactly the same." "Not at all. The fact that you got a little happier today doesn't change the fact that you also became a little sadder. Every day you become a little more of both, which means that right now, at this exact moment, you're the happiest and the saddest you've ever been in your whole life." "How do you know?" "Think about it. Have you ever been happier than right now, lying here in the grass?" "I guess not. No." "And have you ever been sadder?" "No." "It isn't like that for everyone, you know. Some people, like your sister, just get happier and happier everyday. And some people, like Beyla Asch, just get sadder and sadder. And some people, like you, get both." "What about you? Are you the happiest and saddest right now that you've ever been?" "Of course I am." "Why?" "Because nothing makes me happier and nothing makes me sadder than you.")

My tears fell on the picture frame. Luckily there was glass.

I'd love to stay here reminiscing, Bernard said, *but I really should go. All those people out there.* He gestured. *Let me know if you need anything.* I nodded. He closed the door behind him, and then, God help me, I took the photograph and shoved it in my pants. Down the stairs I went, and out the door. In the driveway I knocked on the window of one of the limousines. The driver roused himself from sleep.

I'm ready to go back now, I said.

To my surprise, he got out, opened the door, and helped me in.

When I got back to my apartment, I thought I'd been robbed. The furniture was overturned, and the floor was dusted with white powder. I grabbed the baseball bat I keep in the umbrella stand and followed the trail of footsteps to the kitchen. Every surface was covered with pots and pans and dirty bowls. It seemed that whoever had broken in to rob me had taken time to make a meal. I stood with the photograph down my pants. There was a crash behind me, and I turned and swung blindly. But it was just a pot that had slipped from the counter and rolled across the floor. On the kitchen table, next to my typewriter, was a large cake, sunk in the middle. Standing, nonetheless. It was frosted with yellow icing, and across the top, in sloppy pink letters, it read, *LOOK WHO BAKED A CAKE.* On the other side of my typewriter was a note: *WAITED ALL DAY.*

I couldn't help it, I smiled. I put the baseball bat away, upturned the furniture that I remembered I had knocked over the night before, took out the picture frame, breathed on the glass, rubbed it with my shirt, and set it up on my night table. I climbed the stairs to Bruno's floor. I was about to knock when I saw the note on the door. It said: *DO NOT DISTURB. GIFT UNDER YOUR PILLOW.*

It had been a long time since anyone had given me a gift. A feeling of happiness nudged my heart. That I can wake up each morning and warm my hands on a hot cup of tea. That I can watch the pigeons fly. That at the end of my life, Bruno has not forgotten me.

Back down the stairs I went. To delay the pleasure I knew was coming my way, I stopped to pick up my mail. I let myself back into my apartment. Bruno had managed to leave a dusting of flour over the entire floor of the place. Maybe a wind had blown in, who knows. In the bedroom I saw that he had gotten down on the floor and made an angel in the flour. I stepped around it, not wanting to ruin what had been made so lovingly. I lifted my pillow.

It was a large brown envelope. On the outside was my name, written in a handwriting I didn't recognize. I opened it. Inside was a stack of printed pages. I began to read. The words were familiar. For a moment I couldn't place them. Then I realized they were my own.

MY FATHER'S TENT

1. MY FATHER DID NOT LIKE TO WRITE LETTERS

The old Cadbury tin full of my mother's letters doesn't contain any of his replies. I've looked for them everywhere, but never found them. Also, he didn't leave me a letter to open when I get older. I know because I asked my mother if he did, and she said No. She said he was not that sort of man. When I asked her what sort of man he was she thought for a minute. Her forehead creased. She thought some more. Then she said he was the sort of man who liked to challenge authority. "Also," she said, "he couldn't sit still." This is not the way I remember him. I remember him sitting in chairs or lying in beds. Except for when I was very little and thought that being an "engineer" meant he drove a train. Then I imagined him in the seat of an engine car the color of coal, a string of shiny passenger cars trailing behind. One day my father laughed and corrected me. Everything snapped into focus. It's one of those unforgettable moments that happen as a child, when you discover that all along the world has been betraying you.

2. HE GAVE ME A PEN THAT COULD WORK WITHOUT GRAVITY

"It can work without gravity," my father said, as I examined it in its velvet box with the NASA insignia. It was my seventh birthday. He was lying in a hospital bed wearing a hat because he had no hair. Shiny wrapping paper lay crumpled on his blanket. He held my hand and told me a story about when he was six and threw a rock at a kid's head who was bullying his brother, and how after that no one had ever bothered either of them again. "You have to stick up for yourself," he told me. "But it's bad to throw rocks," I said. "I know," he said. "You're smarter than me. You'll find something better than rocks." When the nurse came, I went to look out the window. The 59th Street Bridge shone in the dark. I counted the boats passing on the river. When I got bored, I went to look at the old man whose bed was on the other side of the curtain. He slept most of the time, and when he was awake his hands shook. I showed him the pen. I told him that it could work without gravity, but he didn't understand. I tried to explain again, but he was still confused. Finally I said, "It's to use when I'm in outer space." He nodded and closed his eyes.

3. THE MAN WHO COULDN'T ESCAPE GRAVITY

Then my father died, and I put the pen away in a drawer. Years passed, and then I was eleven and got a Russian pen pal. It was arranged through our Hebrew School by the local chapter of Hadassah. At first we were supposed to write to Russian Jews who had just immigrated to Israel, but when that fell through we were assigned regular Russian Jews. On Sukkot we sent our pen pals' class an etrog with our first letters. Mine was named Tatiana. She lived in St. Petersburg, near the Field of Mars. I liked to pretend she lived in outer space. Tatiana's English wasn't very good, and often I couldn't understand her letters. But I waited for them eagerly. *Father is mathematician*, she wrote. *My father could survive in the wild*, I wrote back. For every one of her letters, I wrote two. *Do you have a dog? How many people use your bathroom? Do you own anything that belonged to the Czar?* One day a letter came. She wanted to know if I had ever been to Sears Roebuck. At the end there was a P.S. It said: *Boy in my class is moved to New York. Maybe you want write him because he knows anybody.* That was the last I ever heard from her.

4. I SEARCHED OUT OTHER FORMS OF LIFE

"Where's Brighton Beach?" I asked. "In England," my mother said, searching the kitchen cabinets for something she'd misplaced. "I mean the one in New York." "Near Coney Island, I think." "How far is Coney Island?" "Maybe half an hour." "Driving or walking?" "You can take the subway." "How many stops?" "I don't know. Why are you so interested in Brighton Beach?" "I have a friend there. His name is Misha and he's Russian," I said with admiration. "Just Russian?" my mother asked from inside the cabinet under the kitchen sink. "What do you mean, *just* Russian?" She stood up and turned to me. "Nothing," she said, looking at me with the expression she sometimes gets when she's just thought of something amazingly fascinating. "It's just that you, for example, are one-quarter Russian, one-quarter Hungarian, one-quarter Polish, and one-quarter German." I didn't say anything. She opened a drawer, then closed it. "Actually," she said, "you could say you're three-quarters Polish and one-quarter Hungarian, since Bubbe's parents were from Poland before they moved to Nuremberg, and Grandma Sasha's town was originally in Belarus, or White Russia, before it became part of Poland." She opened another cabinet stuffed with plastic bags and started rooting around in it. I turned to go. "Now that I'm thinking about it," she said, "I suppose you could also say you're three-quarters Polish and one-quarter Czech, because the town Zeyde came from was in Hungary before 1918, and in Czechoslovakia after, although the Hungarians continued to consider themselves Hungarian, and briefly even became Hungarian again during the Second World War. Of course, you could always just say you're half Polish, one-quarter Hungarian, and one-quarter English, since Grandpa Simon left Poland and moved to London when he was nine." She grabbed a piece of paper from the pad by the telephone and started to write vigorously. A minute passed while she scratched away at the page. "Look!" she said, pushing the paper over so I could see it. "You can actually make *sixteen different* pie

charts, each of them accurate!" I looked at the
paper. It said:

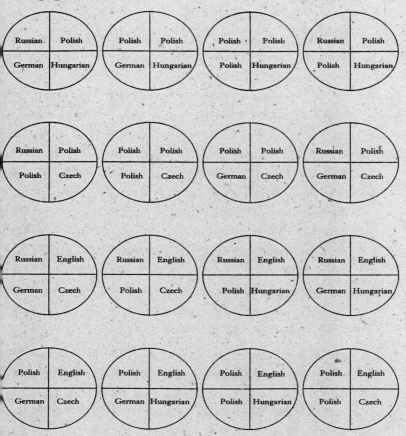

Russian	Polish		Polish	Polish		Polish	Polish		Russian	Polish
German	Hungarian		German	Hungarian		Polish	Hungarian		Polish	Hungarian

Russian	Polish		Polish	Polish		Polish	Polish		Russian	Polish
Polish	Czech		Polish	Czech		German	Czech		German	Czech

Russian	English		Russian	English		Russian	English		Russian	English
German	Czech		Polish	Czech		Polish	Hungarian		German	Hungarian

Polish	English		Polish	English		Polish	English		Polish	English
German	Czech		German	Hungarian		Polish	Hungarian		Polish	Czech

"Then again, you could always just stick with
half English and half Israeli, since—" "I'M
AMERICAN!" I shouted. My mother blinked.

"Suit yourself," she said, and went to put the kettle on to boil. From the corner of the room where he was looking at the pictures in a magazine, Bird muttered: "No, you're not. You're Jewish."

5. ONCE I USED THE PEN TO WRITE TO MY FATHER

We were in Jerusalem for my Bat Mitzvah. My mother wanted to have it at the Wailing Wall so Bubbe and Zeyde, my father's parents, could attend. When Zeyde came to Palestine in 1938 he said he wasn't ever going to leave, and he never did. Anyone who wanted to see him had to come to their apartment in the tall building in Kiryat Wolfson, overlooking the Knesset. It was filled with the old dark furniture and old dark photographs they'd brought from Europe. In the afternoon they lowered the metal blinds to protect it all from the blinding light, because nothing they owned was made to survive in that weather.

My mother looked for weeks for cheap tickets, and finally found three $700 tickets on El Al. It was still a lot of money for us, but she said it was a good thing to spend it on. The day before my Bat Mitzvah, Mom took us to the Dead Sea. Bubbe came, too, wearing a straw hat that stayed on with a band under her chin. When she came out of the changing room, she was fascinating in her bathing suit, her skin wrinkled and puckered and covered with blue veins. We watched her face flush in the hot sulfur springs, beads of sweat forming on her upper lip. When she got out, water streamed off of her. We followed her down to the edge of the water. Bird stood in the mud, crossing his legs. "If you have to go, go in the water," Bubbe said in a loud voice. A group of heavy Russian women coated in the black mineral clay turned to look. If Bubbe noticed, she didn't care. We floated on our backs while she kept watch over us from under the wide brim of her hat. My eyes were closed, but I felt her shadow over me. "You don't have a bosom? Vat happened?" I felt my face get hot and pretended not to have heard. "You have boyfriends?" she asked. Bird perked up. "No," I muttered. "Vat?" "*No.*" "Vy not?" "I'm twelve." "So vat! Ven I vas your age I had three, maybe four. You're young and pretty, *keynehore.*" I paddled out to get some distance from her giant, imposing bosom. Her voice followed me. "But it von't last forever!" I tried to stand, and slipped in the clay. I scanned the flat water for my mother until I caught sight of her. She'd swum out beyond the farthest bather, and was still going.

The next morning I stood at the Wailing Wall,

still stinking of sulfur. The cracks between the massive stones were filled with tiny crumpled papers. The rabbi told me that if I wanted I could write a note to God and add it to the cracks. I didn't believe in God, so I wrote to my father instead: *Dear Dad, I'm writing this with the pen you gave me. Yesterday Bird asked if you could do the Heimlich and I told him yes. I also told him you could fly a hovercraft. By the way, I found your tent in the basement. I guess Mom didn't notice it when she threw out everything that belonged to you. It smells of mildew, but it doesn't have any leaks. Sometimes I set it up in the backyard and lie inside thinking about how you used to lie in it, too. I'm writing this but I know that you can't read it. Love, Alma.* Bubbe wrote one, too. When I tried to stuff mine into the wall, hers fell out. She was busy praying, so I picked it up and unfolded it. It said: *Baruch Hashem, I and my husband should live to see tomorrow and that my Alma should grow up to be blessed with health and happiness and what would be so terrible some nice breasts.*

6. IF I HAD A RUSSIAN ACCENT EVERYTHING WOULD BE DIFFERENT

When I got back to New York, Misha's first letter was waiting. *Dear Alma,* it began. *Greetings! I am very happy for your welcome!* He was almost thirteen, five months older than I. His English was better than Tatiana's because he'd memorized the lyrics of almost all the Beatles songs. He sang them while accompanying himself on the accordion his grandfather gave him, the one who'd moved in after Misha's grandmother died and, according to Misha, her soul descended on the Summer Gardens in St. Petersburg in the form of a flock of geese. It stayed for two weeks straight, honking in the rain, and when it left the grass was covered with turds. His grandfather arrived a few weeks later, dragging behind him a battered suitcase filled with the eighteen volumes of *The History of the Jews.* He moved into the already cramped room Misha shared with his older sister, Svetlana, took out his accordion, and began to produce his life's work. At first he just wrote variations on Russian folk songs mixed with Jewish riffs. Later he moved on to darker, wilder versions, and at the very end he stopped playing things they recognized altogether, and as he held the long notes he wept, and no one needed to tell Misha and Svetya, even thick-headed as they were, that at last he'd become the composer he'd always wanted to be. He had a beat-up car that sat in the alley behind their apartment. The way Misha tells it, he drove like a blind man, giving

the car almost full independence to feel its way
along, bumping off things, only giving the wheel
a spin with the tips of his fingers when the situation verged on life-threatening. When their
grandfather came to pick them up from school,
Misha and Svetlana would shield their ears and
try to look away. When he revved the motor and
became impossible to ignore, they'd hurry toward
the car with their heads down and slide into the
back seat. They'd huddle together in the back
while their grandfather sat at the wheel, humming
along to a tape of their cousin Lev's punk band,
Pussy Ass Mother Fucker. But he always got the
words wrong. For *"Got into a fight, smashed his
face on the car door,"* he might sing, *"You are my
knight and you wear shining ar-mor,"* and for *"You're
a louse, but you're so pretty,"* he'd sing, *"Take it up
to the house, in a jitney."* When Misha and his sister
pointed out his mistakes, their grandfather acted
surprised and turned up the volume to hear better,
but the next time around he'd sing the same thing.
When he died, he left Svetya the eighteen
volumes of *The History of the Jews*, and Misha the
accordion. Around the same time, Lev's sister,
who wore blue eye shadow, invited Misha into
her room, played him "Let it Be," and taught him
how to kiss.

7. THE BOY WITH THE ACCORDION

Misha and I wrote twenty-one letters back and forth. This was the year I was twelve, two years before Jacob Marcus wrote to my mother asking her to translate *The History of Love*. Misha's letters were filled with exclamation points and questions like, *What does mean, your ass is grassy?* and mine were filled with questions about life in Russia. Then he invited me to his Bar Mitzvah party.

My mother braided my hair, lent me her red shawl, and drove me to his apartment house in Brighton Beach. I rang the buzzer and waited for Misha to come down. My mother waved to me from the car. I shivered in the cold. A tall boy with dark fuzz on his upper lip came out. "Alma?" he asked. I nodded. "Welcome, my friend!" he said. I waved to my mother and followed him inside. The lobby smelled like sour cabbage. Upstairs, the apartment was packed with people eating and shouting in Russian. There was a band set up in a corner of the dining room, and people kept trying to dance even though there was no room. Misha was busy talking to everyone and stuffing envelopes in his pocket, so I spent most of the party sitting in the corner of the couch with a plate of giant shrimp. I don't even eat shrimp but it was the only thing I recognized. If anyone talked to me, I had to explain that I didn't speak Russian. An old man offered me some vodka. Just then Misha rushed out of the kitchen strapped into his accordion, which was plugged into an amplifier, and broke into song. "You say it's your birthday!" he shouted. The crowd looked nervous. "Well it's my birthday, too!" he yelled, and the accordion shrieked to life. This led into "Sgt. Pepper's Lonely Heart's Club Band," which led into "Here Comes the Sun," and eventually, after five or six songs, the Beatles broke into "Hava Nagila," and the crowd went wild, everyone singing along and trying to dance. When the music finally stopped, Misha came to find me, his face pink and sweaty. He grabbed my hand, and I followed him out of the apartment, down the hall, up five flights of stairs, through a door, and out onto the roof. You could see the ocean in the distance, the lights of Coney Island, and after that an abandoned roller coaster. My teeth started to chatter, and Misha took off his jacket and put it around my shoulders. It was warm and smelled of sweat.

8. БЛЯДЬ

I told Misha everything. About how my father had died, and my mother's loneliness, and Bird's unshakable belief in God. I told him about the three volumes of *How to Survive in the Wild*, and the English editor and his regatta, and Henry Lavender and his Philippine shells, and the veterinarian, Tucci. I told him about Dr. Eldridge and *Life as We Don't Know It*, and later—two years after we started to write to each other, seven years after my dad died, and 3.9 billion years after the first life on earth—when Jacob Marcus's first letter arrived from Venice, I told Misha about *The History of Love*. Mostly we wrote or talked on the phone, but sometimes on the weekends we'd get to see each other. I liked going to Brighton Beach better, because Mrs. Shklovsky would bring us tea with sweet cherries in china cups, and Mr. Shklovsky, whose armpits always had dark circles of sweat, taught me how to curse in Russian. Sometimes we'd rent movies, especially spy stories or thrillers. Our favorites were *Rear Window*, *Strangers on a Train*, and *North by Northwest*, which we'd watched ten times. When I wrote to Jacob Marcus pretending to be my mother, it was Misha I told about it, reading the final draft to him over the phone. "What do you think?" I asked. "I think your ass is—" "Forget it," I said.

9. THE MAN WHO SEARCHED FOR A STONE

A week went by after I sent my letter, or my mother's letter, or whatever you want to call it. Another week went by and I wondered if maybe Jacob Marcus was out of the country, possibly Cairo, or maybe Tokyo. A week went by and I thought maybe he'd somehow figured out the truth. Four days went by and I studied my mother's face for signs of anger. It was already the end of July. A day went by and I thought maybe I should write to Jacob Marcus and apologize. The next day his letter came.

My mother's name, Charlotte Singer, was written across the front in fountain pen. I slipped it into the waist of my shorts just as the telephone rang. "Hello?" I said impatiently. "Is the *Moshiach* home?" said the voice on the other end. "*Who?*" "The *Moshiach*," the kid said, and I heard muffled laughter in the background. It sounded a little like Louis, who lived one block over, and used to be Bird's friend until he met other friends he liked better, and stopped talking to Bird. "Leave him alone," I said, and hung up, wishing I'd thought of something better.

I ran up the block to the park, holding my side so the envelope wouldn't slip. It was hot out and I was already sweating. I tore the letter open next to a trash can in Long Meadow. The first page was about how much Jacob Marcus liked the chapters my mother had sent. I skimmed it until, on the second page, I got to the sentence that read: *I still haven't mentioned your letter.* He wrote:

I'm flattered by your curiosity. I wish I had more interesting answers to all your questions. I have to say, these days I spend a lot of time just sitting here and looking out the window. I used to love to travel. But the trip to Venice was harder than I thought, and I doubt I'll do it again. My life, for reasons beyond my control, has been pared down to the simplest elements. For example, here on my desk is a stone. A dark gray piece of granite cut in half by a vein of white. It took me most of the morning to find it. Many stones were rejected first. I didn't set out with a particular idea of the stone in my mind. I thought I'd recognize it when I found it. As I searched I developed certain requirements. It had to fit comfortably in the palm, be smooth, preferably gray, etc. So that was my morning. I've spent the last few hours recovering.

It wasn't always like this. It used to be that a day was worthless to me if I hadn't produced a certain amount of work. That I noticed or didn't notice the gardener's limp, the ice on the lake, the long, solemn outings of my neighbor's child who appears to have no friends—these things were beside the point. But that's changed now.

You asked if I was married. I was once, but that was a long time ago, and we were clever or stupid enough not to have a child. We met each other when we were young, before we knew enough about disappointment, and once we did we found we reminded each other of it. I guess you could say that I wear a little Russian astronaut on my lapel, too. I live alone now, which doesn't bother me. Or maybe just a little. But it would take an unusual woman to want to keep me company now that I can hardly walk down to the bottom of the driveway and back to pick up the mail. I still do it, though. Twice a week a friend brings by some groceries, and my neighbor looks in once a day with the excuse of wanting to check on the strawberries she planted in my garden. I don't even like strawberries.

I'm making it sound worse than it is.
I don't even know you yet, and I'm already
fishing for sympathy.

You also asked what I do. I read. This
morning I finished *The Street of Crocodiles*
for the third time. I found it almost unbearably beautiful.

Also, I watch movies. My brother got
me a DVD player. You wouldn't believe
how many movies I've watched in the last
month. That's what I do. Watch movies
and read. Sometimes I even pretend to
write, but I'm not fooling anyone. Oh, and
I go to the mailbox.

Enough. I loved your book. Please
send me some more.

JM

10. I READ THE LETTER ONE HUNDRED TIMES

And each time I read it, I felt I knew a little less
about Jacob Marcus. He said he spent the morning looking for a rock, but he never said anything
more about why *The History of Love* was so important to him. Of course it didn't escape me that
he'd written: *I don't even know you yet*. Yet! Meaning

he was expecting to get to know us better, or at least our mother, since he didn't know about Bird and me. (Yet!) But why could he hardly walk to the mailbox and back? And why would it take an unusual woman to keep him company? And why was he wearing a Russian astronaut on his lapel?

I decided to make a list of clues. I went home, closed my bedroom door, and took out the third volume of *How to Survive in the Wild*. I turned to a new page. I decided to write everything in code, in case anyone decided to snoop around in my things. I remembered Saint-Ex. At the top I wrote *How to Survive if Your Parachute Fails to Open*. Then I wrote:

1. *Search for a stone*
2. *Live near a lake*
3. *Have a gardener with a limp*
4. *Read* The Street of Crocodiles
5. *Need an unusual woman*
6. *Have trouble just walking to the mailbox*

Those were all the clues I could come up with from his letter, so I snuck into my mother's study while she was downstairs and got his other letters out of her desk drawer. I read these for more clues. That's when I remembered that his first letter began with a quote from my mother's introduction about Nicanor Parra, the one about how he wore a little Russian astronaut on his lapel and carried in his pockets the letters of a woman who left him for another. When Jacob Marcus wrote that he also wore a Russian astronaut, did it mean that his wife had left him for someone else? Because I wasn't sure, I didn't put this down as a clue. Instead I wrote:

7. *Take a trip to Venice*
8. *A long time ago, have someone read to you from* The History of Love *while you're falling asleep.*
9. *Never forget it.*

I looked over my clues. None of them helped.

11. HOW I AM

I decided that if I really wanted to find out who Jacob Marcus was, and why it was so important to him to have the book translated, the only place left to look was *The History of Love*.

I snuck upstairs to my mother's study, to see if I could print the chapters she'd translated off her computer. The only problem was that she was sitting in front of it. "Hello," she said. "Hello," I said, trying to sound casual. "How are you?" she asked. "Finethankyouhowareyou?" I answered, because that's what she taught me to say, as well as how to hold my knife and fork properly, how to balance a teacup between two fingers, and the best way to dig out a piece of food between my teeth without drawing attention to myself, on the off chance that the Queen happened to invite me for high tea. When I pointed out that no one I know holds their knife and fork properly, she looked unhappy and said she was trying to be a good mother, and if she didn't teach me, who would? I wish she hadn't, though, because sometimes being polite is worse than being not-polite, like the time Greg Feldman passed me in the hall at school and said, "Hey, Alma, what's up?" and I said, "Finethankyouhowareyou?" and he stopped and gave me a look like I'd just parachuted down from Mars, and said, "Why can't you ever just say, *Not much*?"

12. NOT MUCH

It got dark out, and my mother said there was nothing to eat in the house, and did we want to order some Thai food, or maybe West Indian, or how about Cambodian. "Why can't we cook?" I asked. "Macaroni and cheese?" my mother asked. "Mrs. Shklovsky makes a very good Chicken L'Orange," I said. My mother looked doubtful. "Chili?" I said. While she was at the supermarket, I went up to her study and printed out chapters one through fifteen of *The History of Love*, which was as far as she'd gotten. I took the pages downstairs and hid them in my survival backpack under the bed. A few minutes later my mother came home with one pound of ground turkey, one head of broccoli, three apples, a jar of pickles, and a box of marzipan imported from Spain.

13. THE ETERNAL DISAPPOINTMENT OF LIFE AS IT IS

After a dinner of microwaved fake-meat chicken nuggets, I went to bed early and read what my mother had translated of *The History of Love* under the covers by flashlight. There was the chapter about how people used to talk with their hands, and the chapter about the man who thought he was made of glass, and a chapter I hadn't read called "The Birth of Feeling." *Feelings are not as old as time*, it began.

Just as there was a first instant when someone rubbed two sticks together to make a
spark, there was a first time joy was felt, and
a first time for sadness. For a while, new feelings were being invented all the time. Desire
was born early, as was regret. When stub-
bornness was felt for the first time, it started
a chain reaction, creating the feeling of
resentment on the one hand, and alienation
and loneliness on the other. It might have
been a certain counterclockwise movement
of the hips that marked the birth of ecstasy;
a bolt of lightning that caused the first feeling of awe. Or maybe it was the body of a
girl named Alma. Contrary to logic, the feeling of surprise wasn't born immediately. It
only came after people had enough time to
get used to things as they were. And when
enough time *had* passed, and someone felt
the first feeling of surprise, someone, somewhere else, felt the first pang of nostalgia.

It's also true that sometimes people felt
things and, because there was no word for
them, they went unmentioned. The oldest
emotion in the world may be that of being
moved; but to describe it—just to name
it—must have been like trying to catch
something invisible.

(Then again, the oldest feeling in the world might simply have been confusion.)

Having begun to feel, people's desire to feel grew. They wanted to feel more, feel deeper, despite how much it sometimes hurt. People became addicted to feeling. They struggled to uncover new emotions. It's possible that this is how art was born. New kinds of joy were forged, along with new kinds of sadness: The eternal disappointment of life as it is; the relief of unexpected reprieve; the fear of dying.

Even now, all possible feelings do not yet exist. There are still those that lie beyond our capacity and our imagination. From time to time, when a piece of music no one has ever written, or a painting no one has ever painted, or something else impossible to predict, fathom, or yet describe takes place, a new feeling enters the world. And then, for the millionth time in the history of feeling, the heart surges, and absorbs the impact.

All of the chapters were sort of like this, and none of them really told me anything about why the book was so important to Jacob Marcus. Instead I found myself thinking about my father.

About how much *The History of Love* must have meant to him if he gave it to my mother only two weeks after they met, even though he knew she couldn't read Spanish yet. Why? Because he was falling in love with her, of course.

Then I thought of something else. What if my father had written something inside the copy of *The History of Love* he gave to my mother? It hadn't ever occurred to me to look.

I got out of bed and went upstairs. Mom's study was empty and the book was next to her computer. I lifted it up and opened to the title page. In handwriting I didn't recognize, it said: *For Charlotte, my Alma. This is the book I would have written for you if I could write. Love, David*

I went back to bed and thought about my father, and those twenty words, for a long time.

And then I started to think about her. Alma. Who was she? My mother would say she was everyone, every girl and every woman that anyone ever loved. But the more I thought about it, the more I thought that she also must have been *someone*. Because how could Litvinoff have written so much about love without being in love himself? With someone in particular. And that someone must have been named—

Under the nine clues I'd already written, I added one more:

10. Alma

14. THE BIRTH OF FEELING

I raced down to the kitchen, but it was empty. Outside the window, in the middle of our backyard overgrown and full of weeds, was my mother. I pushed open the screen door. "Alma," I said, catching my breath. "Hmm?" my mother said. She was holding a gardening trowel. I didn't have time to stop and think about why she was holding a gardening trowel since it was my father, not her, who'd gardened, and since it was already nine-thirty at night. "What's her last name?" I asked. "What are you talking about?" my mother said. "Alma," I said impatiently. "The girl in the book. What's her last name?" My mother wiped her forehead, leaving a smear of dirt. "Actually, now that you mention it—one of the chapters does mention a surname. But it's strange, because while all the other names in the book are Spanish, her surname is—" My mother frowned. "What?" I said, excited. "Hers is what?" "Mereminski," my mother said. "Mereminski," I repeated. She nodded. "M-E-R-E-M-I-N-S-K-I. Mereminski. Polish. It's one of the few clues Litvinoff left about where he came from."

I ran back upstairs, climbed into bed, turned

on my flashlight, and opened the third volume of *How to Survive in the Wild*. Next to *Alma*, I wrote *Mereminski*.

The next day, I started to look for her.

THE TROUBLE WITH THINKING

If Litvinoff coughed more and more as the years passed—a hacking cough that shook his whole body, causing him to bend over double, and made it necessary for him to excuse himself from dinner tables, refuse phone calls, and turn down the occasional invitation to speak—it wasn't so much because he was ill, as that there was something he wished to say. The more time passed, the more he longed to say it, and the more impossible saying it became. Sometimes he woke in a panic from his dreams. *Rosa!* he'd shout. But before the words were out of his mouth he'd feel her hand on his chest, and at the sound of her voice— *What is it? What's wrong, sweetheart?*—he'd lose his courage, overcome with fear of the consequences. And so instead of saying what he wanted to say, he said: *It's nothing. Just a bad dream,* and waited for her to fall back asleep before pushing off the covers and stepping out to the balcony.

When he was young, Litvinoff had a friend. Not his best friend, but a good one. The last time he saw this friend was the day he left Poland. The friend was standing on a street corner. They'd already parted ways, but both turned back to see the other go. For a long time they stood there. His friend's cap was gathered in a fist held to his chest. He raised his hand, saluted Litvinoff, and smiled. Then he pulled his cap down over his eyes, turned, and disappeared empty-handed into the crowd. Not a day went by now that Litvinoff did not think about that moment, or that friend.

On nights when he couldn't sleep, Litvinoff would sometimes go to his study and take out his copy of *The History of Love*. He'd reread the fourteenth chapter, "The Age of String," so many times that now the binding opened to it automatically:

So many words get lost. They leave the mouth and lose their courage, wandering aimlessly until they are swept into the gutter like dead leaves. On rainy days you can hear their chorus rushing past: *IwasabeautifulgirlPleasedon'tgo-ItoobelievemybodyismadeofglassI'veneverloved-anyoneIthinkofmyselfasfunnyForgive me . . .*

There was a time when it wasn't uncommon to use a piece of string to guide words that otherwise might falter on the way to their destinations. Shy people carried a little bundle of string in their pockets, but people considered loudmouths had no less need for it, since those used to being overheard by everyone were often at a loss for how to make themselves heard by someone. The physical distance between two people using a string was often small; sometimes the smaller the distance, the greater the need for the string.

The practice of attaching cups to the ends of the string came much later. Some say it is related to the irrepressible urge to press shells to our ears, to hear the still-surviving echo of the world's first expression. Others say it was started by a man who held the end of a string that was unraveled across the ocean by a girl who left for America.

When the world grew bigger, and there wasn't enough string to keep the things people wanted to say from disappearing into the vastness, the telephone was invented.

Sometimes no length of string is long enough to say the thing that needs to be said. In such cases all the string can do, in whatever its form, is conduct a person's silence.

Litvinoff coughed. The printed book in his hands was a copy of a copy of a copy of a copy of the original, which no longer existed, except in his head. Not the "original" as in the ideal book a writer imagines before sitting down to write. The original that existed in Litvinoff's head was the memory of the manuscript handwritten in his mother tongue, the one he'd held in his hands the day he'd said goodbye to his friend for the last time. They hadn't known it was going to be the last. But in their hearts, each had wondered.

In those days, Litvinoff had been a journalist. He'd worked at a daily, writing obituaries. From time to time, in the evening after work, he went to a café populated by artists and philosophers. Because Litvinoff didn't know many people there, he usually just ordered a drink and pretended to read a newspaper he'd already read, listening to the conversations around him:

> *The thought of time outside of our experience is*
> *intolerable!*
> *Marx, my ass.*
> *The novel is dead!*
> *Before we declare our consent we must carefully*
> *examine—*
> *Liberation is just the means of attaining free-*
> *dom; it's not synonymous with it!*
> *Malevich? My snot is more interesting than*
> *that butthole.*
> *And that, my friend, is the trouble with thinking!*

Sometimes Litvinoff found himself disagreeing with someone's argument, and in his head he delivered a brilliant rebuttal.

One night he heard a voice behind him: "Must be a good article—you've been reading it for the last half hour." Litvinoff jumped, and when he looked up, the familiar face of his old childhood friend was smiling down at him. They embraced, and took in the slight changes time had enacted on the other's appearance. Litvinoff had always felt a certain affinity with this friend, and he was anxious to know what he'd been doing the last few years. "Working, like everyone else," his friend said, pulling up a chair. "And your writing?" Litvinoff asked. His friend shrugged. "It's quiet at night. No one bothers me. The landlord's cat comes and sits on my lap. Usually I fall asleep at my desk, and wake when the cat stalks off at the first sign of daylight." And then, for no reason, they both laughed.

From then on, they met every evening at the café. With growing horror they discussed the movements of Hitler's armies and the rumored actions being taken against the Jews until they became too depressed to speak. "But perhaps something more cheerful," his friend would finally say, and Litvinoff would happily change the subject, eager to test out one of his philosophical theories on his old friend, or to run by him a new fast-cash plan involving ladies' stockings and the black market, or to describe the pretty girl who lived across the street from him. His friend, in turn, occasionally showed Litvinoff bits of what he was working on. Small things, a paragraph here and there. But Litvinoff was always moved. With the first page he read, he recognized that, in the time since they had been schoolboys together, his friend had grown into a real writer.

A few months later, when it was learned that Isaac Babel had been killed by Moscow's secret police, it fell to Litvinoff to write the obituary. It was an important assignment and he worked hard on it, trying to strike the right tone for a great writer's tragic death. He didn't leave the office until midnight, but as he walked home through the cold night he smiled to himself, believing the obituary was one of his finest. So often the material he had to work with was thin and paltry, and he had to patch something together with a few superlatives, clichés, and false notes of glory in order to commemorate the life, and bolster a sense of loss over the death. But not this time. This time it had been necessary to rise to the material, to struggle to find words for a man who had been a master of words, who had devoted his entire existence to resisting the cliché in the hope of introducing to the world a new way of thinking and writing; a new way, even, of feeling. And whose reward for his labors was death by firing squad.

The next day it appeared in the newspaper. His

editor called him into his office to congratulate him on his work. A few of his colleagues also complimented him. When he saw his friend that evening in the café, he, too, praised the piece. Litvinoff ordered them a round of vodka, feeling happy and proud.

A few weeks later, his friend didn't show up at the café as usual. Litvinoff waited an hour and a half and then gave up and went home. The next evening he waited again, and again his friend didn't come. Worried, Litvinoff set out for the house where his friend boarded. He'd never been, but he knew the address. When he got there, he was surprised by how dingy and run-down the house was, by the oily walls in the entryway and the smell of something stale. He knocked on the first door he came to. A woman answered. Litvinoff asked after his friend. "Yeah, sure," she said, "the big writer." She jerked her thumb upwards. "Top floor on the right."

Litvinoff knocked for five minutes before he finally heard his friend's heavy steps on the other side. When the door opened, his friend stood in his bedclothes looking pale and haggard. "What happened?" Litvinoff asked. His friend shrugged and coughed, "Watch out or you'll catch it, too," he said, dragging himself back to bed. Litvinoff stood awkwardly in his friend's cramped room wanting to help, but not knowing how. At last a voice came from the pillows: "A cup of tea would be nice." Litvinoff hurried to the corner where a makeshift kitchen was set up, and banged around looking for the kettle ("On the stove," his friend called weakly). While the water boiled, he opened the window to let in a little fresh air, and washed the dirty dishes. When he brought the steaming cup of tea to his friend, he saw that he was shivering with a fever, so he closed the window and went downstairs to ask the landlady for an extra blanket. Eventually his friend fell asleep. Not knowing what else to do, Litvinoff sat down in the only chair in the room and waited. After a quarter of an hour, a cat meowed at the door. Litvinoff let it in, but when she saw that her midnight companion was indisposed she stalked out.

In front of the chair was a wooden desk. Pages were scattered across the surface. One caught Litvinoff's eye and, glancing over to make sure his friend was soundly asleep, he picked it up. Across the top it said: *THE DEATH OF ISAAC BABEL.*

Only after they charged him with the crime of silence did Babel discover how many kinds of silences existed. When he heard music he no longer listened to the notes, but the silences in between. When he read a book he gave himself over entirely to commas and semicolons, to the space after the period and before the capital letter of the next sentence.

He discovered the places in a room where silence gathered; the folds of curtain drapes, the deep bowls of the family silver. When people spoke to him, he heard less and less of what they were saying, and more and more of what they were not. He learned to decipher the meaning of certain silences, which is like solving a tough case without any clues, with only intuition. And no one could accuse him of not being prolific in his chosen métier. Daily, he turned out whole epics of silence. In the beginning it had been difficult. Imagine the burden of keeping silent when your child asks you whether God exists, or the woman you love asks if you love her back. At first Babel longed for the use of just two words: Yes and No. But he knew that just to utter a single word would be to destroy the delicate fluency of silence.

Even after they arrested him and burned all of his manuscripts, which were all blank pages, he refused to speak. Not even a groan when they gave him a blow to the head, a boot tip in the groin. Only at the last possible moment, as he faced the firing squad, did the writer Babel suddenly sense the possibility of his error. As the rifles were pointed at his chest he wondered if what he had taken for the richness of silence was really the poverty of never being heard. He had thought the possibilities of human silence were endless. But as the bullets tore from the rifles, his body was riddled with the truth. And a small part of him laughed bitterly because, anyway, how could he have forgotten what he had always known: There's no match for the silence of God.

Litvinoff dropped the page. He was furious. How could his friend, who could have his pick of what to write about, steal the one subject about which he, Litvinoff, happened to have written something of which he was proud? He felt mocked and humiliated. He wanted to drag his friend out of bed and demand what he'd meant by it. But after a moment he cooled down and read it again, and as he did he recognized the truth. His friend hadn't stolen anything that belonged to him. How could he have? A person's death belongs to no one but the one who's died.

A feeling of sadness came over him. All these years Litvinoff had imagined he was so much like his friend. He'd prided himself on what he considered their similarities. But the truth was that he was no more like the man fighting a fever in the bed ten feet away than he was like the cat that had just slunk off: they were different species. It was obvious, Litvinoff thought. All you had to do was look at how each had approached the same subject. Where he saw a page of words, his friend saw the field of hesitations, black holes, and possibilities between the words. Where his friend saw dappled light, the felicity of flight, the sadness of gravity, he saw the solid form of a common sparrow. Litvinoff's life was defined by a delight in the weight of the real; his friend's by a rejection of reality, with its army of flat-footed facts. Looking at his reflection in the dark window, Litvinoff believed something had been peeled away and a truth revealed to him: He was an average man. A man willing to accept things as they were, and, because of this, he lacked the potential to be in any way original. And though he was wrong in every way about this, after that night nothing could dissuade him.

Beneath THE DEATH OF ISAAC BABEL was another page. With tears of self-pity stinging his sinuses, Litvinoff read on.

FRANZ KAFKA IS DEAD

He died in a tree from which he wouldn't come down. "Come down!" they cried to him. "Come down! Come down!" Silence filled the night, and the night filled the silence, while they waited for Kafka to speak. "I can't," he finally said, with a note of wistfulness. "Why?" they cried. Stars spilled across the black sky.

"Because then you'll stop asking for me." The people whispered and nodded among themselves. They put their arms around each other, and touched their children's hair. They took off their hats and raised them to the small, sickly man with the ears of a strange animal, sitting in his black velvet suit in the dark tree. Then they turned and started for home under the canopy of leaves. Children were carried on their fathers' shoulders, sleepy from having been taken to see the man who wrote his books on pieces of bark he tore off the tree from which he refused to come down. In his delicate, beautiful, illegible handwriting. And they admired those books, and they admired his will and stamina. After all: who doesn't wish to make a spectacle of his loneliness? One by one, families broke off with a goodnight and a squeeze of the hands, suddenly grateful for the company of neighbors. Doors closed to warm houses. Candles were lit in windows. Far off, in his perch in the trees, Kafka listened to it all: the rustle of clothes being dropped to the floor, of lips fluttering along naked shoulders, beds creaking under the weight of tenderness. **It all caught in the delicate pointed shells of his ears and rolled like pinballs through the great hall of his mind.**

That night, a freezing wind blew in. When the children woke up, they went to the windows and found the world encased in ice. One child, the smallest, shrieked out in delight and her cry tore through the silence and exploded the ice of a giant oak tree. The world shone.

They found him frozen on the ground like a bird. It's said that when they put their ears to the shell of his ears, they could hear themselves.

Beneath that page was another page, titled *THE DEATH OF TOLSTOY*, and beneath that was one for Osip Mandelstam, who died at the bitter end of 1938 in a transit camp near Vladivostok, and beneath that, six or eight more. Only the last page was different. It said: *THE DEATH OF LEOPOLD GURSKY*. Litvinoff felt a gust of cold in his heart. He glanced at his friend, who was breathing heavily. He started to read. When he got to the end he shook his head and read it again. And again after that. He read it over and over, mouthing the words as if they were not an announcement of death, but a prayer for life. As if just by saying them, he could keep his friend safe from the angel of death, the force of his breath alone keeping its wings pinned for a moment more, a moment more—until it gave up and left his friend alone. All night, Litvinoff watched over his friend, and all night he moved his lips. And for the first time in as long as he could remember, he did not feel useless.

As morning broke, Litvinoff saw with relief that the color had returned to his friend's face. He was sleeping the restful sleep of recovery. When the sun had climbed to the position of eight o'clock, he stood. His legs were stiff. His insides felt scraped out. But he was filled with happiness. He folded THE DEATH OF LEOPOLD GURSKY in half. And here is another thing no one knows about Zvi Litvinoff: for the rest of his life he carried in his breast pocket the page he'd protected all night from becoming real, so that he could buy a little more time—for his friend, for life.

UNTIL THE WRITING HAND HURTS

The pages I'd written so long ago slipped from my hands and scattered on the floor. I thought: Who? And how? I thought: After all these—What? Years.

I fell back into my memories. The night passed in a fog. By morning I was still shocked. It was noon before I was able to go on. I knelt down in the flour. I gathered the pages up one by one. Page ten gave me a paper cut. Page twenty-two a pang in the kidneys. Page four a blockage in the heart.

A bitter joke came to mind. *Words failed me.* And yet. I clutched the pages, afraid my mind was playing tricks on me, that I would look down and find them blank.

I made my way to the kitchen. The cake sagged on the table. Ladies and gentlemen. We are gathered today to celebrate the mysteries of life. What? No, stone throwing is not allowed. Only flowers. Or **money.**

I wiped the egg shells and spilled sugar off my chair and sat down at the table. Outside, my loyal pigeon cooed and fluttered its wings against the glass. Perhaps I should have given him a name. Why not, I've taken pains to name plenty of things less real than he. I tried to think of a name that would give me pleasure to call. I glanced around. My eye came to rest on the menu from the Chinese take-out. They haven't changed it for years. *MR. TONG'S FAMOUS CANTONESE, SZECHUAN AND HUMAN CUISINE.* I tapped the window. The pigeon flapped off. *Goodbye, Mr. Tong.*

It took me most of the afternoon to read. Memories crowded in. My eyes blurred, I had trouble focusing. I thought: I'm seeing things. I pushed back my chair and stood. I thought: Mazel tov, Gursky, you've finally lost it completely. I watered the plant. *To lose you have to have had.* Ah? So *now* you're a stickler for details? Have, didn't have! Listen to you! You made a profession out of losing. A champion loser you were. And yet. Where's the proof you ever had her? Where's the proof that she was yours to have?

I filled the sink with soapy water and washed the dirty pots. And with each pot and pan and spoon I put away, I also put away a thought I couldn't bear, until my kitchen and my mind returned to a state of mutual organization. And yet.

Shlomo Wasserman had become Ignacio da Silva.

The character I called Duddelsach was now
Rodriguez. Feingold was De Biedma. So-called
Slonim became Buenos Aires, a town I'd never heard
of now stood in for Minsk. It was almost funny. But
I didn't laugh.

I studied the handwriting on the envelope. There
was no note. Believe me: I checked five or six times.
No return address. I would have interrogated Bruno
if I'd thought he'd have anything to tell. If there's a
package, the super leaves it on the table in the lobby.
No doubt Bruno saw it and picked it up. It's a big
event when something comes for either of us that can't
fit in the mailbox. If I'm not mistaken, the last time
was two years ago. Bruno had ordered a studded dog
collar. Perhaps it doesn't go without saying that he'd
recently brought home a dog. It was small and warm
and something to love. He called it Bibi. *Come, Bibi,
come!* I'd hear him call. But Bibi never came. Then
one day he took it to the dog run. *Vamos, Chico!* someone called to their dog, and Bibi took off toward the
Puerto Rican. *Come, Bibi, come!* Bruno cried, but to no
avail. He switched tactics. *Vamos, Bibi!* he shrieked at
the top of his lungs. And lo and behold, Bibi came
running. She barked all night and shat over the floor,
but he loved her.

One day Bruno took her to the dog run. She frol-
icked and shat and sniffed while Bruno looked on with
pride. The gate opened for an Irish setter. Bibi glanced

up. Before Bruno knew what was happening, she shot through the open gate and disappeared down the street. He tried to chase her. *Run!* he said to himself. The memory of speed flooded his system, but his body revolted. With his first steps his legs tangled and wilted. *Vamos Bibi!* he cried. And yet. No one came. In his hour of need—crumpled on the sidewalk while Bibi betrayed him by being what she was: an animal— I was at home pecking away at my typewriter. He came home, devastated. That evening we went back to the dog run to wait for her. *She'll come back*, I said. But. She never came back. That was two years ago, and still he goes to wait.

I tried to make sense of things. Now that I think about it, I have always tried. It could be my epitaph. LEO GURSKY: HE TRIED TO MAKE SENSE.

Night fell and still I was lost. I hadn't eaten all day. I called Mr. Tong. The Chinese take-out, not the bird. Twenty minutes later, I was alone with my spring rolls. I turned on the radio. They were asking for pledges. In return you got a plunger that said WNYC.

There are things I find hard to describe. And yet I persist like a stubborn mule in my efforts. Once Bruno came downstairs and saw me sitting at the kitchen table in front of the typewriter. *That thing again?* The earphones had slipped down to rest like a half-halo on the back of his head. I kneaded my knuckles over the steam from my teacup. *A regular Vladimir*

Horowitz, he remarked as he passed on his way to the refrigerator. He hunched over, digging around for whatever it was he wanted in there. I rolled a new page into my machine. He turned around, the refrigerator door still open, a milk mustache on his upper lip. *Play on, Maestro,* he said, then pulled the earphones onto his ears and shuffled out the door, turning on the light above the table as he passed. I watched the light chain swing as I listened to the voice of Molly Bloom blasting his ears, THERE'S NOTHING LIKE A KISS LONG AND HOT DOWN TO YOUR SOUL ALMOST PARALYSES YOU, it's only her Bruno listens to now, wearing down the magnetic strip.

Over and over, I read the pages of the book I'd written as a young man. It was so long ago. I was naïve. A twenty-year-old in love. A swollen heart and a head to match. I thought I could do anything! Strange as that might seem, now that I've done all I'm going to do.

I thought: How did it survive? As far as I knew, the only copy was lost in a flood. I mean, if you don't count the excerpts I sent in letters to the girl I loved after she left for America. I couldn't resist sending her my best pages. But. It was only a few parts. And here in my hands was almost the whole book! Somehow in English! With Spanish names! It boggled the mind.

I sat shiva for Isaac, and while I sat, I tried to understand. Alone in my apartment, the pages on my lap. Night became day became night became day. I fell in and out of sleep. But. I didn't get any closer to solving the mystery. Story of my life: I was a lock-smith. I could unlock every door in the city. And yet I couldn't unlock anything I wanted to unlock.

I decided to make a list of all the people I knew who were alive, in case I was forgetting someone. I busied myself looking for paper and pen. Then I sat down, smoothed down the page, and brought the nib to meet it. But. My mind drew a blank.

Instead I wrote: *Questions for the Sender*. This I underlined twice. I continued:

1. *Who are you?*
2. *Where did you find this?*
3. *How did it survive?*
4. *Why is it in english?*
5. *Who else has read it?*
6. ~~*Did they like it?*~~
6. *Is the number of readers greater or less than—*

I paused and deliberated. Was there a number that wouldn't disappoint me?

I looked out the window. Across the street, a tree tossed in the wind. It was the afternoon, the children were shouting. I like to listen to their songs. *This is a game! Of concentration!* the girls sing and clap. *No repeats! Or hesitations! Starting with:* I wait on tenterhooks. *Animals!* they shout. Animals! I think. *Horse!* one says. *Monkey!* says the other. Back and forth it goes. *Cow!* shouts the first. *Tiger!* cries the second, because a moment of hesitation ruins the rhythm and ends the game. *Pony! Kangaroo! Mouse! Lion! Giraffe!* One girl fumbles. *YAK!* I shout.

I looked down at my page of questions. What would it take, I wondered, for a book I wrote sixty years ago to arrive in my mailbox, in a different language?

Suddenly I was struck by a thought. It came to me in Yiddish, I'll do my best to paraphrase, it was something along the lines of: COULD I BE FAMOUS WITH-OUT KNOWING IT? I felt dizzy. I drank down a glass of cold water and took some aspirin. Don't be an idiot, I told myself. And yet.

I grabbed my coat. The first drops of rain pelted the window, so I put on my galoshes. Bruno calls them rubbers. But that's his business. Outside, a howling wind. I struggled through the streets, locked in a battle with my umbrella. Three times it blew itself inside out. I hung on. Once it slammed me against the side of a building. Twice I was airborne.

I reached the library, my face lashed by rain. Water dripped from my nose. The beast my umbrella was shattered, so I discarded it in the stand. I made my way to the librarian's desk. Scamper, stop and pant, hike up trouser legs, step, drag, step, drag, etcetera.

The librarian's chair was vacant. I quote unquote hurried around the reading room. Finally I found someone. She was reshelving. I had difficulty restraining myself.

I'd like everything you have by the writer Leo Gursky! I shouted.

She turned to look at me. So did everyone else.

Excuse me?

Everything you have by the writer Leo Gursky, I repeated.

I'm in the middle of something. You'll have to wait a minute.

I waited a minute.

Leo Gursky, I said. *G-U-R-*

She shoved her cart along. *I know how to spell it.*

I followed her to the computer. She typed in my name. My heart raced. I may be old. But. My heart can still get it up.

There's a book about bullfighting by a Leonard Gursky, she said.

Not him, I said. *What about a Leopold?*

Leopold, Leopold, she said. *Here it is.*

I clutched the nearest stable object. Drumroll, please:

The Incredible, Fantastic Adventures of Frankie, Toothless Girl Wonder, she said, and grinned. I fought the urge to smack her over the head with my galosh. Off she went for the book in the children's section. I didn't stop her. Instead I died a little death. She sat me down with it. *Enjoy*, she said.

Once Bruno said that if I bought a pigeon, halfway down the street it would become a dove, on the bus home a parrot, and in my apartment, the moment before I took it out of the cage, a phoenix. *That's you*, he said, brushing some crumbs that weren't there from the table. A few minutes passed. *No it's not*, I said. He shrugged and looked out the window. *Whoever heard of a phoenix?* I said. *A peacock, maybe. But a phoenix I don't think so*. His face was turned away but I thought I saw his mouth twitch in a smile.

But now I couldn't do anything to turn the nothing the librarian had found into something.

In the days after my heart attack and before I began to write again, all I could think about was dying. I'd been spared again, and only after the danger had passed did I allow my thoughts to unravel to their inevitable end. I imagined all the ways I could go. Blood clot to the brain. Infarction. Thrombosis. Pneumonia. Grand mal obstruction to the vena cava. I saw myself foaming at the mouth, writhing on the floor. I'd wake up in the night, gripping my throat. And yet. No matter how often I imagined the possible failure of my organs, I found the consequence inconceivable. That it could happen to me. I forced myself to picture the last moments. The penultimate breath. A final sigh. And yet. It was always followed by another.

I remember the first time I understood what it was to die. I was nine. My uncle, my father's brother, may his memory be a blessing, died in his sleep. There was no explanation. A huge, strapping man who ate like a horse and went out in the freezing cold to break blocks of ice with his bare hands. Gone, kaput. He used to call me Leopo. He said it like this: *Lay-o-po*. Behind my aunt's back he would sneak me and my cousins a cube of sugar. He used to do an imitation of Stalin that could make your sides split.

My aunt found him in the morning, the body already stiff. Three men were needed to carry him to the *khevra kadisha*. My brother and I slipped in to behold the great heap. The body was more remarkable to us in death than it had been in life—the forest of fur on the back of his hands, the flat yellowed nails, the thick rime on the soles of his feet. He seemed so human. And yet. Horribly not. Once I came in to bring my father a glass of tea. He was sitting with the body, which couldn't be left alone for even a minute. *I have to go to the bathroom*, he told me. *Wait here until I come back*. Before I could protest that I hadn't even been Bar Mitzvahed, he rushed out to relieve himself. The next few minutes passed like hours. My uncle was laid out on a slab of stone the color of raw meat with white veins. Once I thought I saw his chest rise a fraction and almost shrieked. But. It wasn't only him I was afraid of. I was afraid for myself. In that cold room,

I sensed my own death. In the corner was a sink with cracked tiles. Down that drain had gone all the clipped nails, hairs, and grains of dirt washed from the dead. The faucet had a leak, and with every drip I felt my life ebbing away. One day it would be all gone. The joy of being alive became so concentrated in me I wanted to scream. I was never a religious child. But. Suddenly I felt the need to beg God to spare me as long as possible. When my father came back he found his son on his knees on the floor, with eyes squeezed shut and knuckles white.

From then on, I was terrified that I or one of my parents were going to die. My mother worried me the most. She was the force around which our world turned. Unlike our father, who spent his life in the clouds, my mother was propelled through the universe by the brute force of reason. She was the judge in all of our arguments. One disapproving word from her was enough to send us off to hide in a corner, where we would cry and fantasize our own martyrdom. And yet. One kiss could restore us to princedom. Without her, our lives would dissolve into chaos.

The fear of death haunted me for a year. I cried whenever anyone dropped a glass or broke a plate. But even when that passed, I was left with a sadness that couldn't be rubbed off. It wasn't that something new had happened. It was worse: I'd become aware of what had been with me all along without my notice.

I dragged this new awareness around like a stone tied
to my ankle. Wherever I went, it followed. I used to
make up little sad songs in my head. I eulogized the
falling leaves. I imagined my death in a hundred different ways, but the funeral was always the same: from
somewhere in my imagination, out rolled a red carpet.
Because after every secret death I died, my greatness
was always discovered.

Things might have gone on like that.

One morning, having wasted time over my breakfast and then stopped to examine Mrs. Stanislawski's
giant underwear drying on the line, I was late to
school. The bell had rung, but a girl in my class was
kneeling in the dusty schoolyard. Her hair was braided
down her back. She was cupping her hands around
something. I asked her what it was. *I caught a moth*,
she said, without looking at me. *What do you want with
a moth?* I asked. *What kind of question is that?* she said.
I rethought my question. *Well if it was a butterfly that
would be one thing*, I said. *No it wouldn't*, she said.
It would be another thing. You should let it go, I said. *It's
a very rare moth*, she said. *How do you know?* I asked.
I have a feeling, she said. I pointed out that the bell
had already rung. *Then go in*, she said. *No one's stopping you. Not unless you let it go. Then you might have
to wait forever.*

She opened the space between her thumbs and
looked in. *Let me see*, I said. She didn't say anything.

Can I please see it? She looked at me. Her eyes were green and sharp. *All right. But be careful.* She lifted her clasped hands to my face and parted her two thumbs a half inch. I could smell the soap on her skin. All I could see was a little bit of brown wing, so I pulled on her thumb to get a better look. And yet. She must have thought I was trying to free the moth, because suddenly she clapped her hands shut. We looked at each other in horror. When she peeled her hands apart again, the moth jumped feebly in her palm. One wing had come off. She made a little gasp. *I didn't do it*, I said. When I looked at her eyes, I saw they were filled with tears. A feeling I didn't yet know was longing clenched my stomach. *I'm sorry*, I whispered. I felt an urge to hug her, to kiss away the moth and the broken wing. She said nothing. Our eyes were locked in a stare.

It was as if we shared a guilty secret. I'd seen her every day in school, and never felt anything particular for her before. If anything, I found her bossy. She could be charming. But. She was a poor loser. More than once she'd refused to talk to me on the rare occasions when I managed to answer one of the teacher's trivia questions faster than her. *The King of England is George!* I'd shout, and for the rest of the day I'd have to defend myself against her icy silence.

But now she seemed different to me. I became aware of her special powers. How she seemed to pull light and gravity to the place where she stood. I noticed, as I had never before, the way her toes pointed slightly inward. The dirt on her bare knees. The way her coat fit neatly across her narrow shoulders. As if my eyes had been given magnifying powers, I saw her more closely yet. The black beauty mark, like a fleck of ink above her lip. The pink, translucent shell of her ear. The blond down on her cheeks. Inch by inch she revealed herself to me. I half expected that in another moment I'd be able to make out the cells of her skin as if under a microscope, and a thought crossed my mind that had to do with the familiar worry that I'd inherited too much from my father. But it didn't last long, because at the same time that I was becoming conscious of her body, I was becoming aware of my own. The sensation almost knocked the breath out of me. A tingling feeling caught fire in my nerves and spread. The whole thing must have happened in less than thirty seconds. And yet. When it was over, I'd been initiated into the mystery that stands at the beginning of the end of childhood. It was years before I'd spent all the joy and pain born in me in that less than half a minute.

Without another word, she dropped the broken moth and ran inside. The heavy iron door swung closed behind her with a thud.

Alma.

It's been a long time since I uttered that name.

I resolved to make her love me, whatever the cost. But. I knew enough not to attack right away. I watched her every move for the next couple of weeks. Patience had always been one of my virtues. Once I hid for four whole hours under the outhouse behind the rabbi's house to find out if the famous *tzaddik* who'd come to visit from Baranowicze really took shits like the rest of us. The answer was yes. In my enthusiasm for the coarse miracles of life, I shot out from under the outhouse shouting an affirmative. For this I got five raps on the knuckles and had to kneel on corncobs until my knees were bloody. But. It was worth it.

I considered myself a spy infiltrating an alien world: the domain of the female. With the excuse of gathering evidence, I stole Mrs. Stanislawski's enormous panties off the clothesline. Alone in the outhouse, I sniffed them with abandon. I buried my face in the crotch. I put them on my head. I raised them and let them balloon in the breeze like the flag of a new nation. When my mother pushed open the door, I was trying them on for size. They could have fit three of me.

With one lethal look—and the humiliating punishment of having to knock on Stanislawski's door and hand back her underwear—my mother put an end to the general portion of my research. And yet. I continued in the specific. There, my research was exhaustive. I found out that Alma was the youngest of four children, and her father's favorite. I knew her birthday was the twenty-first of February (making her older than me by five months and twenty-eight days), that she loved the sour cherries in syrup that were smuggled from across the border in Russia, and that once she had consumed half a jar of these in secret, and when her mother found out she made her eat the other half, thinking it would make her sick and turn her off the cherries forever. But it didn't. She ate the whole thing up and even claimed to a girl in our class that she could have eaten more. I knew that her father wanted her to learn how to play the piano, but that she wanted to learn the violin, and that this dispute remained unsettled, with both sides standing their ground, until Alma got hold of an empty violin case (she claimed to have found it discarded by the road) and started carrying it around in her father's presence, sometimes even pretending to play the phantom violin, and that this was the straw that broke the camel's back, her father caved in and arranged for a violin to be brought back from Vilna by one of her brothers who was studying at the *Gymnasium*, and the new violin arrived in a shiny black leather case lined with purple velvet, and that every song Alma learned to play on it, no matter how sad, possessed the unmistakable tone of victory. I knew because I heard her play while I stood outside her window, waiting for the secret to her heart to be revealed to me with the same ardor with which I'd waited for the great *tzaddik*'s shit.

But. It never happened. One day she marched around the side of the house and confronted me. *I've seen you out there every day for the past week, and everyone knows you stare at me all day in school, if you have something you want to say to me why don't you just say it to my face instead of sneaking around like a crook?* I considered my options. Either I could run away and never go back to school again, maybe even leave the country as a stowaway on a ship bound for Australia. Or I could risk everything and confess to her. The answer was obvious: I was going to Australia. I opened my mouth to say goodbye forever. And yet. What I said was: *I want to know if you'll marry me.*

She was expressionless. But. Her eyes had the same gleam they got when she removed her violin from its case. A long moment passed. We were locked in a brutal stare. *I'll think about it*, she said at last, and marched back around the corner of the house. I heard the door slam. A moment later, the opening notes of "Songs My Mother Taught Me," by Dvořák. And though she didn't say yes, from then on I knew I had a chance.

That, in a nutshell, was the end of my preoccupation with death. Not that I stopped fearing it. I just stopped thinking about it. If I'd had any extra time on my hands that wasn't spent thinking about Alma, I might have spent them worrying about death. But the truth was that I learned to put a wall up against such thoughts. Each new thing I learned about the world was a stone in that wall, until one day I understood I'd exiled myself from a place I could never go back to. And yet. The wall also protected me from the painful clarity of childhood. Even during the years when I hid in the forest, in trees, holes, and cellars, with death breathing down my neck, I still never thought about the truth: that I was going to die. Only after my heart attack, when the stones of the wall that separated me from childhood began to crumble at last, did the fear of death return to me. And it was just as frightening as it ever was.

I SAT HUNCHED over *The Incredible, Fantastic Adventures of Frankie, Toothless Girl Wonder* by a Leopold Gursky who wasn't me. I didn't open the cover. I listened to the rain running through the roof gutters.

I left the library. Crossing the street, I was hit head-on by a brutal loneliness. I felt dark and hollow. Abandoned, unnoticed, forgotten, I stood on the sidewalk, a nothing, a gatherer of dust. People hurried past me. And everyone who walked by was happier than I. I felt the old envy. I would have given anything to be one of them.

There was a woman I once knew. She was locked out and I helped her. She saw one of my cards, I used to scatter them behind me like bread crumbs. She called, and I got there as fast as I could. It was Thanksgiving, and no one had to say that neither of us had anyplace to go. The lock sprung open under my touch. Maybe she thought it was the sign of a different kind of talent. Inside, a lingering smell of fried onions, a poster of Matisse, or maybe Monet. No! Modigliani. I remember now because it was a naked woman, and to flatter her I said: *Is it you?* It had been a long time since I'd been with a woman. I could smell the grease on my hands, and the smell of my armpits. She invited me to sit down and cooked us a meal. I excused myself to comb my hair and try to wash myself in the bathroom. When I came out she was standing in her underwear in the dark. There was a neon sign across the street, and it cast a blue shadow on her legs. I wanted to tell her that it was OK if she didn't want to look at my face.

A few months later, she called me again. She asked me to make a copy of her key. I was happy for her. That she wouldn't be alone anymore. It's not that I felt sorry for myself. But I wanted to say to her, *It would be easier if you just asked him, the one who the key is for, to take it to the hardware store.* And yet. I made two copies. One I gave to her, and one I kept. For a long time I carried it in my pocket, just to pretend.

One day it struck me that I could let myself in
anywhere. I'd never thought about it before. I was an
immigrant, it took a long time to get over the fear
that they'd send me back. I lived in fear of making a
mistake. Once I missed six trains because I couldn't
figure out how to ask for a ticket. Another man might
have just got on board. But. Not a Jew from Poland
who's afraid that if he even so much as forgets to flush
the toilet he'll get deported. I tried to keep my head
down. I locked and unlocked and that's what I did.
For picking a lock where I came from I was a thief,
but here in America I was a professional.

With time I became more comfortable. Here and
there I added a little flourish to my work. A half twist
at the end that lacked purpose but added a certain
sophistication. I stopped being nervous and became
sly instead. On every lock I installed, I inscribed my
initials. A signature, very small, above the keyway. It
didn't matter that no one would ever notice. It was
enough that I knew. I kept track of all the locks I'd
inscribed with a map of the city folded and refolded
so many times that certain streets had rubbed off in
the creases.

One evening I went to see a movie. Before the
main picture they showed a reel about Houdini. This
was a man who could slip out of a straitjacket while
buried underground. They'd put him in a chest locked
with chains, drop it in the water, and out he'd pop.

They showed how he did exercises and timed himself. He would practice over and over until he got it down to a matter of seconds. From then on, I took an even greater pride in my work. I'd bring the most difficult locks home and time myself. Then I'd cut the time in half and practice until I got there. I'd keep at it until I couldn't feel my fingers.

I was lying in bed dreaming up more and more difficult challenges when it dawned on me: if I could pick the lock to a stranger's apartment, why couldn't I pick the lock to Kossar's Bialys? Or the public library? Or Woolworth's? Hypothetically speaking, what was stopping me from picking the lock to . . . Carnegie Hall?

My thoughts raced while my body tingled with excitement. All I would do is let myself in, and then let myself back out. Perhaps leave a small signature.

I planned for weeks. I staked out the premises. There was no stone I left unturned. Suffice to say: I did it. Through the backstage door on 56th Street in the early hours of the morning. It took me 103 seconds. At home the same lock only took me 48. But it was cold out and my fingers were heavy.

The great Arthur Rubinstein was scheduled to play that night. The piano was set up alone on the stage, a glossy black Steinway grand. I stepped out from behind the curtains. I could just make out the endless rows of seats in the glow of the exit signs. I sat down on the

bench, and pushed down a pedal with the tip of my shoe.
I didn't dare lay a finger on the keys.

When I looked up, she was standing there. Plain
as day, a girl of fifteen, her hair in a braid, not five
feet from me. She lifted her violin, the one her brother
had brought her from Vilna, and lowered her chin to
meet it. I tried to say her name. But. It lodged in my
throat. Besides, I knew she couldn't hear me. She
raised her bow. I heard the opening notes of the
Dvořák. Her eyes were closed. The music spilled from
her fingers. She played it flawlessly, as she'd never
played it in life.

When the last note faded, she was gone. My claps
echoed in the empty auditorium. I stopped and the
silence thundered in my ears. I took one last look out
at the empty theater. Then I hurried out the way I
came.

I never did it again. I'd proven it to myself, and
that was enough. From time to time I'd find myself
passing the entrance of a certain private club, I won't
name names, and I'd think to myself, Shalom, shit-
heads, here's a Jew you can't keep out. But after that
night, I never pushed my luck again. If they threw me
in jail, they'd find out the truth: I'm no Houdini. And
yet. In my loneliness it comforts me to think that the
world's doors, however closed, are never truly locked
to me.

Such was the comfort I groped for standing in the

pouring-rain outside the library while strangers hurried past. After all, wasn't this the real reason my cousin had taught me the trade? He knew I couldn't stay invisible forever. *Show me a Jew that survives,* he once said as I watched a lock give way in his hands, *and I'll show you a magician.*

I stood on the street and let the rain trickle down my neck. I squeezed my eyes shut. Door after door after door after door after door after door swung open.

AFTER THE LIBRARY, after the nothing of *The Incredible, Fantastic Adventures of Frankie, Toothless Girl Wonder,* I went home. I took off my coat and hung it to dry. Put the water on to boil. Behind me someone cleared his throat. I nearly jumped out of my skin. But it was only Bruno, sitting in the dark. *What are you trying to do, give me a conniption?* I yelped, turning on the light. The pages of the book I wrote when I was a boy were scattered on the floor. *Oh no,* I said. *It's not what you—*

He didn't give me a chance.

Not bad, he said. *Not how I would have chosen to describe her. But, what can I say, that's your business.*

Look, I said.

You don't need to explain, he said. *It's a good book. I like the writing. Aside from the bits you stole—very inventive. If we're talking in purely literary terms—*

It took me a moment. And then I realized the difference. He was speaking to me in Yiddish.

—in purely literary terms, what's not to like? Anyway, I'd always wondered what you were working on. Now, after all these years, I know.

But I wondered what you were working on, I said, remembering a lifetime ago when we were both twenty and wanted to be writers.

He shrugged, like only Bruno can. *The same as you.*

The same?

Of course the same.

A book about her?

A book about her, Bruno said. He looked away, out the window. Then I saw he was holding the photograph in his lap, the one of her and me in front of the tree on which she'd never known I'd carved our initials. A + L. You can barely see them. But. They're there.

He said, *She was good at keeping secrets.*

It came back to me then. That day, sixty years ago, when I'd left her house in tears and caught sight of him standing against a tree holding a notebook, waiting to go to her after I'd gone. A few months earlier, we'd been the closest of friends. We'd stay up half the night with a couple of other boys, smoking and arguing about books. And yet. By the time I caught sight of him that afternoon, we were no longer friends.

We weren't even talking. I walked right past him as if he weren't there.

Just one question, Bruno said now, sixty years later. *I always wanted to know.*

What?

He coughed. Then he looked up at me. *Did she tell you you were a better writer than I?*

No, I lied. And then I told him the truth. *No one had to tell me.*

There was a long silence.

It's strange. I always thought—— He broke off.

What? I said.

I thought we were fighting for something more than her love, he said.

Now it was my turn to look out the window.

What is more than her love? I asked.

We sat in silence.

I lied, Bruno said. *I have another question.*

What is it?

Why are you still standing here like a fool?

What do you mean?

Your book, he said.

What about it?

Go get it back.

I knelt on the floor and began to gather up the pages.

Not this one!

Which one?

Oy vey! Bruno said, slapping his forehead. *Do I have to tell you everything?*

A slow smile spread on my lips.

Three hundred and one, said Bruno. He shrugged and looked away, but I thought I saw him smile. *It's not nothing.*

FLOOD

HOW TO MAKE A FIRE WITHOUT MATCHES

I did a search on the internet for Alma Mereminski. I thought someone might have written about her, or that I might find information about her life. I typed in her name and pressed return. But all that came up was a list of immigrants who'd arrived in New York City in 1891 (Mendel Mereminski), and a list of Holocaust victims recorded at Yad Vashem (Adam Mereminski, Fanny Mereminski, Nacham, Zellig, Hershel, Bluma, Ida, but, to my relief, because I didn't want to lose her before I'd even begun to look, no Alma).

2. ALL THE TIME MY BROTHER SAVES MY LIFE

Uncle Julian came to stay with us. He was in New York for as long as it took him to do the final research for a book he'd been writing for five years on the sculptor and painter Alberto Giacometti. Aunt Frances stayed behind in London to take care of the dog. Uncle Julian slept in Bird's bed, Bird slept in mine, and I slept on the floor in my one-hundred-percent down sleeping bag, even though a real expert wouldn't need one, since in emergency conditions she could just kill some birds and stuff their feathers under her clothing for warmth.

Sometimes at night I would hear my brother talking in his sleep. Half phrases, nothing I could make out. Except for once, when he spoke so loudly I thought he was awake. "Don't step there," he said. "What?" I said, sitting up. "It's too deep," he muttered, and turned his face to the wall.

3. BUT WHY

One Saturday, Bird and I went with Uncle Julian to the Museum of Modern Art. Bird insisted on

paying for himself from his lemonade profits. We
wandered around while Uncle Julian went to talk
to a curator upstairs. Bird asked one of the security guards how many water fountains there were
in the building. (Five.) He made weird video game
noises until I told him to be quiet. Then he
counted the number of people with exposed
tattoos. (Eight.) We stood in front of a painting
of a bunch of people collapsed on the floor. "Why
are they lying there like that?" he asked. "Someone
killed them," I said, even though I didn't really
know why they were lying there, or if they were
even people. I went to look at another painting
across the room. Bird followed me. "But why did
someone kill them?" he asked. "Because they
needed money and robbed a house," I said, and
got on the escalator going down.

On the subway home, Bird touched my shoulder. "But why did they need the money?"

4. LOST AT SEA

"What makes you to think this Alma in *History of
Love* is real person?" Misha asked. We were sitting
on the beach behind his apartment building with
our feet buried in the sand, eating Mrs. Shklovsky's
roast beef and horseradish sandwiches. " 'A,' " I

said. "A what?" "*A* real person." "OK," Misha said.
"Answer the question." "Of course she's real." "But
how do you know?" "Because there's only one way
to explain why Litvinoff, who wrote the book,
didn't give her a Spanish name like everyone else."
"Why?" "He couldn't." "Why not?" "Don't you see?"
I said. "He could change every detail, but he could-
n't change her." "But *why*?" His obtuseness frus-
trated me. "Because he was *in love* with her!" I said.
"Because, to him, she was the only thing that was
real." Misha chewed a bite of roast beef. "I'm thinking you watch too many movies," he said. But I
knew I was right. It didn't take a genius to read
The History of Love and guess that much.

5. THE THINGS I WANT TO SAY GET STUCK IN MY MOUTH

We walked down the boardwalk toward Coney
Island. It was boiling hot and a trickle of sweat
dripped down Misha's temple. When we passed
some old people playing cards, Misha greeted
them. A wrinkled old man wearing a tiny bathing
suit waved back. "They think you're my girlfriend," Misha announced. Just then my toe
caught and I tripped. I felt my face get hot, and
thought, I am the most awkward person on earth.

"Well I'm not," I said, which wasn't what I wanted to say. I looked away, pretending to take interest in a kid dragging a blow-up shark toward the water's edge. "*I* know," Misha said. "But they don't." He'd turned fifteen, grown almost four inches, and started to shave the dark hairs above his lip. When we went into the ocean, I watched his body as he dove into the waves, and it gave me a feeling in my stomach that wasn't an ache but something different.

"I bet you a hundred dollars she's listed," I said. There was no part of me that actually believed this, but it was all I could think of to change the subject.

6. LOOKING FOR SOMEONE WHO MOST LIKELY DOESN'T EXIST

"I'm looking for a number for Alma Mereminski?" I said. "M-E-R-E-M-I-N-S-K-I." "What borough?" the woman said. "I don't know," I said. There was a pause and I heard the clicking of keys. Misha watched a girl in a turquoise bikini Rollerblade past. The woman on the phone was saying something. "Excuse me?" I said. "I said I have an A. Mereminski on 147th in the Bronx," she said. "Hold for the number."

I scrawled it on my hand. Misha walked over.
"So?". "Do you have a quarter?" I asked. It was
silly, but I'd already gone so far. He raised his
eyebrows, and reached into the pocket of his
shorts. I dialed the number written on my palm.
A man answered. "Is Alma there?" I asked.
"Who?" he said. "I'm looking for Alma Mereminski." "There's no Alma here," he told me. "You
got the wrong number. This is Artie," he said, and
hung up.

We walked back to Misha's apartment. I went
to the bathroom, which smelled of his sister's
perfume and was crowded with his father's gray-
ish underwear drying on a line. When I came out,
Misha was shirtless in his room, reading a book
in Russian. I waited on his bed while he took a
shower, flipping through the pages of Cyrillic. I
could hear the water falling, and the song he was
singing, but not the words. When I lay on his
pillow, it smelled of him.

7. IF THINGS GO ON LIKE THIS

When Misha was young his family went to their
dacha every summer, and he and his father would
take the nets down from the attic and try to catch
the migrating butterflies that filled the air. The

old house was filled with his grandmother's china that really came from China, and the framed butterflies three generations of Shklovskys had caught as boys. Over time their scales fell away, and if you ran barefoot through the house the china would rattle and your feet would pick up wing dust.

A few months back, the night before his fifteenth birthday, I'd decided to make Misha a card with a butterfly on it. I went online for a picture of a Russian butterfly, but instead I found an article reporting that most butterfly species had declined in numbers over the last two decades, and that their extinction rate was about 10,000 times higher than it should be. It also said that an average of seventy-four species of insects, plants, and animals become extinct every day. Based on these and other frightening statistics, the article reported, scientists believe that we are in the midst of the sixth mass extinction in the history of life on earth. Almost a quarter of the world's mammals face extinction within thirty years. One out of eight species of birds will soon be extinct. Ninety percent of the world's largest fish have disappeared in the last half century.

I did a search on mass extinctions.

The last mass extinction happened about 65 million years ago, when an asteroid probably collided with our planet, killing all the dinosaurs and about half of the marine animals. Before that was the Triassic extinction (also caused by an asteroid, or possibly volcanoes), which wiped out up to ninety-five percent of the species, and before that was the Late Devonian extinction. The current mass extinction will be the quickest in earth's 4.5-billion-year history and, unlike those other extinctions, isn't caused by natural events, but by the ignorance of human beings. If things go on like this, half of all species on earth will be gone in a hundred years.

For this reason, I did not put any butterflies on Misha's card.

8.   INTERGLACIAL

The same February my mother got the letter asking her to translate *The History of Love* it snowed almost two feet, and Misha and I built a snow cave in the park. We worked for hours, and our fingers turned numb, but we kept digging. When it was finished, we crawled inside. A blue light came in through the entrance. We sat shoulder to shoulder. "Maybe one day I'll bring you to Russia," said Misha. "We could go camping in the Ural Mountains," I said. "Or just the Kazakh Steppes."

Our breath made little clouds when we spoke. "I'll take you to the room where I lived with my grandfather," said Misha, "and teach you to skate on the Neva." "I could learn Russian." Misha nodded. "I'll teach you. First word. *Dai*." "*Dai*." "Second word. *Ruku*." "What does it mean?" "Say it first." "*Ruku*." "*Dai ruku*." "*Dai ruku*. What does it mean?" Misha took my hand and held it.

9. IF SHE'S REAL

"What is giving you idea Alma came to New York?" Misha asked. We'd played the tenth round of gin rummy and now we were lying on the floor of his bedroom looking up at the ceiling. There was sand in my bathing suit and between my teeth. Misha's hair was still wet, and I could smell his deodorant.

"In the fourteenth chapter, Litvinoff writes about a string stretching across the ocean held by a girl who left for America. He was from Poland, right, and my mom said he escaped before the Germans invaded. The Nazis killed pretty much everyone in his village. So if he hadn't escaped, there'd be no *History of Love*. And if Alma was also from the same village, which I bet you a hundred dollars she was—"

"You already owe me hundred dollars."

"The point is that in the parts I've read, there are stories about Alma when she was very young, like ten. So if she's real, which I think she is, Litvinoff must have known her as a child. Which means they were probably from the same village. And Yad Vashem doesn't list any Alma Mereminski from Poland who died in the Holocaust."

"Who is Yad Vashem?"

"The Holocaust museum in Israel."

"Okay so maybe she's not even Jewish. And even if she is—even if she's real, and Polish, and Jewish, AND came to America—how do you know she didn't go to some other city? Like Ann Arbor." "Ann *Arbor*?" "I have one cousin there," Misha said. "Anyway, I thought you were looking for Jacob Marcus, not this Alma."

"I am," I said. I felt the back of his hand brush my thigh. I didn't know how to say that even though I'd started out looking for someone who could make my mother happy again, now I was looking for something else, too. About the woman I was named after. And about me.

"Maybe the reason Jacob Marcus wants the book translated has something to do with Alma," I said, not because I believed it, but because I didn't know what else to say. "Maybe he knew her. Or maybe he's trying to find her."

I was glad Misha didn't ask me why, if Litvinoff had been so in love with Alma, he hadn't followed her to America; why he'd gone to Chile instead and married someone named Rosa. The only reason I could think of was that he didn't have a choice.

On the other side of the wall, Misha's mother shouted something at his father. Misha propped himself up on his elbow and looked down at me. I thought of the time, the summer before, when we were thirteen and stood on the roof of his building, the tar soft under our feet, our tongues in each other's mouths while he gave me a lesson in the Shklovsky school of Russian kissing. Now we'd known each other for two years, the side of my calf was touching his shins, and his stomach was against my ribs. He said, "I don't think it's end of world to be my girlfriend." I opened my mouth, but nothing came out. It took seven languages to make me; it would be nice if I could have spoken just one. But I couldn't, so he leaned down and kissed me.

10. THEN

His tongue was in my mouth. I didn't know if I should touch my tongue to his, or leave it off to the side so his tongue could move unconstrained by mine. Before I could decide, he took his tongue out and closed his mouth and I accidentally left my mouth open, which seemed like a mistake. I thought that might be the end of it, but then he opened his mouth again and I didn't realize he was going to, so he ended up licking my lips. Then I opened my lips and stuck out my tongue, but it was too late because his tongue was back in his mouth. Then we got it right, sort of, opening our mouths at the same time like we were both trying to say something, and I put my hand around the back of his neck like Eva Marie Saint does to Cary Grant in the train car scene in *North by Northwest*. We rolled around a little, and his crotch sort of rubbed against my crotch, but only for a second, because then my shoulder got accidentally mashed against his accordion. There was saliva all around my mouth and it was hard to breathe. Outside the window, an airplane passed on the way to JFK. His father started to shout back at his mother. "What are they fighting about?" I asked. Misha pulled his head back. A thought crossed his face in a language I couldn't understand. I wondered if things were going to change between us. "*Merde*," he said. "What does that mean?" I asked, and he said, "It's French." He tucked a strand of my hair around my ear, and started to kiss me again. "Misha?" I whispered. "Shh," he said, and slipped his hand under my shirt around my waist. "Don't," I said, and sat up. And then I said: "I like someone else." As soon as I said it I regretted it. When it was clear there was nothing more to say, I put my sneakers on, which were filled with sand. "My mother is probably wondering where I am," I said, which we both knew wasn't true. When I stood, there was the sound of sand scattering.

11. A WEEK PASSED AND MISHA AND I DIDN'T SPEAK

I studied *Edible Plants and Flowers in North America* again for old time's sake. I went up to the roof of our house to see if I could identify any constellations, but there were too many lights, so I went back down to the backyard and practiced setting up Dad's tent in the dark, which I did in three minutes and fifty-four seconds, beating my record by almost a minute. When I was finished, I lay down in it and tried to remember as many things as I could about Dad.

12. MEMORIES PASSED DOWN TO ME FROM MY FATHER

echad	The taste of raw sugar cane
shtayim	The dirt streets in Tel Aviv when Israel was still a new country, and beyond them the fields of wild cyclamen
shalosh	The rock he threw at a boy's head who bullied his older brother, gaining him respect among the other kids
arba	Buying chickens with his father at the *moshav*, and watching their legs move after their necks were cut
hamesh	The sound of cards being shuffled by his mother and her friends when they played canasta on Saturday nights after Shabbat
shesh	The Falls of Iguaçu, which he traveled to alone, at great effort and personal expense
sheva	The first time he saw the woman who would become his wife, my mother, reading a book on the grass of Kibbutz Yavne, wearing yellow shorts
shmone	The sound of cicadas at night, and also the silence

tesha	The smell of jasmine, hibiscus, and orange flower
eser	The paleness of my mother's skin

13. TWO WEEKS PASSED, MISHA AND I STILL HADN'T SPOKEN, UNCLE JULIAN HADN'T LEFT, AND IT WAS ALMOST THE END OF AUGUST

The History of Love has thirty-nine chapters and my mother had finished another eleven since she'd sent Jacob Marcus the first ten, bringing her to a total of twenty-one. This meant she was more than halfway through and would be sending him another package soon.

I locked myself in the bathroom, the only place I could get any privacy, and tried to work on a second letter to Jacob Marcus, but everything I tried to write sounded wrong, or trite, or like a lie. Which it was.

I was sitting on the toilet with a notepad on my knees. Next to my ankle was the waste bin, and in the waste bin was a crumpled piece of paper. I took it out. *Dog, Frances?* it said. *Dog? Your words are cutting. But I suppose that's what you intended. I am not "in love" with Flo, as you say. We've been colleagues for years, and she happens to be someone who* *cares about the things I care about. ART, Fran, remember art, which, let's be honest, you couldn't give a rat's ass about anymore? You've made such a sport out of criticizing me that you haven't even noticed how much you've changed, how you hardly bear any resemblance at all to the girl I once—*The letter broke off. I crumpled it back up carefully, and replaced it in the waste bin. I shut my eyes tightly. I thought maybe Uncle Julian wouldn't be finishing his research on Alberto Giacometti anytime soon.

14. THEN I HAD AN IDEA

They must record all the deaths somewhere. The births and the deaths—there must be a place, an office or a bureau somewhere in the city that keeps track of them all. There must be files. Files upon files of people who'd been born and died in New York City. Sometimes, driving along the BQE as the sun is going down, you get a view of all those thousands of gravestones as the skyline goes up in lights and the sky glows orange, and you get the weird feeling that the city's electrical power is generated from everyone buried there.

And so I thought, Maybe they have a record of her.

15. THE NEXT DAY WAS SUNDAY

It was raining outside, so I sat around reading *The Street of Crocodiles,* which I'd checked out of the library, and wondering if Misha was going to call. I knew I was on to something when the introduction said that the author was from a village in Poland. I thought: Either Jacob Marcus really likes Polish writers, or he's dropping me a clue. I mean my-mother.

The book wasn't long, and I finished it that afternoon. At five, Bird came home drenched. "It's starting," he said, touching the mezuzah on the kitchen door and kissing his hand. "What's starting?" I asked. "The rain." "It's supposed to stop tomorrow," I said. He poured himself a glass of orange juice, drank it down, and went back through the door, kissing a total of four mezuzahs before he reached his room.

Uncle Julian came in from his day at the museum. "Have you seen Bird's clubhouse?" he asked, picking a banana off the counter and peeling it over the trash. "It's rather impressive, don't you think?"

But Monday the rain didn't stop and Misha didn't call, so I put my raincoat on, found an umbrella, and headed out for the New York City

Municipal Archives, which, according to the internet, is where they keep the records of births and deaths.

16. 31 CHAMBERS STREET, ROOM 103

"Mereminski," I said to the man with round black glasses behind the desk. "M-E-R-E-M-I-N-S-K-I." "M-E-R," the man said, writing it down. "E-M-I-N-S-K-I," I said. "I-S-K-Y," the man said. "No," I said. "M-E-R—" "M-E-R," he said. "E-M-I-N," I said, and he said, "E-Y-N." "No!" I said, "E-*M-I-N*." He stared at me blankly. So I said, "Why don't I write it for you?"

He looked at the name. Then he asked me if Alma M-E-R-E-M-I-N-S-K-I was my grandmother or great-grandmother. "Yes," I said, because I thought it might speed up the process. "Which?" he said. "Great," I said. He looked at me and chewed on a cuticle, then went into the back and came out with a box of microfilm. When I fed the first roll in, it got caught. I tried to get the man's attention by waving and pointing at the tangle of film. He came over, sighed, and threaded it through. After the third roll I got the hang of it. I scrolled through all fifteen. There was no Alma Mereminski in that box, so he brought out another, and another after that. I had to go to the bathroom and on the way out I got a package of Twinkies and a Coke from the machine. The man came out and got a Snickers bar. To make conversation, I said: "Do you know anything about how to survive in the wild?" His face twitched and he pushed his glasses up his nose. "What do you mean?" "For example, do you know that almost all Arctic vegetation is edible? Except for certain mushrooms, of course." He raised his eyebrows, so I said, "Well did you know that you can starve by just eating rabbit meat? It's a documented fact that people who are trying to survive have died by eating too much rabbit. If you eat a lot of any kind of lean meat, like rabbit, you get, you know— Anyway, it can kill you." The man threw out the rest of his Snickers.

Back inside, he brought out a fourth box. Two hours later my eyes hurt and I was still there. "Is it possible she died after 1948?" the man asked, visibly flustered. I told him it was possible. "Well why didn't you say! In that case her death certificate wouldn't be here." "Where would it be?" "New York City Department of Health, Division of Vital Records," he said, "125 Worth Street, Room 133. They have all the deaths after '48." I thought: Great.

17. THE WORST MISTAKE MY MOTHER EVER MADE

When I got home, my mother was curled up on the couch reading a book. "What are you reading?" I asked. "Cervantes," she said. "Cervantes?" I asked. "The most famous Spanish writer," my mother said, turning the page. I rolled my eyes at her. Sometimes I wonder why she didn't just marry a famous writer instead of a wilderness-loving engineer. If she had, none of this would have ever happened. Right now, at this very moment, she'd probably be sitting at the dinner table with her famous-writer husband, talking about the pros and cons of other famous writers, while making the difficult decision of who was worthy of a Posthumous Nobel.

That night I dialed Misha's number, but hung up on the first ring.

18. THEN IT WAS TUESDAY

It was still raining. On the way to the subway I passed the vacant lot where Bird had hung a tarp over the pile of junk that had grown to six feet tall, with trash bags and old ropes strung off the sides. A pole rose up from out of the mass, possibly waiting for a flag.

The lemonade stand was also still there, as was the sign that said LEMON-AID 50 CENTS PLEASE POUR YOURSELF (SPRAINED WRIST), followed by a new addition: ALL PROFITS GO TO CHARITY. But the table was empty, and there was no sign of Bird anywhere.

On the subway, somewhere between Carroll and Bergen, I made up my mind to call Misha and pretend nothing had happened. When I got off the train, I found a pay phone that worked and dialed his number. My heart sped up when it started to ring. His mother answered. "Hi, Mrs. Shklovsky," I said, trying to sound casual. "Is Misha there?" I heard her call him. After what felt like a long time he picked up. "Hi," I said. "Hi." "How are you?" "Good." "What are you doing?" "Reading." "What?" "Comics." "Ask me where I am." "Where?" "Outside the New York City Department of Health." "Why?" "I'm going to look for Alma Mereminski's records." "Still searching," said Misha. "Yeah," I said. There was an awkward silence. I said, "Well I was calling to see if you want to rent *Topaz* tonight." "Can't." "Why?" "I have plans." "What plans?" "I'm going to see a movie." "With who?" "Girl I know." My stomach turned itself inside out. "What girl?" I thought: Please don't let it be—_"Luba," he said. "Maybe you remember, you met her once." Of course I remembered. How can you forget a girl who is five-foot-nine, blond, and claims to be a descendant of Catherine the Great?

It was turning out to be a bad day.

"M-E-R-E-M-I-N-S-K-I," I said to the woman behind the desk in Room 133. I thought, How could he like a girl who couldn't do the Universal Edibility Test if her life depended on it? "M-E-R-E," the woman said, so I said, "M-I-N-S—" thinking, She probably hasn't ever heard of *Rear Window*. "M-Y-M-S," the woman said. "No," I said. "M-*I*-N-S." "M-*I*-N-S," the woman said. "K-I," I said. And she said, "K-I."

An hour passed and we didn't find any death certificate for Alma Mereminski. Another half hour passed and we still didn't find it. Loneliness turned into depression. After two hours, the woman said she was absolutely one-hundred-percent positive there was no Alma Mereminski who died in New York City after 1948.

That night I rented *North by Northwest* again and watched it for the eleventh time. Then I went to sleep.

19. LONELY PEOPLE ARE ALWAYS UP IN THE MIDDLE OF THE NIGHT

When I opened my eyes, Uncle Julian was standing above me. "How old are you?" he asked. "Fourteen. I'll be fifteen next month." "Fifteen next month," he said, as if he were turning a math problem over in his head. "What do you want to be when you grow up?" He was still wearing his raincoat, which was soaking wet. A drop of water fell in my eye. "I don't know." "Come on, there must be something." I sat up in my sleeping bag, rubbed my eye, and looked at my digital watch. There's a button you can press to make the numbers glow. It also has a built-in compass. "It's three-twenty-four in the morning," I said. Bird was asleep in my bed. "I know. I was just wondering. Tell me and I promise I'll let you go back to sleep. What do you want to be?" I thought, Someone who can survive in subzero temperatures and forage for food and build a snow cave and start a fire out of nothing. "I don't know. Maybe a painter," I said, to make him happy so he'd let me go back to sleep. "It's funny," he said. "That's what I was hoping you'd say."

20. AWAKE IN THE DARK

I thought about Misha and Luba, and my father and mother, and why Zvi Litvinoff had moved to Chile and married Rosa, instead of Alma, the one he'd really loved.

I heard Uncle Julian cough in his sleep across the hall.

Then I thought: Wait a minute.

21. SHE MUST HAVE GOTTEN MARRIED!

That was it! That's why I hadn't found the death certificate for Alma Mereminski. Why hadn't I thought of it before?

22. BEING NORMAL

I reached under my bed and pulled out the flash-light from my survival backpack, along with the third volume of *How to Survive in the Wild*. When I turned the flashlight on, something caught my eye. It was stuck between the bed frame and the wall, near the floor. I slid under the bed and shone my flashlight to get a better look. It was a black-and-white composition book. On the front it said יהוה. Next to that it said PRIVATE. Once Misha told me there was no word in Russian for privacy. I opened it.

April 9

יהוה

I have been a normal person for three days in a row. What this means is that I have not climbed on top of any buildings or written G-d's name on anything that doesn't belong to me or answered a perfectly normal question with a saying from the Torah. It also means I have not done anything where the answer would be NO to the question: WOULD A NORMAL PERSON DO THIS? So far it hasn't been that hard.

April 10

יהוה

This is the fourth day in a row that I've acted normal. In gym class Josh K. pinned me against the wall and asked if I thought I was a big fat genius so I told him I did not think I was a big fat genius. Because I did not want to ruin a whole normal day, I did not tell him that what I might

be is the Moshiach. Also my wrist is getting better.
If you want to know how I sprained it, I sprained
it by climbing up on the roof because I got to Hebrew
School early and the door was locked and there was
a ladder attached to the side of the building. The
ladder was rusty but otherwise it was not that
hard. There was a big puddle of water in the middle
of the roof so I decided to see what would happen
if I bounced my jack ball in it and tried to catch
it. It was fun! I did it about fifteen more times
until I lost it when it went over the edge. Then I
lay on my back and looked up at the sky. I counted
three airplanes. When I got bored I decided to go
down. It was harder than going up because I had
to go backwards. Halfway I passed the windows of
one of the classrooms. I could see Mrs. Zucker at
the front so I knew it was the Daleds. (If you want
to know, this year I'm a Hay.) I couldn't hear
what Mrs. Zucker was saying so I tried to read
her lips. I had to lean off of the ladder very far to
get a good view. I pressed my face right against
the window and suddenly everyone turned to look
at me so I waved and that's when I lost my balance.
I fell and Rabbi Wizner said it was a miracle that
I didn't break anything but deep inside I knew I
was safe the whole time and that G-d wouldn't let
anything happen to me because I am almost definitely a lamed vovnik.

April 11

יהוה

*Today was my fifth day of being normal. Alma
says that if I were normal it would make my life
easier not to mention everyone else's life. I got to
take the ace bandage off my wrist, and now it only
hurts a little. It probably hurt a lot more when I
broke my wrist when I was six but I don't
remember.*

I skipped ahead until I came to:

June 27

יהוה

*So far I've made $295.50 from selling lemon-
aid. That's 591 cups! My best customer is Mr.
Goldstein who buys ten cups at one time because
he's extremely thirsty. Also Uncle Julian who
tipped me 20 dollars once. Only $384.50 to go.*

June 28

יהוה

*Today I almost did something not normal. I was
passing a building on 4th Street and there was a
plank of wood leaning against the scaffolding and
no one was around and I really wanted to take
it. It wouldn't have been like regular stealing since*

the special thing I am building will help people and G-d wants me to build it. But I also know that if I stole it and someone found out I would get in trouble and then Alma would have to come get me and she would be angry. But I bet she won't be angry anymore when it starts to rain and I finally tell her what the special thing is that I've started to build. I've already collected a lot of stuff for it, mostly things that people have thrown away with the garbage. One thing I need a lot of that's hard to find is styrofoam because it floats. Right now I don't have that much. Sometimes I worry that it will start raining before I am finished building.

If Alma knew about what is going to happen, I also don't think she'd be so upset that I wrote יהוה on her notebook. I have read all three volumes of How to Survive in the Wild and they are very good and filled with interesting and useful facts. One part is all about what to do if there is a nuclear bomb. Even though I don't think there is going to be a nuclear bomb just in case I read it very carefully. Then I decided that if there is a nuclear bomb before I get to Israel and ashes fall everywhere like snow, I'm going to make angels. I'll walk through anyone's house I want because everyone will be gone. I won't be able to go to school, but it doesn't really matter since we *never learn anything important anyway like what happens after you die. Anyway I'm just joking because there's not going to be a bomb. What there's going to be is a flood.*

23. OUTSIDE, IT WAS STILL COMING DOWN

HERE WE ARE TOGETHER

On his last morning in Poland, after his friend pulled his hat down over his eyes and disappeared around the corner, Litvinoff walked back to his room. It was already empty, the furniture sold or given away. His suitcases stood at the door. He took out the brown paper package he'd been holding inside his coat. It was sealed, and on the front, in his friend's familiar handwriting, was written: *To be held for Leopold Gursky until you see him again.* Litvinoff slipped it into the pocket of his suitcase. He walked to the window and looked out at the tiny square of sky for the last time. Church bells rang in the distance as they'd rung hundreds of times while he worked or slept, so often that they felt like the workings of his own mind. He ran his fingers across the wall, pitted with tack marks where the pictures and articles he'd cut out of the newspaper used to hang. He paused to examine himself in the mirror so that later he would be able to recall exactly how he'd looked on that day. He felt a lump in his throat. For the umpteenth time, he checked his pocket for his passport and tickets. Then he glanced at his watch, sighed, lifted his suitcases, and walked out the door.

If Litvinoff didn't think much about his friend at first, it was because too many other things were on his mind. Through the machinations of his father, who was owed a favor by someone who knew someone, he had been granted a visa from Spain. From Spain he would travel to Lisbon, and from Lisbon he intended to take a boat to Chile, where his father's cousin lived. Once he got on the boat, other things jostled for his attention: bouts of seasickness, his fear of dark water, meditations on the horizon, speculations about life on the ocean floor, attacks of nostalgia, the sighting of a whale, the sighting of a pretty French brunette.

When the ship finally arrived in the port of Valparaíso and Litvinoff shakily disembarked ("sea legs," he told himself, even years later, when the shakiness sometimes returned without explanation), there were other things to occupy him. His first months in Chile were spent working whatever jobs he could get; first in a sausage factory, from which he was fired on his third day when he took the wrong streetcar and arrived fifteen minutes late, and, after that, in a grocery shop. Once, on his way to speak to a foreman he'd been told was hiring,

Litvinoff got lost and found himself standing outside the offices of the city newspaper. The windows were open, and he could hear the clatter of typewriters inside. He felt a pang of longing. He thought of his colleagues at the daily, which reminded him of his desk with the divots in the wood he used to finger to help him think, which reminded him of his typewriter with the sticky *S* so that his copy always had sentences like *hisss death leavesss a hole in the livesss of thossse he helped*, which reminded him of the smell of his boss's cheap cigars, which reminded him of his promotion from stringer to obituary writer, which reminded him of Isaac Babel, which was as far as he allowed himself to get before he stopped his longing in its tracks and hurried away down the street.

In the end, he found work in a pharmacy—his father had been a pharmacist, and Litvinoff had picked up enough along the way to assist the old German Jew who ran a tidy shop in a quiet part of town. Only then, when he could afford to rent a room of his own, was Litvinoff finally able to unpack his suitcases. In the pocket of one he found the brown paper package with his friend's handwriting on the front. A wave of sadness broke over his head. For no reason, he suddenly remembered a white shirt he had left drying on the clothesline in the courtyard in Minsk.

He tried to remember how his face had looked in

the mirror that last day. But he couldn't. Closing his eyes, he willed the memory back. But all that came to mind was the expression on his friend's face as he stood on the street corner. Sighing, Litvinoff put the envelope back in the empty suitcase, zipped it up, and put it away on the closet shelf.

Whatever money was left after his room and board, Litvinoff saved to bring over his younger sister, Miriam. As the closest siblings in age and appearance, they often had been mistaken for twins when they were little, even though Miriam was fairer, and wore tortoiseshell glasses. She'd been in law school in Warsaw until she'd been forbidden to attend classes.

The only expense Litvinoff allowed himself was a shortwave radio. Every night he spun the dial between his fingers, roaming the continent of South America until he found the new station, *The Voice of America.* He only spoke a little English, but it was enough. He listened with horror to the progress of the Nazis. Hitler broke his pact with Russia and invaded Poland. Things went from bad to terrifying.

The few letters from friends and relatives came less and less often, and it was difficult to know what was really happening. Folded inside the second-to-last letter he received from his sister—in which she told him that she'd fallen in love with another law student and gotten married—was a photograph taken when

she and Zvi were children. On the back she'd written
Here we are together.

In the mornings, Litvinoff made the coffee listening to stray dogs fight in the alley. He waited for the
streetcar, already baking in the early sun. He ate lunch
in the back of the pharmacy, surrounded by boxes of
pills and powders and cherry syrup and hair ribbons,
and at night, after he'd finished mopping the floor
and polishing all the jars until he could see his sister's
face in them, he came home. He didn't make many
friends. He was no longer in the business of making
friends. When he wasn't working, he was listening to
the radio. He listened until he was exhausted and fell
asleep in his chair, and even then he listened, his
dreams taking shape around the voice of the broad-
cast. There were other refugees around him experi-
encing the same fears and helplessness, but Litvinoff
didn't find any comfort in this because there are two
types of people in the world: those who prefer to be
sad among others, and those who prefer to be sad
alone. Litvinoff preferred to be alone. When people
invited him for dinner he begged off with some excuse.
Once, when his landlady invited him for tea on a
Sunday, he told her he had to finish something he was
writing. "You write?" she asked, surprised. "What do
you write?" As far as Litvinoff was concerned one
was just as good as another, and so, without giving it
much thought, he said: "Poems."

A rumor got started that he was a poet. And Litvinoff, secretly flattered, did nothing to quash it. He even bought a hat of the kind worn by Alberto Santos-Dumont, who the Brazilians claim made the first-ever successful flight, and whose panama hat, Litvinoff had heard, warped from fanning the plane's engine, was still popular among literary types.

Time passed. The old German Jew died in his sleep, the pharmacy was closed, and, partly on the strength of rumors of his literary prowess, Litvinoff was hired as a teacher at a Jewish day school. The War ended. Bit by bit, Litvinoff learned what had happened to his sister Miriam, and to his parents, and to four of his other siblings (what had become of his oldest brother, Andre, he could only piece together from probabilities). He learned to live with the truth. Not to accept it, but to live with it. It was like living with an elephant. His room was tiny, and every morning he had to squeeze around the truth just to get to the bathroom. To reach the armoire to get a pair of underpants he had to crawl under the truth, praying it wouldn't choose that moment to sit on his face. At night, when he closed his eyes, he felt it looming above him.

He lost weight. Everything about him seemed to shrink, except his ears and nose, which sagged and grew longer, giving him a melancholy look. The year he turned thirty-two, his hair came out in fistfuls. He abandoned the warped panama hat and took to wearing a heavy coat everywhere, in whose inside pocket he kept a worn and wrinkled piece of paper that he'd carried with him for years, and which had begun to rip at the folds. At the school, the children gave themselves cootie shots behind his back if he brushed up against them.

It was in this state that Rosa first began to notice Litvinoff at the cafés along the water. He went in the afternoons with the excuse of reading a novel or a poetry journal (first out of duty to his reputation, and later out of growing interest). But really he just wanted to steal a little more time before he had to go home again where the truth would be waiting. At the café, Litvinoff allowed himself to forget a little. He meditated on the waves and watched the students, sometimes eavesdropping on their arguments, which were the same arguments he'd had when he'd been a student a hundred years ago (i.e., twelve). He even knew some of their names. Including Rosa's. How could he not? People were always calling it.

The afternoon she approached his table and, instead of continuing past to greet some young man, stopped with an abrupt gracefulness and asked if she could join him, Litvinoff thought it was a joke. Her hair was shiny and black and cropped just below her chin, emphasizing her strong nose. She was wearing a green dress (later Rosa would argue that it was red,

red with black polka dots, but Litvinoff refused to relinquish the memory of a sleeveless emerald chiffon). Only after she'd been sitting with him for half an hour and her friends had lost interest and turned back to their conversations did Litvinoff realize that her gesture had been sincere. There was an awkward pause in the conversation. Rosa smiled.

"I haven't even introduced myself," she said.

"You're Rosa," Litvinoff said.

The next afternoon, Rosa turned up for a second meeting just as she'd promised. When she glanced at her watch and realized how late it had got they planned a third meeting, and after that it went without saying that there'd be a fourth. The fifth time they met, under the spell of Rosa's youthful spontaneity—halfway through a heated discussion about who was a greater poet, Neruda or Darío—Litvinoff surprised himself by proposing they go hear a concert together. When Rosa jumped to agree, it dawned on him that, miracle of miracles, this lovely girl might actually be developing *feelings* for him. It was as if someone had struck a gong in his chest. His whole body reverberated with the news.

A few days after the date at the concert, they met in the park and had a picnic. This was followed the next Sunday by a bicycle ride. On their seventh date they saw a movie. When it was over, Litvinoff walked Rosa home. They were standing together, discussing the merits of Grace Kelly's acting versus her unbelievable beauty, when all of a sudden Rosa leaned forward and kissed him. Or at least she tried to kiss him, but Litvinoff, taken off guard, backed away, leaving Rosa tipped forward at an awkward angle, neck outstretched. All night, he'd been monitoring the ebb and flow of distance between their various body parts with growing pleasure. But the shifting measurements had been so fractional that this sudden charge by Rosa's nose almost reduced him to tears. Realizing his mistake, he blindly stuck his neck out into the gulf. But by then, Rosa had already counted her losses and pulled back into safer territory. Litvinoff hung in the balance. Enough time for a waft of Rosa's perfume to tickle his nose, and then he beat a hasty retreat. Or he began to beat a hasty retreat, when Rosa, not wanting to take any more chances, shotput her lips into the contested space, momentarily forgetting that appendage, her nose, which she remembered a fraction of a second later when it collided with Litvinoff's at the instant his lips mashed against hers, so that with their first kiss they became blood relatives.

Litvinoff was giddy on the bus ride home. He flashed a smile at anyone who looked his way. He walked down his street whistling. But as he slipped the key into his lock, a coolness entered his heart. He stood in his dark room without turning on the lamp.

For God's sake, he thought. *Where is your head? What in the world could you offer a girl like that, don't be a fool, you've let yourself fall apart, the pieces have got lost, and now there's nothing left to give, you can't hide it forever, sooner or later she'll figure out the truth: you're a shell of a man, all she has to do is knock against you to find out you're empty.*

For a long time he stood with his head against the window, thinking about everything. Then he took off his clothes. Feeling in the dark, he washed out his underwear and hung them to dry on the radiator. He turned the dial on the radio, which glowed and came to life, but a minute later turned it off again and a tango broke off into silence. He sat naked in his chair. A fly landed on his shriveled penis. He mumbled some words. And because it felt good to mumble, he mumbled some more. They were words he knew by heart because he'd been carrying them on a piece of paper folded in his breast pocket since that night, all those years ago, when he'd watched over his friend, praying for him not to die. He'd said them so many times, even when he didn't know he was saying them, that sometimes he actually forgot that the words weren't his.

That night, Litvinoff went to the closet and brought down his suitcase. Reaching a hand into the pocket, he felt around for a thick paper envelope. He pulled it out, sat back down in his chair, and placed

it on his lap. Although he'd never opened it, of course
he knew what was in it. Closing his eyes to shield them
from the brightness, he reached up and turned on the
lamp.

To be held for Leopold Gursky until you see him again.

Later, no matter how many times he tried to bury
that sentence in the trash under orange peels and
coffee filters, it always seemed to rise again to the
surface. So one morning Litvinoff fished out the empty
envelope, whose contents now sat safely on his desk.
Then, choking back tears, he lit a match and watched
his friend's handwriting burn.

DIE LAUGHING

What does it say?

We stood under the stars at Grand Central, or so I have to assume, since I could sooner hook my ankles over my ears than tilt back my head for an unobstructed view of what lies above.

What does it say? Bruno repeated, jabbing his elbow into my ribs as I raised my chin another notch toward the departures board. My upper lip parted from the lower, to be liberated from the weight of the jaw. *Hurry up*, Bruno said. *Hold your horses*, I told him, except that with my mouth open it came out as, *Old-yer arses*. I could just make out the numbers. *9:45*, I said, or rather, *Nine-orty-I. What time is it now?* Bruno demanded. I worked my gaze back down to my watch. *9:43*, I said.

We started to run. Not run, but move in such a way that two people who've worn away all manner of balls and sockets move if they want to catch a train. I had the lead, but Bruno was hot on my heels. Then

Bruno, who'd hit upon a way to pump his arms for speed that defies all description, edged me out, and for a moment I coasted while he quote unquote broke the wind. I was concentrating on the back of his neck when, without warning, it plummeted from view. I looked behind. He was in a pile on the floor, one shoe on, one off. *Go!* he shouted at me. I floundered, not knowing what to do. *GO!* he shouted again, so I went, and next thing I knew he'd cut a corner and pulled out ahead again, shoe in hand, pumping rapidly.

All aboard track 22.

Bruno headed down the stairs toward the platform. I was right behind. There was every reason to believe we'd make it. And yet. In an unexpected change of plans, he skidded to a halt just as he reached the train. Unable to break my speed, I barreled past him into the car. The doors closed behind me. He smiled at me through the glass. I banged the window with my fist. *Damn you, Bruno.* He waved. He knew I wouldn't have gone alone. And yet. He knew I needed to go. Alone. The train started to pull away. His lips moved. I tried to read them. *Good*, they said. His lips paused. What is good? I wanted to shout. Tell me what is good? And they said: *Luck.* The train lurched out of the station and into the dark.

Five days after the brown envelope had arrived with the pages of the book I'd written half a century

ago, I was on my way to get back the book I'd written half a century later. Or, to say it differently: a week
after my son died, I was on my way to his house. Either
way, I was on my own.

I found a seat by the window and tried to catch
my breath. We sped through the tunnel. I leaned my
head against the glass. Someone had scratched "nice
boobs" into the surface. Impossible not to wonder:
Whose? The train broke into the dirty light and rain.
It was the first time in my life I'd gotten on a train
without a ticket.

A man got on at Yonkers and sat down next to
me. He took out a paperback. My stomach growled.
I hadn't put anything in it yet, if you didn't count the
coffee I drank with Bruno that morning at Dunkin'
Donuts. It was early. We'd been the first customers.
Give me a jelly and a powdered, Bruno said. *Give him a
jelly and a powdered*, I said. *And I'll have a small coffee*.
The man in the paper hat paused. *It's cheaper if you get
a medium.* America, God bless it. *All right*, I said. *Make
it a medium*. The man went off and came back with
the coffee. *Give me a Bavarian Kreme and a glazed*,
Bruno said. I shot him a look. *What?* he said, shrug-
ging. *Give him a Bavarian Kreme—*I said. *And a vanilla*,
said Bruno. I turned to glare at him. *Mea culpa*, he
said. *Vanilla. Go sit down*, I told him. He stood there.
SIT, I said. *Make it a cruller*, he said. The Bavarian
Kreme was gone in four bites. He licked his fingers,

then held the cruller up to the light. *It's a donut, not a diamond*, I said. *It's stale*, said Bruno. *Eat it anyway*, I told him. *Change it for an Apple Spice*, he said.

The train left the city behind. Green fields fell away to either side. It had been raining for days, and it kept raining.

Many times I'd imagined where Isaac lived. I'd found it on a map. Once I even called up Information: *If I want to get from Manhattan to my son*, I asked, *how do I go?* I'd pictured it all, down to the last detail. Happy days! I'd come bearing a gift. A pot of jam, perhaps. We wouldn't stand on ceremony. Too late for all that. Maybe we'd toss a ball around on the lawn. I can't catch. Nor, frankly, can I throw. And yet. We'd talk baseball. I've followed the game since Isaac was a boy. When he rooted for the Dodgers, I, too, was rooting. I wanted to see what he saw, and hear what he heard. I kept abreast, as much as possible, of popular music. The Beatles, the Rolling Stones, Bob Dylan—"Lay, Lady, Lay," you don't need a brass bed to understand it. Each night, I'd come home from work and order from Mr. Tong's. Then I'd pull a record from its sleeve, lift the needle, and listen.

Every time Isaac moved, I mapped out the route between my place and his. The first time he was eleven. I used to stand across the street from his school in Brooklyn and wait for him, just to catch a glimpse maybe, if I was lucky, hear the sound of his voice. One day I waited as usual, but he didn't come out. I thought maybe he'd gotten in trouble and had to stay late. It got dark, they turned off the lights, and still he didn't come. I went back the next day, and again I waited, and again he didn't come. That night I imagined the worst. I couldn't sleep, imagining all the awful things that might have happened to my child. Even though I'd promised myself I never would, the next morning I got up early and went by where he lived. Not went by. Stood across the street. I watched for him, or for Alma, or even that *shlemiel*, her husband. And yet. No one came. Finally I stopped a kid who came out of the building. *You know the Moritz family?* He stared at me. *Yeah. So what?* he said. *They still live here?* I asked. *What's it to you?* he said, and started to go off down the street bouncing a rubber ball. I grabbed him by the collar. There was a look of fear in his eyes. *They moved to Long Island*, he blurted out, and took off running.

A week later a letter arrived from Alma. She had my address, because once a year, on her birthday, I sent her a card. *Happy Birthday*, I'd write, *From Leo*. I tore open her letter. *I know you watch him*, she wrote. *Don't ask me how, but I know. I keep waiting for the day when he'll ask for the truth. Sometimes when I look in his eyes I see you. And I think you're the only one who could answer his questions. I hear your voice like you were next to me.*

I read the letter I don't know how many times. But that's not the point. What mattered was that in the upper left corner of the envelope she'd written the return address: *121 Atlantic Avenue, Long Beach, NY.*

I got out my map and memorized the details of the journey. I used to fantasize about disasters, floods, earthquakes, the world thrown into chaos so that I'd have a reason to go to him and sweep him up under my coat. When I'd given up the hope of extenuating circumstances I started to dream about our being thrown together by chance. I calculated all the ways our lives might casually intersect—finding myself sitting beside him on a train, or in the waiting room of the doctor's office. But in the end, I knew that it was up to me. When Alma was gone, and, two years later, Mordecai, there had been nothing anymore to stop me. And yet.

Two hours later, the train pulled into the station. I asked the person in the ticket booth how I could get a taxi. It had been a long time since I'd been out of the city. I stood in wonder of the greenness of everything.

We drove for some time. We turned off the main road onto a smaller road, then a smaller one yet. At last, up a bumpy wooded drive in the middle of nowhere. It was hard to imagine a son of mine living in such a place. Say he got a craving for a pizza, where would he go? Say he wanted to sit alone in a dark movie theater, or watch some kids kissing in Union Square?

A white house came into view. A little wind was chasing the clouds. Between the branches, I saw a lake. I'd imagined his place many times. But never with a lake. The oversight pained me.

You can drop me here, I said, before we reached the clearing. I half expected someone to be home. As far as I knew, Isaac had lived by himself. But you never know. The taxi came to a halt. I paid and got out, and it backed away down the drive. I made up a story about my car breaking down and needing a phone, took a deep breath, and pulled my collar up against the rain.

I knocked. There was a bell, so I rang it. I knew he was dead, but a small part of me still hoped. I imagined his face as he would pull open the door. What would I have said to him, my only child? Forgive me, your mother didn't love me the way I wanted to be loved; perhaps I didn't love her the way she needed, either? And yet. There was no answer. I waited, just to be sure. When no one came, I walked around to the back. There was a tree on the lawn which reminded me of the tree on which I'd once carved our initials, A + L, and she never knew, just as for five years I never knew that our sum had come to equal a child.

The grass was slippery with mud. In the distance I could see a rowboat tied to the dock. I looked out across the water. Must have been a good swimmer, took after his father, I thought with pride. My own father, who had great respect for nature, had dropped each of us into the river soon after we were born, before our ties to the amphibians, so he claimed, were cut completely. My sister Hanna blamed her lisp on the trauma of this memory. I'd like to think that I would have done it differently. I would have held my son in my arms. I would have told him, *Once upon a time you were a fish. A fish?* he'd have asked. *That's what I'm telling you, a fish. How do you know? Because I was also a fish. You, too? Sure. A long time ago. How long? Long. Anyway, being a fish, you used to know how to swim. I did? Sure. You were a great swimmer. A champion swimmer, you were. You loved the water. Why? What do you mean, why? Why did I love the water? Because it was your life!* And as we talked, I would have let him go one finger at a time, until, without his realizing, he'd be floating without me.

And then I thought: Perhaps that is what it means to be a father—to teach your child to live without you. If so, no one was a greater father than I.

There was a back door with only one lock, a basic pin tumbler, versus the double lock on the front. I knocked one last time, and when there was no answer I got to work. I labored over it for a minute until I could ease it open. I turned the handle and pushed. I stood unmoving in the doorway. *Hello?* I called. There was silence. I felt a chill down my spine. I stepped inside and closed the door behind me. It smelled of wood smoke.

This is Isaac's house, I told myself. I took off my raincoat and hung it on a hook next to another. It was brown tweed, with a brown silk lining. I lifted his sleeve and touched it to my cheek. I thought: This is his coat. I brought it to my nose and inhaled. There was a faint smell of cologne. I took it down and tried it on. The sleeves were too long. But. No matter. I pushed them up. I took off my shoes, which were caked with mud. There was a pair of running sneakers, curled at the toes. I slipped them on my feet like a regular Mr. Rogers. The sneakers were at least a size eleven, maybe eleven and a half. My father had tiny feet, when my sister got married to a boy from a nearby village he spent the whole wedding staring with regret at the size of his new son-in-law's feet. I can only imagine his shock had he lived to see his grandson's.

Like so I entered my son's house: draped in his coat, his shoes on my feet. I was as close as I'd ever been to him. As far away.

I clopped down the narrow hallway that led to the kitchen. Standing in the middle of the room, I waited for the police sirens that didn't come.

There was a dirty dish in the sink. A glass left upside down to dry, a hardened tea bag in a saucer. On the kitchen table there was some spilled salt. A postcard was taped to the window. I took it down and turned it over. *Dear Isaac*, it began. *I'm sending this from Spain, where I've been living for a month. I'm writing to say that I haven't read your book and I'm not going to.*

Behind me there was a bang. I clutched my chest. I thought I was going to turn around and see Isaac's ghost. But it was only the door blown open by the wind. With shaking hands, I put the postcard back where I found it and stood in the silence, my heart in my ears.

The floorboards creaked under my weight. There were books everywhere. There were pens, and a blue glass vase, an ashtray from the Dolder Grand in Zurich, the rusted arrow of a weather vane, a little brass hourglass, sand dollars on the windowsill, a pair of binoculars, an empty wine bottle that served as a candle holder, wax melted down the neck. I touched this thing and that. At the end, all that's left of you are your possessions. Perhaps that's why I've never been able to throw anything away. Perhaps that's why I hoarded the world: with the hope that when I died, the sum total of my things would suggest a life larger than the one I lived.

I felt dizzy and grabbed the mantel for support. I went back into Isaac's kitchen. I didn't have an appetite, but I opened the refrigerator anyway because the doctor told me I shouldn't go without eating, something to do with my blood pressure. A strong odor hit my nostrils. It was some leftover chicken gone bad. I threw it out, along with a couple of brown peaches and some moldy cheese. Then I washed the dirty dish. I don't know how to describe the feeling I had, going through these casual motions in my son's house. I did them with love. The glass I put back in the cabinet. The tea bag I threw away, the saucer I rinsed. There were probably people—the man in the yellow bow tie, or a future biographer—who wanted to leave things exactly as Isaac had. Perhaps one day they would even make a museum of his life, brought to you by the people who saved the glass from which Kafka took his last sip, the plate from which Mandelstam ate his last crumbs. Isaac was a great writer, the writer I could never have been. And yet. He was also my son.

I went upstairs. With every door and cabinet and drawer I opened, I learned something new about Isaac, and with each new thing I learned, his absence became more real, and the more real, the more impossible to believe. I opened his medicine cabinet. Inside were two bottles of talcum powder. I don't even really know what talcum powder is, or why one would use it, but this single fact about his life moved me more than any detail I'd ever imagined. I opened his closet and pushed my face into his shirts. He liked the color blue. I picked up a pair of brown wingtips. The heels were worn down to almost nothing. I put my nose inside and sniffed. I found his watch on the night table and put it on. The leather strap was worn around the hole where he used to buckle it. His wrist had been thicker than mine. When had he grown bigger than me? What had I been doing, and what had he, at the exact moment my son had surpassed me in size?

The bed was neatly made. Had he died in it? Or had he felt it coming, and gotten up to greet his childhood again, only to be struck down? What was the last thing he'd looked at? Was it the watch on my wrist, stopped at 12:38? The lake outside the window? Someone's face? And did he feel pain?

Only once did someone die in my arms. I was working as a janitor in a hospital, this was the winter of 1941. It was only a brief while. In the end I lost the job. But one evening, during my last week, I was mopping the floor when I heard someone gagging. It was coming from the room of a woman who had a disease of the blood. I ran to her. Her body twisted and convulsed. I took her in my arms. I think I can say there was no question in either of our minds about what was about to happen. She had a child. I knew because I'd seen him visit once with his father. A little boy in polished boots and a coat with gold buttons. He'd sat playing with a toy car the whole time, ignoring his mother unless she spoke to him. Perhaps he was angry at her for leaving him alone with his father for so long. As I looked into her face, it was him I thought of, the boy who would grow up without know-

ing how to forgive himself. I felt a certain relief and
pride, even superiority, to be filling the task that he
couldn't. And then, less than a year later, that son
whose mother died without him was me.

There was a noise behind me. A creak. This time
I didn't turn. I squeezed my eyes shut. *Isaac*, I whis-
pered. The sound of my own voice frightened me, but
I didn't stop. *I want to tell you*—and then I broke off.
What do I want to tell you? The truth? What is the
truth? That I mistook your mother for my life? No.
Isaac, I said. *The truth is the thing I invented so I could
live.*

Now I turned and saw myself in the mirror on
Isaac's wall. A fool in fool's clothes. I'd come to get
back my book, but now I didn't care whether I found
it or not. I thought: Let it be lost like the rest. It didn't
matter, not anymore.

And yet.

In the corner of the mirror, reflected from across
the hall, I saw his typewriter. No one had to tell me
it was the same as mine. I'd read in a newspaper inter-
view that he'd been writing on the same manual
Olympia for almost twenty-five years. A few months
later I saw the exact model for sale in a secondhand
shop. The man said it worked, so I bought it. In the
beginning I just liked to look at it, to know that my
son was looking at it, too. Day in and day out it sat
there smiling at me, as if the keys were teeth. Then I

had the heart attack, and still it smiled, so one day I rolled a sheet in and wrote a sentence.

I crossed the hall. I thought: What if I found my book there, on his desk? The strangeness of it hit me. I in his coat, my book on his desk. He with my eyes, I in his shoes.

All I wanted was proof that he'd read it.

I sat down in his chair in front of his typewriter. The house felt cold. I pulled his coat around me. I thought I heard laughter, but told myself it was only the little boat creaking in the storm. I thought I heard footsteps on the roof, but told myself it was only an animal foraging for food. I rocked a little, the way my father used to rock when he prayed. Once my father told me: *When a Jew prays, he is asking God a question that has no end.*

Darkness fell. Rain fell.

I never asked: What question?

And now it's too late. Because I lost you, *Tateh*. One day, in the spring of 1938, on a rainy day that gave way to a break in the clouds, I lost you. You'd gone out to collect specimens for a theory you were hatching about rainfall, instinct, and butterflies. And then you were gone. We found you lying under a tree, your face splashed with mud. We knew you were free then, unbound by disappointing results. And we buried you in the cemetery where your father was buried, and his father, under the shade of a chestnut tree. Three

years later, I lost *Mameh*. The last time I saw her she
was wearing her yellow apron. She was stuffing things
in a suitcase, the house was a wreck. She told me to
go out into the woods. She'd packed me food, and
told me to wear my coat, even though it was July.
"Go," she said. I was too old to listen, but like a child
I listened. She told me she'd follow the next day. We
chose a spot we both knew in the woods. The giant
walnut tree you used to like, *Tateh*, because you said
it had human qualities. I didn't bother to say goodbye. I chose to believe what was easier. I waited. But.
She never came. Since then I've lived with the guilt
of understanding too late that she thought she would
have been a burden to me. I lost Fritzy. He was studying in Vilna, *Tateh*—someone who knew someone told
me he'd last been seen on a train. I lost Sari and
Hanna to the dogs. I lost Herschel to the rain. I lost
Josef to a crack in time. I lost the sound of laughter.
I lost a pair of shoes, I'd taken them off to sleep, the
shoes Herschel gave me, and when I woke they were
gone, I walked barefoot for days and then I broke
down and stole someone else's. I lost the only woman
I ever wanted to love. I lost years. I lost books. I lost
the house where I was born. And I lost Isaac. So who
is to say that somewhere along the way, without my
knowing it, I didn't also lose my mind?

My book was nowhere to be found. Aside from
myself, there was no sign of me.

IF NOT, NOT

1. WHAT I LOOK LIKE NAKED

When I woke up in my sleeping bag the rain had stopped and my bed was empty, the sheets stripped. I looked at my watch. It was 10:03. It was also August 30th, which meant there were only ten days left until school started, a month until I turned fifteen, and only three years left until I was supposed to leave for college to start my life, which, at this point, did not seem very likely. For this and other reasons my stomach ached. I looked across the hall into Bird's room. Uncle Julian was asleep with his glasses on, Volume II of *The Destruction of the European Jews* open on his chest. Bird received the box set as a gift from a cousin of my mother's who lives in Paris, and who took an interest in him after we met her for tea at her hotel. She told us that her husband had fought in the Resistance, and Bird stopped trying to construct a house out of the sugar cubes to say: "Resistancing who?"

In the bathroom I took off my T-shirt and underwear, stood on the toilet, and stared at myself in the mirror. I tried to think of five adjectives to describe what I looked like, and one was *scrawny* and another was *My ears stick out.* I considered a nose ring. When I raised my arms over my head, my chest became concave.

2. MY MOTHER LOOKS RIGHT THROUGH ME

Downstairs, my mother was in her kimono reading the newspaper in the sunlight. "Did anyone call for me?" I asked. "Fine, thank you, and how are you?" she said. "But I didn't say how are you," I said. "I know." "You shouldn't have to always be polite with your family." "Why not?" "It would be better if people just said what they meant." "You mean you don't care how I am?" I glared at her. "Finethankyouhowareyou?" I said. "Fine, thank you," said my mother. "Did anyone call?" "For instance?" "Anyone." "Has something happened between you and Misha?" "No," I said, opening the refrigerator and examining some wilted celery.

I dropped an English muffin into the toaster, an
my mother turned the page of the newspape
scanning the headlines. I wondered if she'd eve
notice if I let it burn to a black crisp.

"*The History of Love* starts when Alma is te
right?" I said. My mother looked up and nodde
"Well how old is she when it ends?" "It's hard t
say. There are so many Almas in the book." "Ho
old is the oldest?" "Not very. Maybe twenty." "S
the book ends when Alma is only twenty?" "In
way. But it's more complicated than that. She isr
even mentioned in some chapters. And the who
sense of time and history in the book is very loose
"But there's no Alma in any of the chapters old
than twenty?" "No," said my mother. "I gue
not."

I made a mental note that if Alma Meremins
was a real person, Litvinoff most likely fell in lo
with her when they were both ten, and that twen
was probably how old they were when she left f
America, which must have been the last time l
saw her. Why else would the book end when sl
was still so young?

I ate the English muffin with peanut butt
standing up in front of the toaster. "Alma?" n
mother said. "What?" "Come give me a hug," sl
said, so I did, even though I didn't feel like it. "Ho
did you get so tall?" I shrugged, hoping sl

wouldn't go on. "I'm going to the library," I told her, which was a lie, but by the way she was looking at me I knew she hadn't really heard, since it wasn't me she saw.

3. ALL THE LIES I'VE EVER TOLD WILL COME BACK TO ME ONE DAY

On the street I passed Herman Cooper sitting on his front stoop. He'd been in Maine all summer, where he'd gotten a tan and his driver's license. He asked me if I wanted to go for a ride sometime. I could have reminded him of the rumor he spread about me when I was six involving being adopted and Puerto Rican, or the one he spread about me when I was ten involving me lifting my skirt in his basement and showing him everything. Instead I told him that I got carsick.

I went back to 31 Chambers Street again, this time to find out if there were any marriage records for Alma Mereminski. The same man with black glasses was sitting behind the desk in room 103. "Hi," I said. He looked up. "Miss Rabbit Meat. How are you?" "Finethankyouhowareyou?" I said. "OK, I guess." He turned the page of a magazine and added, "A little tired, you know, and I think I might be getting a cold, and this morning I woke

up and my cat had puked, which wouldn't be so
bad if she hadn't done it on my shoe." "Oh," I
said. "On top if which, I just found out that they're
cutting off my cable because I happened to be a
little late paying the bill, which means I'm going
to miss all of my shows, plus the plant my mother
gave me for Christmas is going a little brown, and
if it dies I'll never hear the end of it." I waited in
case he was going to continue, but he didn't, so I
said: "Maybe she got married." "Who?" "Alma
Mereminski." He closed the magazine and looked
at me. "You don't know if your own great-
grandmother got married?" I considered my
options. "She wasn't really my great grandmother," I said. "I thought you said—" "We're
actually not even related." He looked confused
and a little upset. "Sorry. It's a long story," I said,
and part of me wanted him to ask me why I was
looking for her, so I could tell him the truth: that
I wasn't really sure, that I had started out looking
for someone to make my mother happy again, and
even though I hadn't given up on finding him yet,
along the way I began to look for something else,
too, which was connected to the first search, but
also different, because it had to do with me. But
he just sighed and said, "Would she have gotten
married before 1937?" "I'm not sure." He sighed
and pushed his glasses up his nose, and told me

they only had records in Room 103 for marriages up until 1937.

We looked anyway, but we didn't find any Alma Mereminski. "You better go to the City Clerk's Office," he said glumly. "That's where they have all the later records." "Where is it?" "One Centre Street, Room 252," he said. I had never heard of Centre Street, so I asked for directions. It wasn't that far so I decided to walk, and while I did I imagined rooms all over the city that housed archives no one has ever heard of, like last words, white lies, and false descendants of Catherine the Great.

4. THE BROKEN LIGHTBULB

The man behind the desk at the City Clerk's Office was old. "How can I help?" he asked when it was my turn. "I want to find out if a woman named Alma Mereminski got married and changed her name," I said. He nodded and wrote something down. "M-E-R," I began, and he said: "E-M-I-N-S-K-I. Or is it Y?" "I," I said. "That's what I thought," he said. "When would she have married?" "I don't know. It could have been anytime after 1937. If she's still alive now, she's probably about eighty." "First marriage?" "I think." He scratched a note into his pad. "Any idea the man maybe she married?" I shook my head. He licked his finger, turned the page, and took another note. "The wedding—would've been civic or a priest or any chance maybe was a rabbi married her?" "Probably a rabbi," I said. "That's what I thought," he said.

He opened a drawer and took out a roll of Life Savers. "Mint?" I shook my head. "*Take*," he said, so I took one. He popped a mint into his mouth and sucked on it. "She came from Poland maybe?" "How did you know?" "Easy," he said. "With such a name." He rolled the mint from one side of his mouth to the other. "It's possible she came '39, '40, before the War? She would have been . . ." he licked his finger and flipped back a page, then took out a calculator and punched the buttons with the eraser of his pencil. "Nineteen, twenty. Most I'd give her is twenty-one."

He wrote these numbers down on his pad. He tutted his tongue and shook his head. "Must have been lonely, poor thing." He glanced up at me with a questioning look. His eyes were pale and watery. "I guess so," I said. "Sure she would have!" he said. "Who does she know? Nobody! Except for maybe a cousin who doesn't want to know from her. He lives in America now, the big *macher*, what does he need with this refugenik? His boy speaks English without an accent, he'll be someday a rich lawyer, the last thing he needs is the *mishpocheh* from Poland, skinny like the dead, knocking at his door." It didn't seem like a good idea to say anything, so I didn't. "Maybe she is lucky once, twice he invites her for *shabbes*, and his wife grumbles because they don't even have for themselves what to eat, she has to beg the butcher to give her again on credit a chicken, This is the last time, she tells her husband, Give a pig a chair, and he'll want to get on the table, which is not even to mention that back in Poland the murderers are killing her family, every last one, may-they-rest-in-peace, from my mouth to God's ear."

I didn't know what to say, but he seemed to be waiting, so I said: "It must have been terrible." "That's what I'm telling you," he said, and then he tutted his tongue again and said, "Poor thing. Was a Goldfarb, Arthur Goldfarb, someone, the grandniece I think it was, came in a couple days ago. A doctor, she had a picture, handsome fellow, was a bad *shiddukh*, turns out he got divorced after a year. Would've been perfect for your Alma." He crunched on the mint and wiped his nose with a handkerchief. "My wife tells me it's no talent to be a matchmaker for the dead, so I tell her if you always drink vinegar, you don't know anything sweeter exists." He got up from his chair. "Wait here, please."

When he came back he was out of breath. He pulled himself back up onto his stool. "Like searching for gold, so hard to find was this Alma." "Did you?" "What?" "Find her?" "Of course I found her, what kind of clerk am I that I can't find a nice girl? Alma Mereminski, here she is. Married in Brooklyn in 1942 to Mordecai Moritz, wedding performed by a Rabbi Greenberg. Lists also the parents' names." "This is really her?" "Who else? Alma Mereminski, right here says she was born in Poland. He was born in Brooklyn, but the parents were from Odessa. Says here his father owned a dress factory, so she didn't do so bad. To be honest, I'm relieved. Maybe was a nice wedding. In those days would break a lightbulb under his foot the *chassan* because no one could spare a glass."

5. THERE ARE NO PAY PHONES IN THE ARCTIC

I found a pay phone and called home. Uncle Julian answered. "Did anyone call for me?" I asked. "I don't think so. Sorry I woke you last night, Al." "It's OK." "I'm glad we had that little talk." "Yeah," I said, hoping he wouldn't bring up becoming a painter again. "What do you say we go out for dinner tonight? Unless you have other plans." "I don't," I said.

I hung up and called Information. "What borough?" "Brooklyn." "What listing?" "Moritz. First name is Alma." "Business or residence?" "Residence." "I have nothing under that listing." "What about Mordecai Moritz?" "No." "Well, how about in Manhattan?" "I have a Mordecai Moritz on 52nd." "You do?" I said. I couldn't believe it. "Hold for the number." "Wait!" I said. "I need the address." "Four-fifty East 52nd," the woman said. I wrote it down on my palm and caught a subway uptown.

6. I KNOCK AND SHE ANSWERS

She's old with long white hair held back by a tortoiseshell comb. Her apartment is flooded with sunlight, and she owns a parrot that talks. I tell her about how my father, David Singer, found *The History of Love* in the window of a bookstore in Buenos Aires when he was twenty-two, while traveling alone with a topographical map, a compass, a Swiss Army knife, and a Spanish-Hebrew dictionary. I also tell her about my mother and her wall of dictionaries, and Emanuel Chaim who goes by the name Bird in honor of his freedom, and his having survived an effort to fly that left behind a scar on his head. She shows me a picture of herself when she was my age. The talking parrot squawks, "Alma!" and both of us turn.

7. I'M SICK OF FAMOUS WRITERS

Daydreaming, I missed my stop and had to walk back ten blocks, and with every block I felt more nervous and less sure. What if Alma—the real, live Alma—actually answered the door? What was I supposed to say to someone who'd walked off the pages of a book? Or what if she'd never heard of *The History of Love*? Or what if she had, but wanted to forget it? I'd been so busy trying to find her that it hadn't occurred to me that maybe she didn't want to be found.

But there was no time left to think, because I was standing at the end of 52nd Street outside her building. "Can I help you?" the doorman asked. "My name is Alma Singer. I'm looking for Mrs. Alma Moritz. Is she home?" I asked. "Mrs. Moritz?" he said. He had a weird expression when he said her name. "Uh," he said. "No." He looked as if he felt sorry for me, and then I felt sorry for myself, because what he said next was that Alma wasn't alive. She'd died five years ago. Which was how I found out that everyone I'm named after is dead. Alma Mereminski, and my father, David Singer, and my great-aunt Dora who died in the Warsaw Ghetto, and for whom I was given my Hebrew name, Devorah. Why do people always get named after dead people? If they have to be named after anything at all, why can't it be things, which have more permanence, like the sky or the sea, or even ideas, which never really die, not even bad ones?

The doorman had been talking, but now he stopped. "Are you OK?" he asked. "Finethankyou," I said, even though I wasn't. "You want to sit down or something?" I shook my head. I don't know why, but I thought of the time Dad took me to see the penguins at the zoo, lifting me up onto his shoulders in the dank and fishy cold so I could press my face against the glass and watch them get fed, and how he taught me to pronounce the word *Antarctica*. Then I wondered if it ever really happened.

Because there was nothing left to say, I said, "Have you ever heard of a book called *The History of Love*?" The doorman shrugged and shook his head. "If you want to talk about books, you should talk to the son." "Alma's son?" "Sure. Isaac. He still comes in sometimes." "Isaac?" "Isaac Moritz. Famous writer. You didn't know that was their son? Sure, he still uses the place when he's in town. You want to leave a message?" he asked. "No, thank you," I said, because I'd never heard of any Isaac Moritz.

8. UNCLE JULIAN

That evening, Uncle Julian ordered a beer for himself and a mango lassi for me, and said, "I know sometimes things are hard with Mum." "She misses Dad," I said, which was like pointing out that a skyscraper is tall. Uncle Julian nodded. "I know you didn't know your grandpa. In lots of ways he was very wonderful. But he was also a difficult man. Controlling would be a nice word for it. He had very strict rules about how your mum and I should live." The reason I didn't know my grandfather very well was because he died of old age while on holiday at a hotel in Bournemouth a few years after I was born. "Charlotte got the brunt of it since she was the eldest and a girl. I think that's why she's always refused to tell you and Bird what to do or how to do it." "Except for our manners," I pointed out. "No, she doesn't restrain herself on the subject of manners, does she? I suppose what I'm trying to say is that I know she may seem distant sometimes. She has her own things she needs to work out. Missing your dad is one. Arguing against her own father is another. But you know how much she loves you, Al, don't you?" I nodded. The way Uncle Julian smiled was always a little lopsided, with one side of his mouth curling up higher than the other, as if part of him refused to cooperate with the rest. "Well, then," he said, and raised his glass. "To you turning fifteen, and to me finishing this bloody book."

We clicked glasses. Then he told me the story about how he fell in love with Alberto Giacometti when he was twenty-five. "How did you fall in love with Aunt Frances?" I asked. "Ah," said Uncle Julian, and mopped his forehead, which was shiny and damp. He was going a little bald, but in a handsome way. "You really want to know?" "Yes." "She was wearing blue tights." "What do you mean?" "I saw her at the zoo in front of the chimpanzee cage, and she was wearing bright blue tights. And I thought: That's the girl I'm going to marry." "Because of her tights?" "Yes. The light was shining on her in a very nice way. And she was completely transfixed by this one chimp. But if it hadn't been for the tights, I don't think I would have ever gone up to her." "Do you ever think about what would have happened if she'd decided not to wear those tights that day?" "All the time," said Uncle Julian. "I might have been a much happier man." I pushed the tikka masala around on my plate. "But probably not," he said. "What if you would have been?" I asked. Julian sighed. "Once I start to think about it, it's hard to imagine any kind of anything—happiness or otherwise—without her. I've lived with Frances for so long that I can't imagine what life would look or feel like with another person." "Like Flo?" I said. Uncle Julian choked on his food. "How do you know about Flo?" "I found the letter you started in the trash bin." His face turned red. I looked up at the map of India on the wall. Every fourteen-year-old should know the exact location of Calcutta. It wouldn't do to go around without the faintest clue of where Calcutta was. "I see," said Uncle Julian. "Well, Flo is a colleague of mine at the Courtauld. And she's a good friend, and Frances has always been a little jealous of that. There are certain things— How to say this, Al? OK. Let me give you an example. Can I give you an example?" "OK." "There's a self-portrait by Rembrandt. It's at Kenwood House, very close to where we live. We took you there when you were little. Do you remember?" "No." "Doesn't matter. The point is, it's one of my favorite paintings. I go to see it quite a lot. I start off on a walk on the Heath, and then I find myself there. It's one

of the last self-portraits he did. He painted it
sometime between 1665 and when he died four
years later, bankrupt and alone. Whole stretches
of the canvas are bare. There's a hurried intensity
in the strokes—you can see where he scratched
into the wet paint with the end of the brush. It's
as if he knew there wasn't much time left. And
yet, there's a serenity in his face, a sense of something that's survived its own ruin." I slid down in
the booth and swung my foot, accidentally kicking Uncle Julian's leg. "What does it have to do
with Aunt Frances and Flo?" I asked. For a
moment Uncle Julian looked lost. "I really don't
know," he said. He mopped his forehead again,
and called for the check. We sat in silence. Uncle
Julian's mouth twitched. He took a twenty out of
his wallet and folded it into a tiny square, then
folded that into an even smaller square. Then very
quickly he said, "Fran couldn't give two shits about
that painting," and put his empty beer glass to his
lips.

"If you want to know, I don't think you're a
dog," I said. Uncle Julian smiled. "Can I ask you
a question?" I said, while the waiter went back for
his change. "Of course." "Did Mom and Dad ever
fight?" "I suppose they did. Certainly, sometimes.
No more than anyone else." "Do you think Dad
would have wanted Mom to fall in love again?"

Uncle Julian gave me one of his lopsided smiles. "I do," he said. "I think he would have wanted that very much."

9. MERDE

When we got home, my mother was out in the backyard. Through the window I saw her kneeling in a pair of muddy overalls, planting flowers in what little light was left. I pushed open the screen door. The dead leaves and the weeds that had been growing for years had been torn out and cleared away, and four black trash bags stood by the iron garden bench that no one ever sat on. "What are you doing?" I called. "Planting mums and asters," she said. "Why?" "I was in the mood." "Why were you in the mood?" "I sent off some more chapters this afternoon, so I thought I'd do something relaxing." "*What?*" "I said, I sent off some more chapters to Jacob Marcus, so I thought I'd relax a bit," she repeated. I couldn't believe it. "You sent the chapters yourself? But you always give me everything to take to the post office!" "Sorry. I didn't know it meant so much to you. Anyway, you were gone all day. And I wanted to get it off. So I just did it myself." DID IT YOUR-SELF? I wanted to shout. My mother, her own species, dropped a flower into a hole and started to fill it with dirt. She turned and looked at me over her shoulder. "Dad used to love to garden," she said, as if I'd never known him at all.

10. MEMORIES PASSED DOWN TO ME FROM MY MOTHER

i   Getting up for school in the pitch-dark

ii   Playing in the rubble of bombed-out buildings near her house in Stamford Hill

iii   The smell of old books her father brought from Poland

iv   The feel of her father's large hand on her head when he blessed her on Friday nights

v   The Turkish boat she took from Marseilles to Haifa; her seasickness

vi   The great silence and the empty fields of Israel, and also the sound of the insects her first night at Kibbutz Yavne, which gave depth and dimension to the silence and emptiness

vii   The time my father took her to the Dead Sea

viii   Finding sand in the pockets of her clothes

ix   The blind photographer

x   My father steering his car with one hand

11. HOW TO RESTORE A HEARTBEAT

Chapters 1 through 28 of *The History of Love* ⸺
in a pile by my mother's computer. I searched t⸺
garbage bin, but there were no drafts of the lette⸺
she'd sent to Marcus. All I found was a crumple⸺
paper that said: *Back in Paris, Alberto began to ha⸺
second thoughts.*

12. I GAVE UP

That was the end of my search to find someo⸺
that would make my mother happy again. I fina⸺
understood that no matter what I did, or who⸺
found, I—he—none of us—would ever be able⸺
win over the memories she had of Dad, memor⸺
that soothed her even while they made her sa⸺
because she'd built a world out of them she kn⸺
how to survive in, even if no one else could.

   I couldn't sleep that night. I knew Bird w⸺
awake, too, by the sound of his breathing. I want⸺
to ask him about the thing he was building in t⸺

vacant lot, and how he knew he was a *lamed vovnik*, and to tell him I was sorry about shouting at him the time he wrote on my notebook. I wanted to say that I was scared, for him and for me, and I wanted to tell him the truth about all the lies I'd been telling him all these years. I whispered his name. "Yeah?" he whispered back. I lay in the dark and the silence, which was nothing like the dark and the silence my father lay in as a boy in a house on a dirt street in Tel Aviv, or the dark and the silence my mother lay in on her first night at Kibbutz Yavne, but which held those darknesses and those silences, too. I tried to think of what it was I wanted to say. "I'm not awake," I finally said. "Me either," said Bird.

Later, after Bird finally fell asleep, I turned on my flashlight and read some more of *The History of Love*. I thought about how, if I read it closely enough, I might find out something true about my father, and the things he would have wanted to tell me if he hadn't died.

The next morning I woke up early. I heard Bird moving around above me. When I opened my eyes he was pushing the sheets into a ball, and the seat of his pajamas was wet.

13. THEN IT WAS SEPTEMBER

And summer was over, and Misha and I were
officially not speaking, and no more letters
arrived from Jacob Marcus, and Uncle Julian
announced that he was going back to London
to try to work things out with Aunt Frances. The
night before he left for the airport and I started
tenth grade, he knocked on my door. "That thing
I said about Frances and the Rembrandt," he
said when I let him in. "Can we pretend I never
said it?" "Said what?" I said. He smiled, showing the gap between his front teeth that we both
inherited from my grandmother. "Thanks," he
said. "Hey, I got you something." He handed
me a large envelope. "What is it?" "Open it."
Inside was a catalogue for an art school in the
city. I looked up at him. "Go on, read it." I
opened the cover, and a piece of paper fluttered
to the floor. Uncle Julian stooped and picked it
up. "Here," he said, mopping his forehead. It
was a registration form. On it was my name, and
the name of a class called "Drawing from Life."
"There's a card, too," he said. I reached inside
the envelope. It was a postcard of a Rembrandt
self-portrait. On the back it said: *Dear Al,*

Wittgenstein once wrote that when the eye sees something beautiful, the hand wants to draw it. I wish I could draw you. Happy early birthday. Love, your Uncle Julian.

THE LAST PAGE

In the beginning it was easy. Litvinoff pretended to be just passing time, doodling in an absentminded way while he listened to the radio, just as his students did while he lectured in class. One thing he did not do was sit down at the drafting table onto which the most important of all Jewish prayers had been carved by his landlady's son, and think to himself: I am going to plagiarize my friend who was murdered by the Nazis. Nor did he think: If she thinks I wrote this, she will love me. He simply copied the first page, which, naturally, led to copying the second.

It wasn't until he got to the third page that Alma's name appeared. He paused. He had already changed a Feingold from Vilna to a De Biedma from Buenos Aires. Would it be so terrible if he switched Alma to Rosa? Three simple letters—the final "A" could remain. He'd already gone so far. He brought the pen to the page. Anyway, he told himself, Rosa was the only one who'd read it.

But if, when he went to write a capital R where there had been a capital A, Litvinoff's hand stalled, perhaps it was because he was the only person, aside from its true author, to have read *The History of Love* and known the real Alma. In fact, he'd known her since they were both children, having gone up through the grades with her before he'd left to study at yeshiva. She was one of a group of girls he'd observed bloom from scraggly weeds into tropical beauties who churned the air around them into a dense humidity. Alma left an indelible impression on his mind, as had the six or seven other girls whose transformations he'd witnessed, and, in the throes of his own puberty, had all taken turns as the object of his desire. Even all those years later, sitting at his desk in Valparaíso, Litvinoff could still remember the original catalogue of bared thighs, inner elbows, and backs of necks that had been the inspiration for countless frenetic variations. That Alma had been taken by someone else in an on-and-off-and-on-again sort of way didn't distract from her participation in Litvinoff's reveries (which relied heavily on the technique of montage). If he ever envied her being taken, it wasn't out of any special feeling for Alma, but out of a wish to be likewise singled out and loved alone.

And if, when he tried a second time to replace her name with another, for the second time his hand froze, perhaps it was because he knew that to remove her name would be like erasing all the punctuation, and the vowels, and every adjective and noun. Because without Alma, there would have been no book.

With his pen stalled above the page, Litvinoff remembered the day, early in the summer of 1936, when he'd returned to Slonim after two years away at yeshiva. Everything looked smaller than he remembered. He walked down the street with his hands in his pockets, wearing the new hat he'd bought with money he'd saved, and which he thought lent him an air of worldly experience. Turning onto a street that led away from the square, he felt that much more time had passed than two years. The same chickens were laying eggs in their coops, the same toothless men were arguing over nothing, but somehow everything seemed smaller and shabbier. Litvinoff knew that inside him something had changed. He had become something else. He passed a tree with a hole in the trunk in which he'd once hidden a dirty picture he'd stolen from the desk of his father's friend. He'd shown it to five or six boys before word got back to his brother, who'd confiscated it for his own purposes. Litvinoff walked toward the tree. And that's when he saw them. They were standing about ten yards away. Gursky was leaning against a fence, and Alma was leaning against him. Litvinoff watched as Gursky took her face in his hands. She paused, and then lifted her face to meet his. And as Litvinoff watched them kiss, he felt that everything that belonged to him was worthless.

Sixteen years later, he watched as each night another chapter of the book written by Gursky reappeared in his own longhand. For the record, he copied it word for word, except for the names, all but one of which he changed.

CHAPTER 18, he wrote on the eighteenth night. *LOVE AMONG THE ANGELS.*

HOW ANGELS SLEEP. Unsoundly. They toss and turn, trying to understand the mystery of the Living. They know so little about what it's like to fill a new prescription for glasses and suddenly see the world again, with a mixture of disappointment and gratitude. The first time a girl named—here Litvinoff paused to crack his knuckles—*Alma puts her hand just below your bottom rib: about this feeling, they have only theories, but no solid ideas. If you gave them a snow globe, they might not even know enough to shake it.*

Also, they don't dream. For this reason, they have one less thing to talk about. In a backward way, when they wake up they feel as if there is something they are forgetting to tell each other. There is disagreement among the angels as to whether this is a result of something vestigial, or whether it is the result of the empathy they feel for the

Living, so powerful it sometimes makes them weep. In general, they fall into these two camps on the subject of dreams. Even among the angels, there is the sadness of division.

At this point, Litvinoff got up to piss, flushing before he was finished in order to see if he could empty his bladder before the bowl refilled with fresh water. Afterwards, he glanced at himself in the mirror, took a pair of tweezers out of the medicine chest, and plucked a stray nose hair. He crossed the hall to the kitchen and rooted around in the cabinet for something to eat. Finding nothing, he put the kettle on to boil, sat down at his desk, and continued copying.

PRIVATE MATTERS. It's true that they don't have a sense of smell, but angels, in their infinite love for the Living, go around smelling everything in emulation. Like dogs, they don't feel bashful about going up and sniffing each other. Sometimes, when they are unable to sleep, they lie in bed with a nose in their armpits, wondering what they smell like.

Litvinoff blew his nose, crumpled the tissue, and dropped it at his feet.

*THE ARGUMENTS BETWEEN ANGELS. Are eternal and lack hope of solution. This is because they argue about what it means to be among the Living, and because they don't know they can only speculate, much the way the Living speculate about the nature (or lack thereof)—*here the kettle began to scream—*of God.*

Litvinoff got up to make a cup of tea. He opened the window and threw away a bruised apple.

BEING ALONE. Like the Living, angels sometimes get tired of each other and want to be alone. Because the houses they live in are crowded, and there's nowhere to go, the only thing an angel can do at such moments is shut his eyes and put his head down on his arms. When an angel does this, the others understand that he is trying to fool himself into feeling alone, and they tiptoe around him. To help things along, they might talk about him as if he weren't there. If they happen to bump into him by accident, they whisper: "It wasn't me."

Litvinoff shook his hand, which had begun to cramp. Then he continued writing:

FOR BETTER OR WORSE. Angels don't get married. To begin with they are too busy, and secondly they don't fall in love with each other. (If you don't know what it feels like to have someone you love put a hand below your bottom rib for the first time, what chance is there for love?)

Litvinoff paused to imagine Rosa's smooth hand on his ribs, and was pleased to find that it gave him goose bumps.

The way they live together is not unlike a fresh litter of pups: blind and grateful and denuded. This is not to say that they don't feel love, because they do; sometimes they feel it so strongly that they think they're having a panic attack. In these moments, their hearts race uncontrollably and they worry that they are going to throw up. But the love they feel is not for their own kind, but for the Living, who they can neither understand, nor smell, nor touch. It is a general love for the Living (though being general doesn't make it any less potent). Only from time to time does an angel find in herself a defect that causes her to fall in love, not in general, but in the specific.

On the day Litvinoff reached the last page, he gathered up his friend Gursky's manuscript, shuffled the pages around, and threw them in the trash bin under the kitchen sink. But Rosa often came over, and it occurred to him that she might find them there. So he took them out again and disposed of them in the metal trash cans behind the house, hidden under a few garbage bags. Then he got ready for bed. But half an hour later, plagued by the fear that someone might find them, he was up again, digging through the bins to retrieve the pages. He stuffed them under his bed and tried to sleep, only the stench of garbage was too bad, so he got up, found a flashlight, took a gardening trowel out of his landlady's shed, dug a hole next to her white hydrangea, dropped the pages in, and buried them. By the time he got into bed again in his muddy pajamas, the sky was already getting light.

That might have been the last of it, if it weren't for the fact that every time he saw his landlady's hydrangea from his window, Litvinoff was reminded of what he wished to forget. When spring arrived, he began to watch the bush obsessively, half expecting it to bloom with the news of his secret. One afternoon he watched in aggravated suspense as his landlady planted some tulips around the base of it. Whenever he would close his eyes to sleep, the huge white flowers would appear in his mind to taunt him. Things only got worse, his conscience tormented him more and more, until the night before he and Rosa were to get married and move to the bungalow on the cliff, Litvinoff got up in a cold sweat, snuck out in the middle of the night, and dug up his burden once and for all. From then on he kept it in a drawer of his desk in the study of the new house, locked with a key he thought he'd hidden.

We always woke at five or six in the morning, Rosa wrote in the final paragraph of her introduction to the second and last printing of *The History of Love. It was a blazing hot January when he died. I wheeled his bed to the open window upstairs. The sun streamed in on us, and he threw back the covers and stripped off everything and got brown in the sun, as we always did every morning, because the nurse came in at eight o'clock, and then the day would become rather hideous. Medical questions, which were not interesting to either of us. Zvi was not in pain. I asked him, "Are you in pain?" And he said, "I've never been so comfortable in my life." And on that morning, we looked out at the sky, which was cloudless and brilliant. Zvi had opened the book of Chinese poems he was reading to a poem he said was for me. It was called "Don't Set Sail." It's very short. It begins,* Don't set sail! / Tomorrow the wind will have dropped; / And then you can go, / And I won't trouble about you. *On the morning he died there'd been a tremendous gale, a storm in the garden all night, but when I opened the window there was the clear sky. Not a drop of wind. I turned and called to him. "Darling, the wind has dropped!" And he said, "Then I can go, and you won't trouble about me?" I thought my heart would stop. But it was true. It was just like that.*

But it wasn't just like that. Not really. The night before Litvinoff died, as the rain pounded on the roof and coursed through the gutters, he'd called out to Rosa. She'd been washing the dishes, and hurried to him. "What is it, darling?" she asked, putting her hand on his forehead. He coughed so hard she thought he was going to spit up blood. When it passed, he said, "There's something I want to tell you." She waited, listening. "I—" he began, but the cough returned, sending him into convulsions. "Shh," Rosa said, covering his lips with her fingers. "Don't speak." Litvinoff took her hand and squeezed it. "I need to," he said, and for once his body complied and was quiet. "Don't you see?" he said. "See what?" she asked. He squeezed his eyes shut and opened them again. She was still there, looking at him with tenderness and care. She patted his hand. "I'm going to go make you some tea," she said, getting up to go. "Rosa!" he called after her. She turned. "I wanted you to love me," he whispered. Rosa looked at him. He seemed to her, just then, like the child they never had. "And I did love you," she said, straightening a lampshade. Then she went out the door, closing it softly behind her. And that was the end of the conversation.

It would be convenient to imagine that those were Litvinoff's last words. But they weren't. Later that night he and Rosa talked about the rain, and Rosa's nephew, and whether or not she should buy a new toaster, since the old one had already caught fire twice. But there was no more mention of *The History of Love*, or its author.

Years before, when *The History of Love* had been accepted by a small publishing house in Santiago, the editor had made a few suggestions, and, wanting to be agreeable, Litvinoff tried to make the requested changes. Sometimes he could even almost convince himself that what he was doing wasn't terrible: Gursky was dead, at least the book would finally be published and read, wasn't that something? To this rhetorical question, his conscience answered with a cold shoulder. Desperate, not knowing what else to do, that night he also made one change the editor hadn't asked for. Locking the door to his study, he reached into his breast pocket and unfolded the piece of paper he had been carrying around with him for years. He took a fresh sheet of paper out of his desk drawer. At the top he wrote, *CHAPTER 39: THE DEATH OF LEOPOLD GURSKY.* Then he copied the page word for word, and, to the best of his ability, translated it into Spanish.

When his editor received the manuscript he wrote back to Litvinoff. *What were you thinking when you added the new last chapter? I'm going to strike it—it has nothing to do with anything.* It was low tide, and Litvinoff looked up from the letter and watched the seagulls fight for something they'd found on the rocks. *If you do,* he wrote back, *I'll pull the book.* A day of silence. *For God's sake!* came the editor's reply. *Don't be so sensitive.* Litvinoff took his pen out of his pocket. *It's not up for discussion,* he wrote back.

Which is why, when the rain at last ceased the next morning, and Litvinoff died quietly in his bed bathed in sunlight, he didn't take his secret with him. Or not entirely. All anyone had to do was turn to the last page, and there they would find, spelled out in black and white, the name of the true author of *The History of Love.*

Among the two, it was Rosa who was better at keeping secrets. For example, she never told anyone about the time she had seen her mother kissing the Portuguese ambassador at a garden party thrown by her uncle. Or the time she had seen the maid drop a gold chain belonging to her sister into the pocket of her apron. Or that her cousin Alfonso, who was extremely popular among the girls because of his green eyes and full lips, preferred boys, or that her father suffered from headaches that made him cry. So it may not be surprising that she also never told anyone about the letter addressed to Litvinoff that had arrived a few months after the publication of *The History of Love*. It was postmarked from America, and Rosa had figured it was a belated rejection letter from one of the publishers in New York. Wishing to shield Litvinoff from any hurt, she slipped it into a drawer and forgot about it. Some months later, looking for an address, she found it again and opened it. To her surprise, it was in Yiddish. *Dear Zvi,* it began. *So you don't get a heart attack, I'll start by saying it's your old friend Leo Gursky. You're probably surprised that I'm alive, and sometimes I am, too. I'm writing from New York, which is where I live now. I don't know if this letter will reach you. A few years ago I sent a letter to the only address I had for you, and it got sent back. It's a long story how I finally tracked down this one. Anyway, there is a lot to say, but it's too hard in a letter. I hope you are well and happy, and have a good life. Of course I have always wondered whether you kept the package I gave you the last time we saw each other. Inside was the book I was writing when you knew me in Minsk. If you do have it, could you please send it back to me? It is not worth anything to anyone but me now. Sending a warm embrace, L.G.*

Slowly, the truth dawned on Rosa: something

terrible had happened. It was grotesque, really; it made her sick to her stomach just to think of it. And she was partly guilty. She remembered now the day she'd discovered the key to his desk drawer, opened it, found the pile of dirty pages in a handwriting she didn't recognize, and chose not to ask. Litvinoff had lied to her, yes. But, with a dreadful feeling, she remembered how it had been her who'd insisted that he publish the book. He'd argued with her, saying it was too personal, a private matter, but she'd pushed and pushed, softening his resistance until he finally broke down and agreed. Because wasn't that what wives of artists were meant to do? Husband their husbands' work into the world, which, without them, would be lost to obscurity?

When the shock wore off, Rosa tore the letter to pieces and flushed them down the toilet. Quickly, she thought of what to do. She sat down at the little desk in the kitchen, took out a piece of blank stationery, and wrote: *Dear Mr. Gursky, I am very sorry to say that my husband, Zvi, is too ill to reply himself. He was overjoyed to receive your letter, however, and to hear that you are alive. Sadly, your manuscript was destroyed when our house was flooded. I hope you can find a way to forgive us.*

The next day she packed a picnic and told Litvinoff they were taking a trip to the mountains. After the excitement surrounding his recent publication, she told him, he needed a rest. She supervised the loading of the provisions into the car. When Litvinoff started the motor, Rosa slapped her forehead. "I almost forgot the strawberries," she said, and ran back into the house.

Inside, she went directly to Litvinoff's study, removed the little key taped to the underside of his desk, slipped it into the drawer, and took out a sheaf of warped, dirty pages that smelled of mold. She placed them on the floor. Then, for extra measure, she took the Yiddish manuscript written in Litvinoff's longhand off a high shelf, and moved it to one closer to the bottom. On her way out, she turned on the tap of the sink and plugged the drain. She paused to watch the water fill the basin until it began to overflow. Then she closed the door to her husband's study behind her, grabbed the basket of strawberries from the hall table, and hurried out to the car.

MY LIFE UNDERWATER

1. THE LONGING THAT EXISTS BETWEEN SPECIES

After Uncle Julian left, my mother became more withdrawn, or maybe a better word would be *obscure*, as in faint, unclear, distant. Empty teacups gathered around her, and dictionary pages fell at her feet. She abandoned the garden, and the mums and asters that had trusted her to see them through to the first frost hung their waterlogged heads. Letters came from her publishers asking if she'd be interested in translating this or that book. These went unanswered. The only phone calls she accepted were from Uncle Julian, and whenever she spoke to him, she closed the door.

Every year, the memories I have of my father become more faint, unclear, and distant. Once they were vivid and true, then they became like photographs, and now they are more like photo-graphs of photographs. But sometimes, at rare moments, a memory of him will return to me with such suddenness and clarity that all the feeling I've pushed down for years springs out like a jack-in-the-box. At these moments, I wonder if this is the way it feels to be my mother.

2. SELF-PORTRAIT WITH BREASTS

Every Tuesday evening I took the subway into the city and attended "Drawing from Life." During the first class I found out what this meant. It meant sketching the hundred percent naked people who were hired to stand still in the center of the circle we made with our chairs. I was the youngest person in the class by far. I tried to be casual, as if I'd been drawing naked people for years. The first model was a woman with sagging breasts, frizzy hair, and red knees. I didn't know where to look. Around me, the class bent over their sketch pads, drawing furiously. I made a few hesitant lines on the paper. "Let's remember nipples, folks," the teacher called out, making her way around the circle. I added nipples. When she got to me, she said, "May I?", and held my drawing up for the rest of the class. Even the model turned to look.

"Do you know what this is?" she said, pointing to my drawing. A few people shook their heads. "A Frisbee with a nipple," she said. "Sorry," I muttered. "Don't be sorry," the teacher said, laying her hand on my shoulder: "*Shade*." Then she demonstrated to the class how to turn my Frisbee into a huge breast.

The model for the second class looked a lot like the model from the first class. Whenever the teacher came by, I hunched over my work and shaded vigorously.

3. HOW TO WATERPROOF YOUR BROTHER

The rain started near the end of September, a few days before my birthday. It rained for a week straight, and just when it seemed like the sun was going to come out it was forced back in, and the rain began again. Some days it came down so hard that Bird had to abandon work on the tower of junk, even though he'd hung a tarp over the cabin starting to take shape at the top. Maybe he was building a meeting house for *lamed vovniks*. Some old boards formed two walls, and he'd stacked cardboard boxes to make the other two. Aside from the sagging tarp, there was no roof yet. One

afternoon I stopped to watch him scramble down
the ladder that leaned against one side of the heap.
He was carrying a large piece of scrap metal. I
wanted to help him, but I didn't know how.

4. THE MORE I THOUGHT ABOUT IT,
THE MORE MY STOMACH HURT

The morning of my fifteenth birthday I woke up
to Bird shouting, "UP AND AT 'EM!" followed by
"For She's a Jolly Good Fellow," a song our
mother used to sing to us on our birthdays when
we were little, and which Bird has taken upon
himself to carry on singing. She came in a little
while later and laid her presents next to Bird's on
my bed. The mood was light and happy until I
opened Bird's gift and it turned out to be an orange
life jacket. There was a moment of silence while
I stared at it, nestled in the wrapping.

"A life jacket!" my mother exclaimed. "What
a great idea. Where did you ever find it, Bird?"
she asked, fingering the straps with genuine
admiration. "So handy," she said.

Handy? I wanted to shout. HANDY?

I was beginning to seriously worry. What if
Bird's religiousness wasn't just a passing phase but
a permanent state of fanaticism? My mother

thought it was his way of dealing with losing Dad,
and that one day he would grow out of it. But
what if age only strengthened his beliefs, despite
the proof against them? What if he never made
any friends? What if he became someone who
wandered around the city in a dirty coat handing
out life jackets, forced to deny the world because
it was inconsistent with his dream?

I tried to find his diary but he'd moved it from
behind the bed, and it wasn't in any of the places
I looked. Instead, mixed in with dirty clothes
under my bed and two weeks overdue, I found
The Street of Crocodiles, by Bruno Schulz.

5. ONCE

I'd casually asked my mother if she'd heard of
Isaac Moritz, the writer the doorman at 450 East
52nd Street had said was Alma's son. She'd been
sitting on the bench in the garden staring at a
huge quince bush like it was about to say something. At first she didn't hear me. "Mom?" I
repeated. She turned, looking surprised. "I said,
have you ever heard of a writer named Isaac
Moritz?" She said Yes. "Have you ever read any
of his books?" I asked. "No." "Well do you think
there's a chance he deserves the Nobel?" "No."

"How do you know if you haven't read any of his books?" "I'm speculating," she said, because she would never admit that she only awards Nobels to dead people. Then she went back to staring at the quince bush.

At the library, I typed "Isaac Moritz" into the computer. It came up with six books. The one they had the most copies of was *The Remedy*. I wrote down the call numbers and when I found his books, I took *The Remedy* off the shelf. On the back cover was a photograph of the author. It felt strange to look at his face, knowing that the person I was named after must have looked a lot like him. He had curly hair, was balding, and had brown eyes that looked small and weak behind his metal glasses. I flipped to the front and opened to the first page. *CHAPTER ONE*, it said. *Jacob Marcus stood waiting for his mother at the corner of Broadway and Graham.*

6.   I READ IT AGAIN

Jacob Marcus stood waiting for his mother at the corner of Broadway and Graham.

7. AND AGAIN

Jacob Marcus stood waiting for his mother

8. AND AGAIN

Jacob Marcus

9. HOLY COW

I flipped back to the photograph. Then I read the whole first page. Then I flipped back to the photograph, read another page, then flipped back and stared at the photograph. Jacob Marcus was just a character in a book! The man who'd been sending letters to my mother the whole time was the writer Isaac Moritz. Alma's *son*. He'd been signing his letters with the character of his most famous book! A line from his letter came back to me: *Sometimes I even pretend to write, but I'm not fooling anyone.*

I got to page fifty-eight before the library closed. It was already dark when I got outside. I stood in front of the entrance with the book under my arm, watching the rain and trying to grasp the situation.

· 10. THE SITUATION

That night while my mother was upstairs translating *The History of Love* for the man whose name
she thought was Jacob Marcus, I finished *The
Remedy*, about a character named Jacob Marcus,
by a writer named Isaac Moritz, who was the son
of the character Alma Mereminski, who also
happened to have been real.

11. WAITING

When I'd finished the last page, I called Misha
and let it ring twice before hanging up. This was
a code we'd used when we wanted to speak to each
other late at night. It had been more than a month
since we'd last talked. I'd made a list in my notebook of all the things I missed about him. The
way he wrinkles his nose when he's thinking was
one. How he holds things was another. But now
I needed to talk to him for real and no list would
substitute. I stood by the phone while my stomach turned itself inside out. During the time I
waited, a whole species of butterfly may have
become extinct, or a large, complex mammal with
feelings like mine.

But he never called back. This probably meant he didn't want to talk to me.

12. ALL THE FRIENDS I EVER HAD

Down the hall in his room my brother was asleep, his *kippah* dropped to the floor. Printed on the lining in gold letters was *Marsha and Joe's Wedding, June 13, 1987,* and though Bird claimed to have found it in the dining room cabinet and was convinced it had belonged to Dad, none of us had ever heard of Marsha or Joe. I sat down next to him. His body was warm, almost hot. I thought about how, if I hadn't made up so many things about Dad, maybe Bird wouldn't have worshipped him so much and believed he himself needed to be something extraordinary.

Rain splashed against windows. "Wake up," I whispered. He opened his eyes and groaned. Light shone in from the hallway. "Bird," I said, touching his arm. He squinted up at me and rubbed his eye. "You have to stop talking about God, OK?" He didn't say anything, but I was pretty sure he was awake now. "You're going to be twelve soon. You have to stop making weird noises, and jumping off things and hurting yourself." I knew I was pleading with him, but I didn't care. "You have to stop wetting your bed," I whispered, and now in the dim light I saw the hurt on his face. "You have to just push your feelings down and try to be normal. If you don't . . ." His mouth tightened, but he didn't speak. "You have to make some friends," I said. "I have a friend," he whispered. "Who?" "Mr. Goldstein." "You have to make more than one." "You don't have more than one," he said. "The only person who ever calls you is Misha." "Yes, I do. I have plenty of friends," I said, and only as the words came out did I realize they weren't true.

13. IN ANOTHER ROOM, MY MOTHER SLEPT CURLED NEXT TO THE WARMTH OF A PILE OF BOOKS

14. I TRIED NOT TO THINK ABOUT

a) Misha Shklovsky
b) Luba the Great
c) Bird
d) My mother
e) Isaac Moritz

15. I SHOULD

Get out more, join some clubs. I should buy some new clothes, dye my hair blue, let Herman Cooper take me on a ride in his father's car, kiss me, and possibly even feel my nonexistent breasts. I should develop some useful skills like public speaking, electric cello, or welding, see a doctor about my stomachaches, find a hero that is not a man who wrote a children's book and crashed his plane, stop trying to set up my father's tent in record time, throw away my notebooks, stand up straight, and cut this habit of answering any question regarding my well-being with a reply fit for a prim English schoolgirl who believes life is nothing but a long preparation for a few finger sandwiches with the Queen.

16. A HUNDRED THINGS CAN CHANGE YOUR LIFE

I opened my desk drawer and turned it upside down in search of the piece of paper on which I'd copied the address for Jacob Marcus who was really Isaac Moritz. Under a report card, I found an old letter from Misha, one of his first. *Dear*

Alma, it said. *How are you knowing me so well? I think we are like two peas in a pod. It is true I like John more than Paul. But I have large respect for Ringo too.*

Saturday morning I printed a map and the directions off the internet, and told my mother I was going to Misha's house for the day. Then I walked up the street and knocked on the Coopers' door. Herman came out with his hair sticking up, wearing a Sex Pistols T-shirt. "Whoa," he said when he saw me. He stepped back from the door. "Do you want to go for a ride?" I asked. "Is this a joke?" "No." "Oookaay," said Herman. "Hold, please." He went upstairs to ask his father for the keys, and when he came down he'd wet his hair and changed into a fresh blue T-shirt.

17. LOOK AT ME

"Where are we going, Canada?" Herman asked when he saw the map. There was a pale band around his wrist where his watch had been all summer. "Connecticut," I said. "Only if you take off that hood," he said. "Why?" "I can't see your face." I pushed it off. He smiled at me. There was still sleep in the corner of his eye. A drop of rain rolled down his forehead. I read him the directions

and we talked about the colleges he was applying
to for next year. He told me he was considering a
major in marine biology because he wanted to live
a life like Jacques Cousteau. I thought maybe we
had more in common than I'd originally thought.
He asked me what I wanted to become and I said
I'd briefly considered paleontology, and then he
asked me what a paleontologist did, so I told him
if he took a complete, illustrated guide to the
Metropolitan Museum of Art, shredded it into a
hundred pieces, cast them into the wind from the
museum's steps, etc., and then he asked me why
I'd changed my mind, and I told him I thought I
wasn't cut out for it, so he asked me what I thought
I was cut out for, and I said, "It's a long story," so
he said, "I have time," so I said, "You really want
to know?" and he said Yes, so I told him the truth,
beginning with my father's Swiss Army knife and
the book of *Edible Plants and Flowers in North
America*, and ending with my plans to one day
explore the Arctic wilderness with nothing but
what I could carry on my back. "I wish you would-
n't," he said. Then we took a wrong exit and
stopped at a gas station to ask for directions and
buy some SweetTarts. "These are on me," Herman
said when I took out my wallet to pay. When he
handed a five-dollar bill across the counter, his
hands were shaking.

18. I TOLD HIM THE WHOLE STORY ABOUT *THE HISTORY OF LOVE*

It was raining so hard that we had to pull over to the side of the road. I took my sneakers off and put my feet up on the dashboard. Herman wrote my name in the fog on the windshield. Then we reminisced about a water fight we'd had a hundred years ago, and I felt a pang of sadness that next year Herman would be gone to start his life.

19. I JUST DO

After looking forever, we finally found the dirt road to Isaac Moritz's house. We must have driven past it two or three times without noticing it. I'd been ready to give up, but Herman wouldn't. My palms started to sweat as we drove up the muddy drive because I'd never met a famous writer before, and definitely not one I'd forged a letter to. The numbers of Isaac Moritz's address were nailed to a big maple tree. "How do you know it's a maple?" Herman asked. "I just do," I said, sparing him the details. Then I saw the lake. Herman pulled up to the house and turned off the car. Suddenly it was very quiet. I leaned down to tie my sneakers. When

I sat up he was looking at me. His face was hopeful and unbelieving and also a little sad, and I wondered if it was anything like my father's face when he looked at my mother all those years ago at the Dead Sea, setting in motion a train of events that had finally brought me here, to the middle of nowhere, with a boy I'd grown up with but hardly knew.

20. SHALLON, SHALOP, SHALLOT, SHALLOW

I got out of the car and took a deep breath.

I thought, My name is Alma Singer you don't know me but I was named after your mother.

21. SHALOM, SHAM, SHAMAN, SHAMBLE

I knocked on the door. There was no answer. I rang the bell, but there was still no answer, so I walked around the house and looked into the windows. It was dark inside. When I came back around to the front, Herman was leaning against the car with his arms crossed over his chest.

22. I DECIDED THERE WAS NOTHING LEFT TO LOSE

We sat together on the porch of Isaac Moritz's house, swinging on a bench and watching the rain. I asked Herman if he'd ever heard of Antoine de Saint-Exupéry and when he said no I asked him if he'd ever heard of *The Little Prince* and he said he thought he had. So I told him about the time Saint-Ex crashed in the Libyan desert, drank the dew off the airplane's wings which he'd gathered with an oil-stained rag, and walked hundreds of miles, dehydrated and delirious from the heat and cold. When I got to the part about how he was found by some Bedouins, Herman slipped his hand into mine, and I thought, An average of seventy-four species become extinct every day, which was one good reason but not the only one to hold someone's hand, and the next thing that happened was we kissed each other, and I found I knew how, and I felt happy and sad in equal parts, because I knew that I was falling in love, but it wasn't with him.

We waited a long time, but Isaac never came. I didn't know what else to do, so I left a note on the door with my telephone number.

A week and a half later—I remember the date,

October 5th—my mother was reading the newspaper and she said, "Remember that writer you
asked me about, Isaac Moritz?" and I said, "Yes,"
and she said, "There's an obituary for him in the
paper."

That evening I went up to her study. She had
five chapters left of *The History of Love*, and she
didn't know that now she wasn't translating them
for anyone but me.

"Mom?" I said. She turned. "Can I talk to you
about something?"

"Of course, darling. Come here."

I took a few steps into the room. There was
so much I wanted to say.

"I need you to be—" I said, and then I started
to cry.

"Be what?" she said, opening her arms.

"Not sad," I said.

ONE NICE THING

September 28

יהוה

Today is the 10th day in a row of rain. Dr. Vishnubakat
said one nice thing to write in my journal is my
thoughts and feelings. He said that if I wanted him to
know something about how I feel but don't want to
talk about it I could just give him my journal. I did
not say haven't you ever heard of the word PRIVATE?
One thought I have is it's very expensive to take a
plane to Israel. I know this because I tried to buy a
ticket at the airport and they said it was 1200 dollars.
When I told the woman that one time my mom bought
a ticket for 700 dollars, she said there were no tickets for 700 dollars anymore. I thought maybe she was
just saying that because she thought I didn't have the
money, so I took out the shoebox and showed her the
741 dollars and fifty cents. She asked me where I got
so much money, so I told her 1500 cups of lemon-aid,

even though it wasn't totally true. Then she asked me why I wanted to go to Israel so much and I asked her if she could keep a secret and she said yes so I told her I was a lamed vovnik and also maybe the Messiah. When she heard this she took me to a special room that is only for employees and gave me an El Al pin. Then the police came and took me home. The way I felt about this was angry.

September 29

יהוה

It's been raining for 11 days. How is anyone supposed to be a lamed vovnik if first it costs 700 dollars to get to Israel and then they change it to 1200 dollars? They should keep the price the same so that people will know how much lemon-aid they have to sell if they want to get to Jerusalem.

Today Dr. Vishnubakat asked me to explain the note I left for Mom and Alma when I thought I was going to Israel. He put it in front of me to refresh my memory. But I did not need my memory freshened because I already knew what it said because I'd done 9 drafts since I wanted to type it for officialness and I kept making mistakes. What it said was "Dear Mom and Alma and Anyone Else, I have to go away and I might be gone for a long time. Please don't try to find me. The reason why is I'm a lamed vovnik and I have to take care of a lot of things. There is going to be a flood but you don't have to worry because I built you an ark. Alma you know where it is. Love, Bird."

Dr. Vishnubakat asked me how I got the name Bird. I told him I just did. If you want to know why Dr. Vishnubakat is called Dr. Vishnubakat it's because he's from India. If you want to remember how to say it just think of Dr. Fishinabucket.

September 30

יהוה

Today the rain stopped and the firemen took down my ark because they said it was a fire hazard. The way this made me feel was sad. I tried not to cry because Mr. Goldstein says that what G-d does is for the best, and also because Alma said I should try to push down my feelings so that I can have friends. Something else Mr. Goldstein says is What the eyes don't see the heart doesn't feel, but I had to see what happened to the ark because all of a sudden I remembered that I had painted יהוה on the back, which no one is allowed to throw away. I made Mom call the firemen to ask where they'd put all the pieces. She told me they'd piled them on the sidewalk for the garbage man, so I made her take me there, but the garbage man had already come and everything was gone. Then I cried and kicked a stone and Mom tried to hug me but I wouldn't let her because she shouldn't have let the firemen take down the ark, and also she should have asked me before she threw away everything that belonged to Dad.

October 1

יהוה

Today I went to see Mr. Goldstein for the first time since I tried to go to Israel. Mom brought me to Hebrew School and waited outside. He wasn't in his office in the basement, or in the sanctuary, but I finally found him outside in the back digging a hole for some siddurs with broken spines. I said Hello Mr. Goldstein and for a long time he didn't say anything or even look at me, so I said Well it's probably going to start raining again tomorrow, and he said Fools and weeds grow without rain, and kept digging. His voice sounded sad and I tried to understand what he wanted to tell me. I stood next to him and watched the hole get deeper. There was dirt on his shoes and I remembered how once someone from the Daleds stuck a sign on his back that said KICK ME, and no one told him, not even me, because I didn't want him to ever know it was there. I watched him wrap three siddurs in an old cloth, and then he kissed them. The circles under his eyes were bluer than ever. I thought maybe Fools and weeds grow without rain meant he was disappointed so I tried to think of why, and when he lay the cloth with the broken siddurs in the hole I said Yisgadal veyisqadash shemei rabbah, Magnified and sanctified may His great name be in the world that He created, and may His kingdom come in your lives and your days, and then I saw that tears were coming out of Mr. Goldstein's eyes. He started to shovel dirt in the hole and I saw that his lips were moving but I couldn't hear what they were saying, so I listened harder, I put my ear right to his mouth, and he said, Chaim, which is the name he calls me, A lamed vovnik is humble and works in secret, and then he turned away, and I understood that the thing he was crying about was me.

October 2

יהוה

It started to rain again today, but I didn't even care because the ark is gone now, and because I disappointed Mr. Goldstein. To be a lamed vovnik means never to tell anyone you're one of the 36 people the world depends on, it means doing good things that help people without anyone ever noticing you. Instead I'd told Alma that I was a lamed vovnik, and Mom, and the woman at El Al, and Louis, and Mr. Hintz, my gym teacher, because he tried to make me take off my kippah and put on shorts, and also a few other people, and the police had to come and get me, and

the firemen came and took down the ark. The way
this makes me feel is like crying. I disappointed Mr.
Goldstein and also G-d. I don't know if this means I
am not a lamed vovnik anymore.

October 3

יהוה

Today Dr. Vishnubakat asked me if I was feeling
depressed so I said What do you mean by depressed
so he said For example do you feel sad and one thing
I did not say is Are you an ignoramus? because that is
not what a lamed vovnik would say. Instead I said If a
horse knew how small a man is compared to it, it would
trample him, which is something Mr. Goldstein sometimes says, and Dr. Vishnubakat said That's interesting, can you elaborate? and I said No. Then we sat in
silence for a few minutes which is something we do
sometimes, but I got bored so I said Corn can grow
on manure which is something else Mr. Goldstein says,
and this seemed to interest Dr. Vishnubakat a lot
because he wrote it down on his pad, so I said Pride
lies on the dung heap. Then Dr. Vishnubakat said Can
I ask you a question and I said Depends and he said
Do you miss your father and I said I don't really
remember him, and he said I think it would be very
hard to lose your father, and I didn't say anything. If
you want to know why I didn't say anything it's because

I don't like it when anyone talks about Dad unless they knew him.

One thing I decided is that from now on before I do anything I will always ask myself WOULD A LAMED VOVNIK DO THIS? For example today Misha called for Alma and I did not say Do you want to French kiss her? because when I asked myself the question WOULD A LAMED VOVNIK DO THIS? the answer was NO. Then Misha said How is she? and I said OK and he said Tell her I was calling to see if she ever found the person she was looking for, and I didn't know what he was talking about so I said Pardon me? and then he said Actually never mind don't tell her I called, and I said OK and didn't tell her because one thing a lamed vovnik is good at is keeping secrets. I did not know Alma was looking for someone and I tried to think of who but I couldn't.

October 4

יהוה

Today something terrible happened. Mr. Goldstein got very sick and fainted and nobody found him for three hours and now he's in the hospital. When Mom told me I went to the bathroom and locked the door and asked G-d to please make sure Mr. Goldstein was going to be OK. When I was almost 100 percent positive that I was a lamed vovnik I used to think G-d could hear me. But I'm not sure anymore. Then I had a very horrible thought which was that maybe Mr. Goldstein got sick because I'd disappointed him. Suddenly I felt very, very sad. I squeezed my eyes shut so that no tears could leak out, and I tried to think of what to do. Then I had an idea. If I could do one good thing to help someone and not tell anyone about it, maybe Mr. Goldstein would get better again, and I would be a real lamed vovnik!

Sometimes if I need to know something I ask G-d. For example I will say If you want me to steal 50 more dollars out of Mom's wallet so I can buy a ticket to Israel even though stealing is bad then let me find 3 blue punch-buggies in a row tomorrow, and if I find 3 blue punch-buggies in a row the answer is yes. But I knew this time I couldn't ask G-d for help because I had to figure it out by myself. So I tried to think of someone who needed help and all of a sudden I knew the answer.

THE LAST TIME I SAW YOU

I was in bed, dreaming a dream that took place in the former Yugoslavia, or maybe it was Bratislava, for all I know it could have been Belarus. The more I think about it, the harder it is to say. *Wake up!* Bruno shouted. Or so I have to assume he shouted, before he resorted to the mug of cold water he emptied onto my face. Perhaps he was getting me back for the time I saved his life. He stripped back the sheets. I regret whatever he may have found there. And yet. Talk about an argument. Every morning it stands at attention, like the lead counsel for the defense.

Look! shouted Bruno. *They wrote about you in a magazine.*

I was in no mood for his practical jokes. Left to my own devices, I'm content to wake myself with a fart. So I tossed my wet pillow on the floor and burrowed headfirst into the sheets. Bruno slapped me upside the head with the magazine. *Get up and look*, he said. I played the part of the deaf-mute, which I've perfected over the years. I heard Bruno's footsteps retreat. A crash from the direction of the hall closet. I braced myself. There was a loud noise, and the screech of feedback. *THEY WROTE ABOUT YOU IN A MAGAZINE*, Bruno said through the bullhorn he'd managed to dig out of my things. Despite my being under the sheets, he managed to locate the precise placement of my ear. *I REPEAT*, the bullhorn shrieked. *YOU: IN A MAGAZINE*. I threw off the sheets and ripped the bullhorn from his lips.

When did you become such a fool? I said.

When did you? said Bruno.

Listen, Gimpel, I said. *I'm going to close my eyes and count to ten. When I open them, I want you to be gone.*

Bruno looked hurt. *You don't mean that,* he said.

Yes, I do, I said, and closed my eyes. *One, two.*

Say you didn't mean it, he said.

With my eyes closed I remembered the first time I ever met Bruno. He was kicking a ball in the dust, a skinny, red-haired boy whose family had just moved to Slonim. I walked up to him. He lifted his eyes and took me in. Without a word, he kicked me the ball. I kicked it back.

Three, four, five, I said. I felt the magazine drop open in my lap and heard Bruno's footsteps moving away down the hall. For a moment they paused. I tried to imagine my life without him. It seemed impossible. And yet. *SEVEN!* I shouted. *EIGHT!!* On nine, I heard

the front door slam. *Ten*, I said, to no one in particular. I opened my eyes and looked down.

There, on the page of the only magazine I
subscribe to, was my name.

I thought: What a coincidence, another Leo
Gursky! Obviously it gave me a thrill, even though it
had to be someone else. It's not an unusual name. And
yet. It isn't common, either.

I read a sentence. And that was all I needed to
read to know it could be no one other than me. I knew
this because I was the one who'd written the sentence.
In my book, the novel of my life. The one I'd started
to write after my heart attack and sent, the morning
after the art class, to Isaac. Whose name, I saw now,
was printed in block letters across the top of the magazine's page. *WORDS FOR EVERYTHING*, it said, the title
I'd finally chosen, and underneath: *ISAAC MORITZ*.

I looked up at the ceiling.

I looked down. Like I said, there are parts I know
by heart. And the sentence I knew by heart was still
there. As were a hundred or so others I knew, also by
heart, only edited a little here and there, in a way that
felt ever-so-slightly sickening. When I turned to read
the contributors' notes, it said that Isaac had died that
month, and the piece they'd published was part of his
last manuscript.

I got out of bed and took the phone book out
from under *Famous Quotations* and *The History of*

Science, with which Bruno likes to boost himself when sitting at my kitchen table. I found the number for the magazine. *Hello*, I said, when the switchboard answered. *Fiction, please.*

It rang three times.

Fiction Department, said a man. He sounded young.

Where did you get this story? I asked.

Excuse me?

Where did you get this story?

Which story, sir?

Words for Everything.

It's from a novel by the late Isaac Moritz, he said.

Ha, ha, I said.

Pardon me?

No, it's not, I said.

Yes, it is, he said.

No, it's not.

I assure you it is.

I assure you it isn't.

Yes, sir. It is.

OK, I said. *It is.*

May I ask whom I'm speaking with? he said.

Leo Gursky, I said.

There was an awkward pause. When he spoke again his voice was less sure.

Is this some sort of joke?

Nope, I said.

But that's the name of the character in the story.

My point exactly, I said.

I'll have to check with the Fact-Checking Department, he said. *Normally they inform us if there's an existing person with the same name.*

Surprise! I shouted.

Please hold, he said.

I hung up the phone.

At most a person has two, three good ideas in a lifetime. And on those magazine pages was one of mine. I read it over again. Here and there, I chuckled aloud and marveled at my own brilliance. And yet. More often, I winced.

I dialed the magazine again and asked for the fiction department.

Guess who? I said.

Leo Gursky? said the man. I could hear the fear in his voice.

Bingo, I said, and then I said: *This so-called book.*

Yes?

When's it coming out?

Please hold, he said.

I held.

In January, he said when he returned.

January! I cried. *So soon!* The calendar on my wall said October 17th. I couldn't help myself, I asked, *Is it any good?*

Some people think it's one of his best.

One of his best! My voice rose an octave and cracked.

Yes, sir.

I'd like an early copy, I said. *I may not live until January to read about myself.*

There was silence on the other end.

Well, he finally said. *I'll see if I can dig one up. What's your address?*

Same as the address of the Leo Gursky in the story, I said, and hung up. Poor kid. He could spend years trying to unravel that mystery.

But I had my own to unravel. Namely, if my manuscript had been found at Isaac's house and mistaken for his, didn't that mean he had read it, or at the very least begun to read it before he died? Because if he had, that would change everything. It would mean—

And yet.

I paced the apartment, at least as much as it was possible to pace, what with a badminton racket here and a stack of *National Geographics* there, and a set of *boules,* a game about which I know nothing, at large on the living room floor.

It was simple: If he'd read my book, he knew the truth.

I was his father.

He was my son.

And now it dawned on me that it was possible there had been a brief window of time in which Isaac and I both lived, each aware of the other's existence.

I went to the bathroom, washed my face with cold water, and went downstairs to check the mail. I thought there was still a chance a letter might arrive from my son, posted before he died. I slipped the key in the box and turned.

And yet. A pile of junk, that was all. The *TV Guide*, a magazine from Bloomingdale's, a letter from the World Wildlife Federation who've remained my loyal companions since I sent them ten dollars in 1979. I took it upstairs to throw it all away. I had my foot on the pedal of the trash bin when I saw it, a little envelope with my name typed across the front. The seventy-five percent of my heart that was still alive started to thunder. I ripped it open.

Dear Leopold Gursky, it said. *Please meet me at 4:00 on Saturday on the benches in front of the entrance to the Central Park zoo. I think you know who I am.*

Overcome with feeling, I shouted out, *I do!*

Sincerely yours, it said.

Sincerely mine, I thought.

Alma.

And then and there I knew my time had come. My hands shook so hard that the paper rattled. I felt my legs giving way. My head got light. So this is how they send the angel. With the name of the girl you always loved.

I banged on the radiator for Bruno. There was no

reply, nor was there one a minute later, or a minute after that, though I banged and banged, three taps means ARE YOU ALIVE?, two means YES, one means NO. I listened for the answer, but there wasn't any. Perhaps I shouldn't have called him a fool, because now when I needed him most there was nothing at all.

WOULD A LAMED VOVNIK DO THIS?

October 5

יהוה

This morning I snuck into Alma's room while she was
in the shower and got How to Survive in the Wild
Volume 3 out of her backpack. Then I got back into
bed and hid it under the covers. When Mom came in
I pretended to be sick. She put her hand on my forehead and said What do you feel? so I said I think I
have swollen glands, so she said You must be coming
down with something, so I said But I have to go to
school, so she said Nothing will happen if you miss a
day, so I said OK. She brought me some chamomile
tea with honey and I drank it with my eyes closed to
show how sick I was. I heard Alma leave for school,
and Mom went upstairs to work. When I heard her
chair creak I took How to Survive in the Wild Volume
3 out and started to read it to see if there were any
clues about who Alma was searching for.

Most of the pages were filled with information like how to make a hot-rock bed, or a lean-to, or how to make water potable which I didn't really understand because I've never seen any water that can't be poured into a pot. (Except maybe ice.) I was starting to wonder if I would find anything about the mystery when I got to a page that said HOW TO SURVIVE IF YOUR PARA-CHUTE FAILS TO OPEN. There were 10 steps but none of them made sense. For example if you are falling through the air and your parachute fails to open I don't think it would help that much to have a gardener with a limp. Also it said search for a stone but why would there be stones unless someone was throwing them at you or you had one in your pocket which most normal people don't? The last step was just a name which was Alma Mereminski.

One thought I had was that Alma was in love with someone named Mr. Mereminski and wanted to marry him. But then I turned the page and it said ALMA MEREMINSKI = ALMA MORITZ. So I thought maybe Alma was in love with Mr. Mereminski AND Mr. Moritz. Then I turned the page and at the top it said THINGS I MISS ABOUT M and there was a list of 15 things, and the first was THE WAY HE HOLDS THINGS. I did not understand how you can miss the way somebody holds things.

I tried to think but it was hard. If Alma was in love with Mr. Mereminski or Mr. Moritz, how come

I'd never met either of them, and how come they never called her like Herman or Misha? And if she loved Mr. Mereminski or Mr. Moritz, why did she miss him?

The rest of the notebook was blank.

The only person I really miss is Dad. Sometimes I get jealous of Alma because she knew Dad more than I did and can remember so much about him. But the weird thing is that when I read Volume 2 of her notebook last year it said, I FEEL SAD BECAUSE I NEVER REALLY KNEW DAD.

I was thinking about why she wrote that when all of a sudden I had a very strange idea. What if Mom had been in love with someone else named Mr. Mereminski or Mr. Moritz, and HE was Alma's father? And what if he died, or went away, which is why Alma never knew him? And then after that Mom met David Singer and had me. And then HE died, which was why Mom was so sad. That would explain why she wrote ALMA MEREMINSKI and ALMA MORITZ but not ALMA SINGER. Maybe she was trying to find her real dad!

I heard Mom get up from her chair so I did my best impression of someone sleeping which I've practiced in front of the mirror 100 times. Mom came in and sat on the edge of my bed and didn't say anything for a long time. But all of a sudden I had to sneeze so I opened my eyes and sneezed and Mom said Poor thing. Then I did something extremely risky. Using my most sleepy voice I said Mom did you ever love someone else before Dad? I was almost 100 percent positive she was going to say no. But instead a funny look came over her face and she said I suppose so, yes! So I said Did he die? and she laughed and said No! Inside I was going crazy but I didn't want to make her too suspicious so I pretended to fall asleep again.

Now I think I know who Alma is looking for. I also know that if I am a real lamed vovnik I will be able to help her.

October 6

יהוה

I pretended to be sick for the second day in a row so I could stay home from school again and also so I don't have to see Dr. Vishnubakat. When Mom went back upstairs I set the alarm on my watch and every 10 minutes I coughed for 5 seconds straight. After half an hour I snuck out of bed so I could look in Alma's backpack for more clues. I didn't see anything besides the things that are always in it like a first aid kit and her Swiss Army knife, but then I took out her sweater and wrapped inside were some pages. I only had to look at them for one second to know that they were from the book Mom is translating called The History of Love, because she is always throwing drafts away in the garbage and I know what they look like. I also know that Alma only keeps very important things in the backpack that she might need in case of an emergency so I tried to figure out why The History of Love was so important to her.

Then I thought of something. Mom always says that Dad was the one who gave her The History of Love. But what if this whole time she meant Alma's dad and not mine? And what if the book held the secret of who he was?

Mom came downstairs and I had to run into the bathroom and pretend I was constipated for 18 minutes so she wouldn't get suspicious. When I came out she gave me the number for Mr. Goldstein at the hospital and said if I felt like calling him I could. His voice sounded very tired, and when I asked him how he felt he said At night all cows are black. I wanted to tell him about the good thing I was going to do, but I knew I couldn't tell anyone, not even him.

I got back into bed and talked to myself to figure out why the identity of Alma's real father had to be a secret. The only reason I could think of was that he was a spy like the blond lady in Alma's favorite movie, the one who was working for the F.B.I. and couldn't reveal her true identity to Roger Thornhill even though she was in love with him. Maybe Alma's real father couldn't reveal his true identity either, not even to Mom. Maybe that's why he had two names! Or even more than two! I felt jealous that my dad wasn't a spy too but then I didn't feel jealous anymore because I remembered that I might be a lamed vovnik which is even better than a spy.

Mom came downstairs to check on me. She said she was going out for an hour, and asked me if I would be OK by myself. After I heard the door close and the key turn in the lock I went to the bathroom to talk to G-d. Then I went to the kitchen to make a peanut butter and jelly sandwich. That's when the telephone rang. I didn't think it was anything special but when I answered it the person on the other end said Hello this is Bernard Moritz, may I please speak with Alma Singer?

That's how I found out G-d can hear me.

My heart was beating like crazy. I had to think very fast. I said She's not here right now but I can take a message. He said Well it's a long story. So I said I can give her a long message.

He said Well I found a note she left on my brother's door. It must have been at least a week ago, he was in the hospital. It said that she knew who he was and that she needed to talk to him about The History of Love. She left this number.

I did not say I knew it! or Did you know he was a spy? I just stayed silent so I wouldn't say the wrong thing.

But then the man said Anyway my brother passed away, he'd been ill for a long time and I wouldn't have called except that before he died he told me that he'd found some letters in our mother's drawer.

I didn't say anything, so the man kept talking.

He said He read the letters and got it into his head that the man who was his real father was the author of a book called The History of Love. I didn't really believe it until I saw Alma's note. She mentioned the book, and you see my mother's name was also Alma. I thought I should talk to her, or at least tell her that Isaac passed away so she wouldn't wonder.

Now I was confused all over again because I thought this Mr. Moritz was Alma's father. The only thing I could think of was that Alma's father had a lot of children who didn't know him. Maybe this man's brother was one and Alma was another, and they were both looking for their father at the same time.

I said Did you say he thought his real father was the author of The History of Love?

The man on the phone said Yes.

So I said Well did he think his father's name was Zvi Litvinoff?

Now the man on the phone sounded confused. He said No he thought it was Leopold Gursky.

I made my voice very calm and said Can you spell that? And he said G-U-R-S-K-Y. I said Why did he think his father's name was Leopold Gursky? And the man said Because that's who sent our mother the letters with parts from the book he was writing called The History of Love.

Inside I was going crazy because even though I didn't understand everything I was sure I was very close to solving the mystery about Alma's father, and that if I could solve it I would be doing something helpful, and if I did something helpful in a secret way I might still be a lamed vovnik, and everything would be OK.

Then the man said Look I think it would be better if I spoke to Ms. Singer myself. I didn't want to make him suspicious, so I said I'll give her the message and hung up the phone.

I sat at the kitchen table trying to think about everything. Now I knew that when Mom said Dad gave her The History of Love what she meant was that Alma's dad gave it to her because he was the one who wrote it.

I squeezed my eyes shut and said to myself If I am a lamed vovnik how do I find Alma's father whose name was Leopold Gursky and also Zvi Litvinoff and also Mr. Mereminski and also Mr. Moritz?

I opened my eyes. I stared at the pad where I'd written G-U-R-S-K-Y. Then I looked up at the phone book on top of the refrigerator. I got the step ladder and climbed up. There was a lot of dust on the cover so I wiped it off and opened it up to G. I didn't really think I was going to find him. I saw GURLAND John. I brought my finger down the page, GUROL, GUROV, GUROVICH, GURRERA, GURRIN, GURSHON, and after GURSHUMOV I saw his name. GURSKY Leopold. It had been right there the whole time. I wrote down his telephone number and his address, 504 Grand Street, closed the phone book, and put the step ladder away.

October 7

יהוה

Today was Saturday so I did not have to pretend I was sick again. Alma got up early and said she was going out, and when Mom asked me how I felt I said Much better. Then she asked if I wanted to do something together like go to the zoo, because Dr. Vishnubakat said it would be good if we did more things together like a family. Even though I wanted to go I knew there was something I had to do. So I told her Maybe tomorrow. Then I went up to her study and turned on the computer and printed out The History of Love. I put it in a brown envelope and on the front I wrote FOR LEOPOLD GURSKY. I told Mom I was going out to play for a while, and she said Play where? and I said Louis's house, even though he's not my friend anymore. Mom said OK but make sure you call me. Then I took 100 dollars out of my lemon-aid money and put it in my pocket. I hid the envelope with The History of Love under my jacket, and went out the door. I did not know where Grand Street was but I'm almost 12 and I knew I would find it.

A + L

The letter arrived in the mail with no return addre
My name, Alma Singer, was typed on the front. T
only letters I'd ever received had all been from Mis
but he'd never used a typewriter. I opened it. It v
only two lines. *Dear Alma*, it said. *Please meet me*
4:00 on Saturday on the benches in front of the entra
to the Central Park zoo. I think you know who I a
Sincerely yours, Leopold Gursky.

I don't know how long I've been sitting on this park bench. The light is almost all gone, but when there was light I was able to admire the statuary. A bear, a hippo, something with cloven hooves I took to be a goat. On my way I passed a fountain. The basin was dry. I looked to see if there were any pennies at the bottom. But there were only dead leaves. They're everywhere now, falling and falling, turning the world back into earth. Sometimes I forget that the world is not on the same schedule as I. That everything is not dying, or that if it is dying it will return to life, what with a little sun and the usual encouragement. Sometimes I think: I am older than this tree, older than this bench, older than the rain. And yet. I'm not older than the rain. It's been falling for years and after I go it will keep on falling.

I read the letter again. *I think you know who I am*
said. But I didn't know anyone named Leopold Gurs

I've made up my mind to sit here and wait. There's nothing more I have to do in life. My buttocks may get sore, but let that be the worst of it. If I get thirsty it wouldn't be a crime if I got down on my knees and licked the grass. I like to imagine my feet taking root in the ground and moss growing over my hands. Maybe I'll take my shoes off to speed the process. Wet earth between the toes, like a boy again. Leaves will grow from my fingers. Maybe a child will climb me. The little boy I watched throwing pebbles into the empty fountain, he wasn't too old to climb trees. You could tell he had too much wisdom for his age. Probably he believed that he wasn't made for this world. I wanted to say to him: *If not you, who?*

Maybe it really was from Misha. It's the sort of thing he might do. I'd go on Saturday, and there he'd be on the bench. It had been two months since that afternoon in his room, with his parents yelling on the other side of the wall. I'd tell him how much I missed him.

Gursky—it sounded Russian.

Maybe it was from Misha.

But probably not.

Sometimes I thought about nothing and sometimes I thought about my life. At least I made a living. What kind of living? A living. I lived. It wasn't easy. And yet. I found out how little is unbearable.

If it wasn't from Misha, maybe it was from the man with glasses who worked at the Municipal Archives at 31 Chambers Street, the one who'd called me Miss Rabbit Meat. I'd never asked his name, but he knew mine, and my address, because I'd had to fill out a form. Maybe he'd found something—a file, or a certificate. Or maybe he thought I was older than fifteen.

There was a time I lived in the forest, or in the forests, plural. I ate worms. I ate bugs. I ate anything that I could put in my mouth. Sometimes I would get sick. My stomach was a mess, but I needed something to chew. I drank water from puddles. Snow. Anything I could get hold of. Sometimes I would sneak into potato cellars that the farmers had around their villages. They were a good hiding place because they were a little warmer in the winter. But there were rodents there. To say that I ate raw rats—yes I did. Apparently, I wanted to live very badly. And there was only one reason: her.

The truth is that she told me she couldn't love me. When she said goodbye, she was saying goodbye forever.

And yet.

I made myself forget. I don't know why. I keep asking myself. But I did.

Or maybe it was from the old Jewish man who worked at the City Clerk's Office at 1 Centre Street. He looked like he could be a Leopold Gursky. Maybe he knew something about Alma Moritz, or Isaac, or *The History of Love*.

I remember the first time I realized I could make myself see something that wasn't there. I was ten years old, walking home from school. Some boys from my class ran by shouting and laughing. I wanted to be like them. And yet. I didn't know how. I'd always felt different from the others, and the difference hurt. And then I turned the corner and saw it. A huge elephant, standing alone in the square. I knew I was imagining it. And yet. I wanted to believe.

So I tried.

And I found I could.

Or maybe the letter was from the doorman at 450 East 52nd Street. Maybe he'd asked Isaac about *The History of Love*. Maybe Isaac had asked him my name. Maybe before he died he'd figured out who I was, and had given the doorman something to give to me.

After that day when I saw the elephant, I let myself see more and believe more. It was a game I played with myself. When I told Alma the things I saw she would laugh and tell me she loved my imagination. For her I changed pebbles into diamonds, shoes into mirrors, I changed glass into water, I gave her wings and pulled birds from her ears and in her pockets she found the feathers, I asked a pear to become a pineapple, a pineapple to become a lightbulb, a lightbulb to become the moon, and the moon to become a coin I flipped for her love, both sides were heads: I knew I couldn't lose.

And now, at the end of my life, I can barely tell the difference between what is real and what I believe. For example, this letter in my hand—I can feel it between my fingers. The paper is smooth, except in the creases. I can unfold it, and fold it again. As certain as I am sitting here now, this letter exists.

And yet.

In my heart, I know my hand is empty.

Or maybe the letter was from Isaac himself, who'd written it before he died. Maybe Leopold Gursky was another character in his book. Maybe there were things he wanted to tell me. And now it was too late— when I went tomorrow, the park bench would be empty.

There are so many ways to be alive, but only one way to be dead. I assumed the position. I thought: At least here they'll find me before I stink up the whole building. After Mrs. Freid died, and nobody found her for three days, they slipped flyers under our doors saying *KEEP YOUR WINDOWS OPEN TODAY, SIGNED, THE MANAGEMENT.* And so we all enjoyed a fresh breeze courtesy of Mrs. Freid who lived a long life with many strange twists she could never have imagined as a child, ending with a final trip to the grocery store to buy a box of cookies she'd yet to open when she lay down to have a rest and her heart stopped.

I thought: Better to wait out in the open. The weather took a turn for the worse, a chill cut the air, the leaves scattered. Sometimes I thought about my life and sometimes I didn't think. From time to time, when the urge struck, I conducted a quick survey: No to the question: Can you feel your legs? No to the question: Buttocks? Yes to the question: Does your heart beat?

And yet.

I was patient. No doubt there were others, on other park benches. Death was busy. So many to tend to. So that it did not think I was crying wolf, I took out the index card I carry in my wallet and safety-pinned it to my jacket.

A hundred things can change your life. And for a few days, between the time I received the letter and the time I went to meet whoever had sent it, anything was possible.

A policeman passed. He read the card pinned to my chest and looked at me. I thought he was going to put a mirror under my nose, but he only asked if I was all right. I said yes, because what was I supposed to say, I've waited my whole life for her, she was the opposite of death—and now I am still here waiting?

Saturday finally came. The only dress I had, the one I wore at the Wailing Wall, was too small. So I put on a skirt and tucked the letter in my pocket. Then I set out.

Now that mine is almost over, I can say that the thing that struck me most about life is the capacity for change. One day you're a person and the next day they tell you you're a dog. At first it's hard to bear, but after a while you learn not to look at it as a loss. There's even a moment when it becomes exhilarating to realize just how little needs to stay the same for you to continue the effort they call, for lack of a better word, being human.

I got out of the subway station and walked toward Central Park. I passed the Plaza Hotel. It was already fall; the leaves were turning brown and dropping.

I entered the park at 59th Street and walked up the path toward the zoo. When I got to the entrance my heart sank. There were about twenty-five benches in a row. People were sitting on seven of them.

How was I supposed to know which was him?

I walked up and down the row. No one gave me a second look. Finally I sat down next to a man. He paid no attention.

My watch said 4:02. Maybe he was late.

Once I was hiding in a potato cellar when the SS came. The entrance was hidden by a thin layer of hay. Their footsteps approached, I could hear them speaking as if they were inside my ears. There were two of them. One said, *My wife is sleeping with another man*, and the other said, *How do you know?* and the first said, *I don't, I only suspect it*, to which the second said, *Why do you suspect it?* while my heart went into cardiac arrest, *It's just a feeling*, the first said and I imagined the bullet that would enter my brain, *I can't think straight*, he said, *I've lost my appetite completely*.

Fifteen minutes passed, then twenty. The man next to me got up and walked away. A woman sat down and opened a book. One bench down, another woman got up. Two benches down a mother sat and rocked her baby's carriage next to an old man. Three benches down a couple laughed and held hands. Then I watched them get up and walk away. The mother stood and pushed her baby away. It was the woman, the old man, and I. Another twenty minutes passed. It was getting late. I figured whoever he was wasn't going to come. The woman closed her book and walked away. The old man and I were the only ones left. I got up to leave. I was disappointed. I don't know what I'd hoped for. I started to leave. I passed the old man. There was a card safety-pinned to his chest. It said: *MY NAME IS LEO GURSKY I HAVE NO FAMILY PLEASE CALL PINELAWN CEMETERY I HAVE A PLOT THERE IN THE JEWISH PART THANK YOU FOR YOUR CONSIDERATION.*

Because of that wife who got tired of waiting for her soldier, I lived. All he had to do was poke the hay to discover that there was nothing beneath it; if he hadn't had so much on his mind I'd have been found. Sometimes I wonder what happened to her. I like to imagine the first time she leaned in to kiss that stranger, how she must have felt herself falling for him, or perhaps simply away from her loneliness, and it's like some tiny nothing that sets off a natural disaster halfway across the world, only this was the opposite of disaster, how by accident she saved me with that thoughtless act of grace, and she never knew, and how that, too, is part of the history of love.

I stood in front of him.
He barely seemed to notice.
I said, "My name is Alma."

And that's when I saw her. It's strange what the mind
can do when the heart is giving the directions. She
looked different than I remembered her. And yet. The
same. The eyes: that's how I knew her. I thought, So
this is how they send the angel. Stalled at the age when
she loved you most.

What do you know, I said. *My favorite name.*

I said, "I was named after every girl in a book called *The History of Love.*"

I said, *I wrote that book.*

"Oh," I said. "I'm serious. It's a real book."

I played along. I said: *I couldn't be more serious.*

I didn't know what to say. He was so old. Maybe he was joking or maybe he was confused. To make conversation I said, "Are you a writer?"

He said, "In a manner of speaking."

I asked the name of his books. He said *The History of Love* was one, and *Words for Everything* was another.

"That's strange," I said. "Maybe there are two books called *The History of Love*."

He didn't say anything. His eyes were shining.

"The one I'm talking about was written by Zvi Litvinoff," I said. "He wrote it in Spanish. My father gave it to my mother when they first met. Then my father died, and she put it away until about eight months ago, when someone wrote asking her to translate it. Now she only has a few chapters left. In *The History of Love* I'm talking about there's a chapter called 'The Age of Silence,' and one called 'The Birth of Feelings,' and one called—"

The oldest man in the world laughed.

He said, "What are you telling me, that you were in love with Zvi, too? It wasn't enough that you loved me, and then you loved me and Bruno, and then you loved only Bruno, and then you loved neither Bruno nor me?"

I was starting to feel nervous. Maybe he was crazy. Or just lonely.

It was getting dark out.

I said, "I'm sorry. I don't understand."

I saw that I'd frightened her. I knew it was too late to argue. Sixty years had passed.

I said, *Forgive me. Tell me which parts you liked. What about "The Age of Glass"? I wanted to make you laugh.*

Her eyes widened.

Also to cry.

Now she looked frightened and surprised.

And then it dawned on me.

It seemed impossible.

And yet.

What if the things I believed were possible were really impossible, and the things I believed were impossible were really not?

For example.

What if the girl sitting next to me on this bench was real?

What if she was named Alma, after my Alma?

The oldest man in the world laughed.

He said, "What are you telling me, that you were in love with Zvi, too? It wasn't enough that you loved me, and then you loved me and Bruno, and then you loved only Bruno, and then you loved neither Bruno nor me?"

I was starting to feel nervous. Maybe he was crazy. Or just lonely.

It was getting dark out.

I said, "I'm sorry. I don't understand."

I saw that I'd frightened her. I knew it was too late to argue. Sixty years had passed.

I said, *Forgive me. Tell me which parts you liked. What about "The Age of Glass"? I wanted to make you laugh.*

Her eyes widened.

Also to cry.

Now she looked frightened and surprised.

on me.

What if my book hadn't been lost in a flood at all?

What if—

A man walked past.

Excuse me, I called to him.

Yes? he said.

Is someone sitting next to me?

The man looked confused.

I don't understand, he said.

Neither do I, I said. *Would you mind answering the question?*

Is someone sitting next to you? he said.

That's what I'm asking.

And he said, *Yes.*

So I said, *Is it a girl, fifteen, possibly sixteen, then again she could be a mature fourteen?*

He laughed and said, *Yes.*

Yes as in the opposite of no?

As in the opposite of no, he said.

Thank you, I said.

He walked away.

I turned to her.

It was true. She was familiar. And yet. She didn't look very much like my Alma, now that I really looked. She was much taller, for one thing. And her hair was black. She had a gap between her front teeth.

Who is Bruno? she asked.

I studied her face. I tried to think of the answer.

Talk about invisible, I said.

To her expression of fright and surprise was now added confusion.

But who is he?

He's the friend I didn't have.

She looked at me, waiting.

He's the greatest character I ever wrote.

She said nothing. I was afraid she was going to get up and leave me. I couldn't think of anything else to say. So I told her the truth.

He's dead.

It hurt to say it. And yet. There was so much more.

He died on a July day in 1941.

I waited for her to stand and walk away. But. She remained there, unblinking.

I'd gone so far.

I thought, Why not a little farther?

And another thing.

I had her attention. It was a joy to behold. She waited, listening.

I had a son who never knew I existed.

A pigeon flapped up into the sky. I said,

His name was Isaac.

And then I realized that I'd been searching for the wrong person.

I looked into the eyes of the oldest man in the world for a boy who fell in love when he was ten.

I said, "Were you ever in love with a girl named Alma?"

He was silent. His lips trembled. I thought he hadn't understood, so I asked him again. "Were you ever in love with a girl named Alma Mereminski?"

He reached out his hand. He tapped me twice on the arm. I knew he was trying to tell me something, but I didn't know what.

I said, "Were you ever in love with a girl named Alma Mereminski who left for America?"

His eyes filled with tears, he tapped my arm twice, then twice again.

I said, "The son you think didn't know you existed, was his name Isaac Moritz?"

I felt my heart surge. I thought: I've lived this long. Please. A little longer won't kill me. I wanted to say her name aloud, it would have given me joy to call, because I knew that in some small way it was my love that named her. And yet. I couldn't speak. I was afraid I'd choose the wrong sentence. She said, *The son you think didn't know*—I tapped her twice. Then twice again. She reached for my hand. With my other I tapped her twice. She squeezed my fingers. I tapped her twice. She put her head on my shoulder. I tapped her twice. She put one arm around me. I tapped her twice. She put both arms around me and hugged me. I stopped tapping.

Alma, I said.

She said, *Yes*.

Alma, I said again.

She said, *Yes*.

Alma, I said.

She tapped me twice.

Alma, I said.
She tapped me twice.

THE DEATH OF LEOPOLD GURSKY

Leopold Gursky started dying on August 18, 1920.
He died learning to walk.
He died standing at the blackboard.
And once, also, carrying a heavy tray.
He died practicing a new way to sign his name.
Opening a window.
Washing his genitals in the bath.

He died alone, because he was too embarrassed to
phone anyone.
Or he died thinking about Alma.
Or when he chose not to.

Really, there isn't much to say.
He was a great writer.
He fell in love.
It was his life.

I said, *I wrote that book.*

"Oh," I said. "I'm serious. It's a real book."